Slice

A novel

By

John Culjak

Slice

ISBN: 978-0-9878223-0-7

Printed in USA by John Culjak
Publisher prefix is: 0-9878223

For Kate, Lachlan and Liz-

Family is more precious than diamonds

Thanks

Kate Morrison's critical eye was invaluable in assisting me to see my characters more clearly … Lachlan's honesty allowed me to improve the dialogue and Liz's support was priceless.

Chapter 1

The brackish water of the pond was deep and dark. It was home for frogs, water boatmen, treaders, and water mites. The insects scattered as Geoff's telescopic ball retriever, extended twelve feet, scraped the bottom in search of his golf ball. The edge of the pond was steep and lined with large boulders causing Geoff to balance himself precariously with his left arm so as to not end up in the water with his ball. His feet were planted between the rocks, scuffing the toes of his brown and white golf shoes. He muttered to himself how bad his tee shot was. He did not like to play golf alone, but the usual partners were not available today. If they were, he thought, he would not have hit the ball so poorly – so he thought – nor would he be scraping the bottom of the pond in search of his ball. The black flies were torturous on this hot humid morning, intensifying his anger. Although it was hot and going to be even hotter, fog hovered over the fairway. Geoff felt some gratification in that no one was with him to observe his humiliation. On his belly, stretching his long scrawny body, reaching as far as his extended retriever would go, "Ah, I think I have it". He slowly drew his arm back, feeling the weight of a ball, perhaps his own. Geoff hoped it was his ball, it felt heavier. He dreaded the thought of losing a ball and being penalized two shots. He wanted to shoot fewer than 90 strokes today to prepare for the coming tournament.

His arm shook as he brought the retriever out of the water. "Damn!" It was a yellow ball, not his own. "Oh well". Geoff reached for the ball and bumping the quivering metal knocked it off the end of the retriever and back into the pond. He let out a sharp sigh of frustration. Geoff could hear the birds chirping brightly as they normally did at this time of the morning, but he did not hear the approaching figure that ended up looming over him. "Did you really expect to find your own ball in that black pool?" The deep voice, not unfamiliar, came from directly above him. Geoff cackled a nervous laugh at being caught in such a ludicrous position. Remaining stretched out; he turned his head only to see who was witnessing his folly. With a silly grin on his face, Geoff first saw a pair of highly polished black shoes, which were definitely not of the golfing variety. The last thing he saw was the bottom of uncuffed gray wool pants before the titanium driver struck his temple with the full force of a swing and a sweet follow through. The crack was dull, unlike the sound of hitting a ball. "Fore," the voice said softly as he watched Geoff's body collapse on the edge of the pond. Blood seeping out of his right eye, his head and right arm found the water. With his foot strategically placed under Geoff's ribs, he pushed and lifted at the same time with his powerful leg and Geoff's body rolled into the pond. The man reached out with his driver and pushed Geoff's head fully under the water, holding it there for half a minute. There were no bubbles.

. . . . .

Lisa, breathing heavily, was reluctantly relieved to feel Philip's weight lift off her body. She brushed the wet strands of her auburn hair from her eye and cheek, smiling contented. "Mmm. You were so hot today, Phil. I'm so glad you came to see me, baby." She rolled over, on top of Philip and kissed him warmly, feeling the beginning of the new growth of his beard scratching her chin. She liked the feel of his soft stomach and chest, which felt cool and wet on her skin. She was glad he was not muscular and tight. Lisa was never impressed with a muscular body. Philip looked into her dark brown eyes. "I am glad I came too," he said laughing. "Pun intended. I was going to play a round of golf today with Geoff, but as soon as I found out that he booked a tee time, I bowed out and called you – to book a time with you." He laughed.

Lisa put her hand over his mouth. "Let's not talk about Geoff. He'll be back soon enough, Philly." She said teasing him. Philip moved her hand away from his mouth, "Do you think he knows about us?" He wondered.

Lisa responded with a smile, exposing her very white teeth, which were too large for her mouth, and said, "He doesn't have a clue."

. . . . .

Philip picked up his number one titanium driver that he left in the hall at the bottom of the stairs when he arrived,

treating the club like a delicate treasured possession and said,
"I'd better not leave this here," referring to the club. "I should
go, Lisa, before Geoff gets back. I don't think it would look
very good if he caught me here with you. It would be hard to
explain why I was here, and not playing golf with him."
She took the club out of his hand and pulled him toward her,
putting her hand under his chin, with her fingers wrapped
around the left side of his cheek, in almost a chokehold. "You
know, Phil, I don't ever want to hear you say anything like
that again. I don't want Geoff to know about us, understand?
If it came to that, I would deny everything. He'd believe me
too. He knows I'd never lie to him, or be unfaithful to him for
that matter. You know that don't you." She smiled looking
intently into his eyes and held on as Phil tried to pull away.
"There is no future for us, Phil, except for a little fun, when
I'm horny. You understand?"
Lisa's hand on his neck and face made him feel
uncomfortable. He pulled away, in a nervous gesture ran his
fingers through his thinning hair, and patted it down. "Don't
worry about Geoff. He won't find out about us. I promise
you that." He said as though it were the definitive answer.
Lisa laughed and looked into his light blue eyes that always
seemed to be teary and vulnerable. At moments like this, she
felt like mothering him. "You are such a little boy, Philip.
Now go home before you get into trouble." Philip lowered
his head and left without saying goodbye. Once outside Philip
looked across the street, both ways to see if anyone noticed
him. He felt awkward; he felt sheepish, like a teenager who

did something naughty. He felt powerless with Lisa, even though he did all that he could to be more aggressive with her. She always ended up taking control. He didn't like the feeling, the position in which she placed him. I am 40 years old and shouldn't feel like a little kid, he thought. He walked to his car, a late model BMW, which was parked a few houses down from Lisa's house, turned to see if anyone was on the street, then got in, satisfied that he was not observed leaving her house. I'll get even with her, he thought, frustrated. I always do. Lisa stood in the doorway, waved and watched Philip as he drove away. She did not want to conceal the fact that a man visited her, in case he was seen leaving her house. Being overly cautious often made it more obvious that she was trying to hide something. At least, that's what she thought.

. . . . .

Driver put his golf bag down, unlocked, and opened the solid wood front door of the Victorian three-story house. The house was painted a traditional white, with silver grey trim. The tree-lined street was quiet, as always. The tall trees arched over the street, creating a covered bridge. Driver liked his privacy and did not want to know who his neighbors were and, as far as he knew, they didn't know him even though he had lived in the house for a year and a half. He cherished his old house in the south end of Halifax and, other than a cosmetic paint job, made no renovations when he bought it.

He closed the door, put the clubs down in the hall, taking the titanium driver from the bag. He looked at the club head, saw what he expected to find, went into the kitchen, and turned on the hot water. He picked up a fingernail brush that was on the back of the counter near the white porcelain sink and put the head of the club under the hot stream coming out of the faucet. He squeezed dish detergent on the brush and scrubbed the face of the club. He rinsed and dried the club thoroughly, examined it, and put it back in the bag, slipping a cover over the head. In the cabinet, under the sink, he found a clean unused shoe brush. He brushed the strands of grass off his shoes, and swiped the bottoms of his trousers to make sure that there was no residue from the links. He went to the pantry for a dustpan and brush, swept up the grass and other bits that came from his shoes and pants and deposited it into the green plastic composter. Driver took a plastic bottle of bleach from the cabinet under the sink and poured some of it into the sink hoping to clear away any of the material that came off the golf club head. However, he was not overly concerned about the club, considering where it came from. He ran the hot water and then paused for a moment, thinking what should be done next. "Ah, yes" he said aloud, and went to his small office, which once might have been used as a front room or a parlor, and was located just off the front entrance hallway. Driver sat down at his computer, which was perched on a small, solid oak postwar desk. Reference books and papers cluttered the top of the desk. He turned the Macintosh power center on and waited briefly for the desktop to appear on the screen. He opened Word and selected a file simply called List. There were six names on the page. Number one was Geoff Jenkins. He moved the cursor over Geoff's name and double clicked to highlight it.

Then he pressed the delete key on the keyboard. "Deleted," he said aloud. "Geoff, you are so deleted. And thank you".

Driver sighed in relief and smiled as he watched the name disappear; five remained.

Chapter 2

Detective Richard "Rick" Redmond, fully aware of the early morning heat and humidity, which he found to be overbearing, labored up the stairs of the recently built police station.

The two-story building, which was built about ten years ago, but still referred to as the new station, looked like a brick fortress, with smoked gray windows, protected by a six-foot overhang. The dark architectural concept made a statement, which was to forewarn people with its gloomy appearance, so everyone thought. Redmond nodded to the officer, who monitored the front door entrance from an enclosed booth. Rick detested using the back entrance, which was the on-duty entry, also used for bookings and which was monitored by video cameras. It frustrated him waiting to be identified before going inside. It was a rigid routine, one in which he refused to participate. So, instead, he always used the front entrance. He was buzzed in and walked through the second set of doors where the older and mostly overweight, former street cops somberly held vigil behind their desks. The front desk sergeant looked up from his work as Redmond walked by. He nodded and gave Redmond an abbreviated wave, which was returned. Redmond liked expensive clothes and wore them well. However, he was a most pugnacious man. His dark brown hair was cut short, and his face looked like he went fifteen rounds with Jake LaMota. Still he possessed a rugged handsomeness to which both men and women were attracted. Once, years ago, he entered a "tough guy" competition at the urging of his colleagues. The bouts were held at the Halifax Metro Centre and Redmond lasted through a series of three fights, winning two and was severely defeated in the third and final match, mainly because of his size; he was 5'10" and he weighed 175 pounds. His opponent weighted more than 235 pounds and it took only two rounds for Redmond to be destroyed. Redmond often worked out after he made detective, and, as tough as he was, could not compete with the heavyweights, who outweighed him by as much as 60 pounds. He smoked and drank too much, too often, so thought almost everyone who knew him. The shape of his nose, somewhat flat and crooked, was attributed to the competition. Besides a few fighting scars from his youth, his cheeks were lightly pocked from pubescent acne. Underneath the scars and twisted nose, lay gentleness and vulnerability. Redmond was unaware that such emotions dwelled within him. If it ever occurred to him that he possessed those emotions, he would deny it vehemently; kindness and compassion were not part of his emotional makeup. He saw himself as a stubborn, macho tough guy who took what he wanted, and would not give an inch. He felt he had to maintain that persona if he were to deal with scumbags on the street. As Redmond climbed the stairs to the Special Investigation Section (SIS), which he headed up and was part of the RCMP/Halifax Regional police integrated major crime unit, he hoped that this day would not require a great deal of energy. He drank far too much last night and his head was as murky as his tongue was fuzzy. Today he felt older than 38. He sat down at his desk, slouched in the chair, and shuffled some papers that were left from the day before without looking at them. Detective Donna Copp approached him with more paper. "This just came in.," she said, handing him the call sheet with some urgency. Rick quickly scanned the sheet.

"Shit! Did Dave see this?"

"No. It just came in. I thought you'd want to see it first." Donna explained.

"Why did they call homicide?" Redmond wanted to know. "How did he die? Was it a heart attack or what?"

"Your guess is as good as mine. I guess they weren't sure what happened. They didn't want to take a chance that he may have been murdered, that's why we were called." Redmond said nothing. "The body was found at a water hazard at Indian Lake Golf Course. Shall we go take a look?" Redmond exhaled a long slow breath. "I sure as hell don't want to go there for nothing." Donna looked at him, rolled her eyes, and shrugged.

"Okay, Copp, let's get our ass to the golf course and get it done with."

"Shall I bring my clubs just in case we want to play a round of golf?" she said smiling. She had an easy, relaxed, unforced smile. Copp, who had been a detective for only about two years, had not been exposed to the brutal slayings and violence that was typical to those who have been on the force for much longer, and the kind of aggressive behavior that soured one's personal life and their perspective on other human beings.

Copp was not a typical cop. She was a psych major at Dalhousie University, with a minor in criminology, before she enrolled in the Police Service training program in Toronto. Her career path turned out to be a great disappointment to her parents. They thought of her as scholarly and expected her to pursue a career in academia. She had other plans, a life of excitement that would deliver a constant adrenalin rush.

It was her degree in psychology and minor in criminology that helped move her up the ranks quickly. After only a few years on the street, she applied for, and made detective, much to the chagrin of other officers who were on the street longer and still remained there. However, she gained the respect of her fellow detectives with her fearless attitude and her excellent investigative abilities and arrest record. Even though Copp was quite attractive and single at 33, she was not subjected to any sexual harassment for the most part, oddly enough.

"Just tell Dave that I want him to come with us, Donna."

. . . . .

Dave Martin and Donna went in Dave's car; a ten-year old black American-made sedan that spewed black fumes out of the exhaust pipe and burned about a quart of oil a month. Rick took an unmarked police issue. It was still early, almost 8:00 a.m., so rush hour traffic was not too heavy, especially since they were going in the opposite direction of the traffic entering the city. The sun was bright and strong, and poured in the drivers' side window as they headed south. It took Rick less than 25 minutes to get to the Indian Lake Golf Course, even though there was a slight delay at the Armdale rotary, a rush hour driver's nightmare. The recent redesigning and construction of the rotary did, however, help the flow somewhat. The Indian Lake Golf Course sign was posted at the intersection of the highway and the unpaved turn-off road. Rick took a right, saw the dust rooster tail behind Dave's car, and followed him about 300 meters to the clubhouse parking lot. Rick slowed his car past the parking lot, through the personnel only gate, and stopped in front of the clubhouse between Dave's car and a standard blue and white with its lights flashing.

Several golfers who were waiting to play a round of golf approached him, obviously having gotten nowhere with the uniforms. They were evidently angry to find the course closed.

"What the hell is going on?" One golfer asked.

"Did someone get hurt?" Another wanted to know.

Ignoring their inquiries, Redmond walked by them and went directly into the clubhouse to find detectives Martin and Copp. Officer Jim Slater, who cordoned off the area with yellow crime tape, blocking access to the first two holes, had been the first to arrive with his partner. The first hole was about fifty yards to the left of the small clubhouse, and the second hole, just to the right, could be seen from the canteen deck. The tee box of the second hole was about 50 feet higher than and 130 yards from the green.

"Hey, Jim. How're ya doing?" Redmond asked Slater.

"Fine as can be."

"So what have we got here?"

"One dead golfer, male in his mid-40s."

"Who found the body?"

Slater, a junior officer, took charge. He was young, fresh, clean-shaven, and anxious to be involved in the work. His uniform was impeccable; clean, pressed, boots highly shined, and he performed by the book. He could easily have been mistaken for a lifer in the military. Slater was black, one of a handful of blacks on the force. He was resourceful, a leader and he was strong, both physically and mentally. Besides being intelligent, he possessed the kind of street smarts that were a positive asset to doing a good job. Slater knew that because he was black he had to be that much better than everyone else, if he was to move up the ladder. He was proud that he was willing and capable of going the extra mile. He did his best to ignore the occasional racial remarks from his fellow policemen. He dismissed the sporadic remarks as ignorant comments made to rouse him and also as an attempt to treat him as inferior.

"He was found on the pond at the third hole by two guys playing behind him. Apparently, the two started their round about fifteen minutes after he did, and were the only players on the course."

"Did you get their statement?"

"Yes, I did, but…" Martin interrupted him, exercising his rank

17

and authority.

"Just a sketchy statement, Rick. I thought you might want to talk to them yourself. I checked the body and it looks like it was no accident."

"Thanks, Dave". Rick said, looking for the witnesses.

"Where are the two who found him?"

"They're in the dining room having a coffee. They're quite upset. Ms Kelder, who manages the place, is with them."

"Dave, you and Donna get their full statement. I'm gong to check the body. Did anyone contact forensics?"

Slater, almost at attention, "I took the liberty of contacting RCMP FIS, the Forensic Inspection Services, Detective." He said adding the formal unit name. "I hope you don't mind. They said they'd have someone here within the hour."

"Good work, Slater. What about the K-9 unit, were they contacted?" The only response was shrugs. "Donna, get them out here immediately. I want to see if the dogs can track the perp's direction in and out. Dave, get a team to canvass the houses on the road coming in. I want to know if anyone saw a car, a person, anything out of the ordinary. I want the entire area scoured, at least 500 yards in every direction from the body. I want to know where the perp came from and where he went."

"I'll get on it, Rick." Copp went directly to Constable Slater's police car to make the calls and Dave made his calls from Rick's car.

"Slater, show me where the body is," Redmond said.

Slater led Rick around the deck and down the steep hill along a gravel path that led to the second hole green. Once at the bottom, they took another gravel path to the left that led to the third hole. About forty yards from the tee box, on the left of the fairway, was the body laying face down along side the boulders that bordered the pond. "Did you ID him, Slater?" "Ms Kelder said his name is Jenkins, Geoff Jenkins. His wallet is intact and his driver license confirmed that. About $90 and plastic all seem to be there. His watch, a Rolex, is still on his wrist and gold wedding band on his finger, so I think we can rule out robbery. Apparently he golfed here a couple of times a week."

"Was a weapon found?"

"Nothing yet, Rick. The only thing we found next to the body was a white wooden tee. It may belong to the Vic. I bagged it. I'll give it to forensics when they get here."

Rick looked at the swollen bloody head without touching it. "Did anyone move or touch anything?" Slater shrugged, "As far as I know no one touched anything...except when I checked his wallet, but I used gloves." Redmond noticed that Jenkins' hair and his golf shirt was wet almost to the waist. His hair was matted with water and blood.

"Looks to me like he was in the water. Someone must have moved him. Shit! With that nasty wound, I don't think he moved himself," Redmond muttered almost to himself. "Did anyone get a fix on the guy? Where he lives, works, relatives?" Rick asked without looking up at Slater.

"Detective Copp called in for a check on him, as soon as she got here.

As far as I know, we didn't get a fix yet."

Redmond stood up and looked around. "That kinda wound couldn't have happened from a fall. It looks like he got clubbed real good with something."

"Bludgeoned," Slater said.

"Yeah, bludgeoned." Redmond said, smiling at the use of the word. Sorta looks like an execution."

"If it was an execution, why didn't they just shoot him? It's quicker and more efficient." Slater asked.

"Too noisy, Jim. The perp probably didn't want to draw attention to him. That would be my guess. Stay here until the forensic boys arrive, and don't touch anything. I'd like to see a photo of that wound, and find out if maybe the perp left anything behind...besides the tee. At least we got a reasonably good fix on the time of death."

. . . . .

Redmond backtracked from the murder site to the clubhouse and went in to talk to the pair that found the body. Karen Kelder, the manager, was sitting with them at a table in the dining room.

"I'm Detective Richard Redmond. Are you the two that found the body on the third hole?" Both men stood up.

"Yes sir, we found him laying face down in the water, just to the left of the fairway, about sixty yards or so from the tee." One of the men said. Redmond motioned them to sit down. He sat down across from them, and took out his note pad.

"Ms Kelder, you're the manager of the clubhouse?"

"Yes, I am...and owner. What a terrible thing to happen to Mr. Jenkins. I can't believe it. He was such a nice man."

"Did anyone talk to you at all, Ms Kelder?" She shook her head indicating that they had not questioned her. Rick did not want to duplicate the inquiry unnecessarily.

"How did you know it was Mr. Jenkins, Ms. Kelder?"

"Well, first of all he was the only one on the course before these gentlemen teed off."

Redmond waited for her to continue, and when she didn't, "and secondly?"

"When Mr. Miller ran back into the clubhouse, almost hysterical, and told me that they found a body in the water at the third hole, I ran down to see who it was. I recognized him immediately. I brought my cell phone with me so I could call 911, which I did." She clutched the top of her blouse, just below her neck, as she spoke, and held it tightly in her grip.

"I wasn't hysterical, Karen, but I was excited", Miller said defensively. "I never saw anyone dead before."

"Did you touch the body, Ms Kelder?"

"I didn't touch anything. I wouldn't do that". Kelder was slender and spry for her 54 years. She had been an amateur golfer who continued to play a round of golf most days. Wrinkles formed in the dry tanned skin around her eyes and mouth and her brown hair was cropped short and naturally highlighted by the time she spent in the sun. When she smiled, her straight white teeth exemplified the youthfulness and beauty that still lingered.

"Someone must have. Didn't you say that the body was in the water?" He asked the two men.

Miller jumped in. "Only his head and shoulders were in the water, not his entire body."

"Then why was his head out of the water when I saw it?" Rick asked.

Miller's head dropped involuntarily, "I thought he had fallen in the water and maybe was drowning, so I pulled him out. Then I saw his head swollen and bloody, and his eye socket crushed. That's when I ran back up to the clubhouse. At first I thought he fell and hit his head on a rock at the edge of the pond."

"Shit! So the scene had been compromised." He said resigned. "Okay, okay. Did either of you see anyone else on the course or near the body?"

They shook their heads. "How'd you pull him out?"

"We grabbed him by the belt and kind of dragged him out of the water. When we saw his face, we just left him there and came back to the clubhouse."

"Mrs. Keller, did you see anyone else besides Mr. Jenkins and these two gentlemen?"

"No, not a soul." As an afterthought, she said, "at least not until the others outside came to sign in and pay for the round they booked."

"Do you know if Mr. Jenkins had any altercations with anyone here? Any problems with anyone?" Redmond directed his question to Karen.

"Not that I know of. He was always smiling, very polite and pleasant. He was so sweet and funny too. If he did have any problems here, I wasn't aware of it. I always looked forward to seeing him here. He was quite a charming man."

Redmond asked Martin and Copp, who returned from making the calls, if they had finished with the witnesses. They had. "If you think of anything else, no matter how insignificant, please call us." He gave each of them his card, and drew Dave and Donna aside. "I would like you to wait for the forensic team and give me a report on their findings, and have the area checked to see if the perp left anything for us. Oh yes, we had better get the witnesses' prints, just in case they show up on the body, and have forensics check their shoes, as well. I don't want to go on a wild goose chase in the event that they left a shoe print. Did I mention I want dogs out here?"

"Yes, you did, Rick."

"Good. Donna, did you get a fix on the victim yet, family, anything?"

"What I have so far is an address, he was 45, and he's married. His wife's name is Lisa. Apparently, they've been married for about 14 years. He was a regular here at the golf club. He also has a sister living in the city. Do you want me to follow up with his wife and sister?"

"No, I'll take that dirty detail. I assume they weren't notified."

"No one has told them yet, as far as I know."

"Okay, I'll talk to his wife first and then get to his sister. Did the Vic have any other relatives?"

"Not that I know of, Rick."

"Okay. We'll meet at my office as soon as you finish up here. Then we'll see what we have. Oh, yes, double check with the golfers who are waiting to play to make sure they arrived after Jenkins was killed, and not before. Also get everyone's name, address, and phone number." Redmond turned to Kelder, "Ms Kelder? Do you know if Mr. Jenkins car is here?"

"One second," she replied and walked through the clubhouse reception area and outside, looking for his car. When she returned she told Redmond that his car was the black Volvo parked in the first spot on the left.

"Donna, Dave, would you check out his car and then have it hauled in for a tight inspection?"

"Sure thing," Dave said.

"Ms Kelder, we are going to have to close down the course for the day, at least." Rick told her.

"What about the back nine? Can we use them?" She pleaded.

"Definitely not today you can't. We don't know if the perp is still on the grounds. We can't take any chances. The course is closed until tomorrow morning." He said, annoyed by her questions. "By the way, do you have a map of the course?"

"Yes, I do. I'll get it for you."

Redmond walked to his car map in hand, angry at having to deal with a murder and struggling with a hangover. He did not like the smell of it. It didn't seem to him to be the run of the mill drug-related hit or a crime of passion. And obviously, it wasn't robbery. He wondered if he missed anything.

. . . . .

24

Driving back into Halifax, he tried to clear the cobwebs from his head; still he could not think straight. It was to be hoped that he covered everything at the site. His fear was that he did not look at all the details, consider all the possibilities. Redmond was concerned that he may have overlooked the obvious and his team would call him on it. This shortcoming so irritated him that he wished he could beat someone with his fists. He was so mad that he wanted to spit.

Chapter 3

Lisa Jenkins tore the sheets off the bed as she typically did whenever she got together with Philip. She was singing to herself, happy, as usual, after having satisfactory sex. She gathered additional dirty clothes, put them in a basket to make a full washer-load, took them to the laundry room, and started the cycle. Her face was still flushed from lovemaking. She wondered why she slept around on Geoff…cheated rather…since she slept with Philip only. She was not in love with Philip. She considered the possibility that her passion for Geoff had evaporated, that she needed variety, and knew that Philip could easily satisfy her sexual appetite. The doorbell rang interrupting her thoughts. She went to the door, pausing to look at her hair in the hallway mirror. She put on her best smile when she saw Redmond and pushed her hair behind her left ear.

"Yes?"

"Ms Jenkins?"

"Yes, may I help you?"

"I'm Rick Redmond, Detective Redmond, Halifax police." He showed her his identification. She glanced at his badge and said nothing. "Umm…may I come in?"

"Sure, I guess." She led him through the wide entry hall and into a large living room, which was divided into two separate sitting areas; the largest one was focused on a tiled fireplace with a granite hearth. The room was painted a shade of desert sand and decorated with a blend of antique and modern furniture and accessories. A large oriental carpet covered part of the oak hardwood floor. The second area was devoted to entertainment, including a TV and a CD player and casual seating. "What is this about? Is something wrong? Did I forget to pay a parking ticket?" She said smiling.

"If you don't mind, can we sit down?" Redmond waited for her to sit, watched her skillfully cross her legs, and then sat across from her.

"Oh god, I hate it when you say something like that, 'can we sit down'. You make it sound like something terrible has happened. Is this about Geoffrey?"

Redmond looks away, squeezing his hands. "Well…"

H expelled a deep sigh of frustration and anticipation.

"For Christ's sake, are you going to tell me or not! Something has happened to Geoffrey, hasn't it?"

"Your husband is dead, Ms Jenkins. He was killed earlier this morning."

"Oh my God! Oh my God!"

Her eyes filled with liquid, began to overflow, and her throat tightened to a narrow passage. Her words were barely audible yet did not indicate how devastated she felt, "What happened? Was it an accident? Did he have an accident…in his car?"

"No, it wasn't an accident. He was…at least we think he was murdered. Anyway that's what it looks like."

Her voice rose and became unstable, and through the

numbness she felt said, "What! It looks like it? You're not sure?" Redmond said nothing. "Was it or wasn't it?" Her heart pounded, she stopped breathing. She felt like her lungs were going to burst.

"Goddammit! This is so crazy. I don't believe it. Please say you're joking."

Redmond stood up and tentatively approached her, reached out and thought about taking her hand but had second thoughts; instead, he put his hand on her shoulder. "I'm sorry, Ms Jenkins. Your husband was killed just minutes after he started his golf game."

Her face went ashen. She felt as though she was struck a blow to her solar plexus, on the verge of collapse.

Why the fuck do I do this, he thought. This is shit. Donna would have managed this better than I have. No, no one could do it better. There is no better way. You can do it a thousand times and it's always the same, difficult and painful. What a shit job.

"If you prefer, we could talk about this later."

"No. No." She collected herself and sat up tall. "Please continue. No doubt I'll have to go through this, if not now, then later."

"Okay. I will have to ask you a few questions." He waited for her response and when none came continued. "Where were you this morning, say for the last two and a half hours?"

"I was here all morning."

"Can anyone verify that?"

"Oh god. Am I a suspect in my own husband's murder?" She

asked overwhelmed.

"Please, Ms Jenkins…this is hard enough"

"A friend of Geoffrey's was here with me for about two hours. In fact, he left about 20 minutes ago."

"And what time did your friend get here?"

"I don't remember, detective, maybe about nine or so."

Redmond looked at her without saying a word, wondering who the friend was, why he was there, and why he stayed for such a long time, typical of his suspicious nature. Lisa responded as if she read his mind.

"He was going to play a round of golf with Geoffrey, but changed his mind. He came here to tell him, but Geoffrey had already left."

"Do you play golf, Ms Jenkins?"

"No, I hate golf. It is a stupid game. If I want to walk around for four hours, I rather do it on a hiking trail." Her voice started to break. "Oh, I'm sorry."

"I don't play either." He said. "I think it's a waste of time and energy. I would rather work out in a gym." He paused, looking directly at her. "What time did Geoff leave this morning?"

"I think it was before eight; maybe between 7:10 and 7:30, I don't know. He had an 8:00 tee time, I think."

Redmond scribbled the times in his notepad. "Did he leave with anyone?"

"No. He was going to play a round with Philip, but Philip didn't show up until later, as I explained before."

"Philip is the friend that was with you?"

"Yes."

"Does Philip have a last name?"

"Don't be smart with me, Detective. This isn't the time to be rude."

"I'm sorry. I didn't mean it the way it sounded." She rolled her eyes.

"I guess that's not an excuse." He said.

"Philip's last name is Nickerson. Philip Nickerson. Philip with one l." Redmond jotted the name in his notepad.

"What time did you say Philip Nickerson got here?"

"Around 8:30 or 9:00, I think."

"Where can I reach Mr. Nickerson?"

"He lives in the south end, not far from here." Lisa gave him the phone number and address from memory, which he noted, and then her body began to slump, and tremble as she attempted to hold herself straight. It was a losing battle, and she gave in, allowing her body to collapse, folding over her thighs, and grief to settle in.

"We can go over this another time if you want."

She pulled herself up. "No, let's continue."

"I will have to go through Geoff's things; his room, his office. Does he have a computer?"

"Yes, he does. Do you want to see it?"

"Not now. I will have someone come to look through his belongings, and perhaps pick up some of his things." A painful sound, between a moan and a primordial cry, emanated from her body.

"Do you know anyone who might have wanted your husband

dead?"

She shrugged weakly and shook her head, and struggled to stand.

"Did your husband use drugs, Ms Jenkins?"

Lisa shook her head. "No, he never used drugs. He hated how drugs could steal your joy, your spirit, and more importantly, your control."

"What about gambling? Did he gamble at all?" He asked.

"I'm not sure if he gambled or not, but I think he didn't. There was no indication that he gambled. If he did, it would have been in such small amounts that it wasn't noticeable. I suppose the way some people play the lottery."

Redmond said, "I believe I have enough information for now. Are you agreeable to another meeting, if it's necessary?"

"Yes, yes, of course" she said without giving it a thought. Lisa stood to show him out.

"That's okay. I'll find my way out. Thank you." He started walking towards the hall, stopped, and turned. "In the meantime, if you think of anything that might be helpful, please call me...anytime. Okay?"

He took a card from his jacket and placed it on the small table in the hallway. "Of course I will," she said.

"And if there is anything that I can do...anyone I can contact..." He shrugged, turned without finishing, and left closing the door behind him.

Chapter 4

Jean Jenkins was shorter than five feet even though she wore two-inch heels. She wore her thick brown hair short and, usually, a hat covered it. Jean was 40 years old, but it was difficult to determine her age. If you looked at her face, you might have thought she was an old looking child. Her intelligent, electric blue eyes belied her age. Everything about Jean appeared to be contradictory. She gave the impression of a little girl playing dress up; her skirt looked too long, hanging at mid-calf, and her shoes too big. It appeared as though she was a child dressed in her mother's clothes. Yet, she possessed the demeanor of an executive or perhaps that of a university professor. She was an odd mixture - an intellectual - a prodigy, perhaps? Jean had been awarded a scholarship to Brown where she excelled in geology, but she decided not to pursue it as a career because of her dislike of the outdoors, which included insects that inhabited the remote areas in which she would have had to work. She had chose Brown because class sizes were small and the city of Providence was similar in size to Halifax; so consequently it was comfortable for her. She was sitting at her computer when the phone rang. She adjusted her hat and let it ring three times before she picked up. "This is Jean speaking." There was a long silence. Jean said nothing. She listened to the dead air. It seemed an eternity before she got a response.

"Hello, Jean." Jean overflowed with disdain at the sound of Lisa's voice.

"Yes?"

"I know you don't like me to call you, but…"

"Lisa, please. I don't need you telling me what I don't like. What do you want?"

"I am sorry…I…"

Interrupting her, "Lisa, I did not schedule your indulgence into my day, so please get to the fucking point."

"Please, bear with me, Jean." Lisa composed herself. "Jean, something terrible has happened."

"More histrionics, Lisa? Just tell me what happened. (Jean listened to the dead air) Lisa? What is it?"

"Geoffrey is dead."

Jean said nothing. She was stung, momentarily paralyzed. Still holding the phone, she took her hat off and put it on the desk.

"Jean? Jean, are you there?" Jean gently placed the receiver down and turned her computer off.

. . . . .

She sat silently, biting down on her lower lip to ease the pain and the emptiness that she felt. Blood began to trickle down her chin from the broken skin. Tears welled up in her eyes like a rising river, flooding over and rolling down her cheeks. There was total silence. The only sound she heard was one that emanated from deep within and escaped the corner of her mouth in a whimper.

Jean sank back into her chair. She clasped her hands together, intertwining her fingers, while her index fingers formed a steeple. She pressed her steepled fingers against her lips as she considered what Lisa had said. She wanted to scream out and say what could not be said, but not a sound was made. She always contained her emotions. Jean longed to be passionate and expressive, but was unable to allow herself that luxury. It was a conflict that would remain with her to the end of her days. She sat and thought. Her face was drained of color.

She remembered Geoff carrying her on his shoulders. She was tiny and weighed only sixty pounds. Geoff paid special attention to Jean. He said sweet things to his sister; he looked after her. Mostly everyone else teased her about her size, calling her cruel names, humiliating her. Geoff made her feel good. He made her laugh, which filled her with indescribable pleasure. It was painful for Geoff to hear derogatory remarks about Jean. He used kindness to take away her pain, and she responded well. Jean adored his smooth tanned face, his mischievous smile, and the fact that he treated her as an equal. Geoff possessed the ability to make her feel like she was exceptional, something special. That gesture of tenderness indicated to her that men or, in Geoff's case, boys could find her interesting, even though it was her brother who provoked such feelings. She was unsure exactly what those feelings were and what they meant. In a manner, she felt guilt, but was uncertain as to explain it. Even now, as she sat at her desk, her face flushed as she thought of Geoff. *Oh God. Oh my God, is it possible?* She sat for what seemed to be an hour thinking about Geoff, tears cascading down her face. She took a tissue from the desk, wiped the blood from her chin and the tears from her cheeks. She picked up the phone and speed dialed Lisa. Lisa picked up after the first ring.

"Is it really true, Lisa? I am so sorry. If only I...no...no...no. Not if only. What is, is done, Lisa." Pulling herself together "Now, what can I do?"

"I don't know, Jean. I don't know. I don't know what to do myself."

Jean's voice was now softer, gentler; more compassionate, and lower than before, "when did it happen, how and where?" The circumstances surrounding Geoff's death flowed out of Lisa's mouth as she reiterated what Detective Redmond had told her. She recounted all the details that she remembered, while Jean remained silent, listened, hanging on to each word. When she was finished, Jean said without hesitation, "Lisa, I will find out who did this. And when I do, I pity the poor son of a bitch."

"Please Jean, don't do anything foolish. Leave it to the police. They know what they're doing." Lisa said, not knowing what else to say to console her, even though her loss needed consoling.

Jean conceded the point, said goodbye and hung up. She decided to talk to Detective Redmond. In reality, she did not intend to do anything to anyone, even if she could. Where would she look? What could she do if confronted by Geoff's

killer, if she were lucky enough to find him or her? She was definitely physically limited by her stature. She pondered the idea of buying a gun, and wondered if that was wise, if she could really shoot someone, even someone who had murdered Geoff. "*Goddamn right I could*, she thought.
I could do it in a minute.
Jean picked up her hat from the desk, held it in her hands, looking at it in wonderment, as though it was the first time she ever saw a hat.
She tilted her head, a dog-like gesture, as if responding to a word of recognition, slipped the hat on, pulled it down decisively, rose from her chair and left the house.

Chapter 5

Detective Redmond sat at his desk. He scooped his eyes with his fingertips several times and rubbed his face; then realized that he hadn't shaved this morning. Redmond often went to work unshaven. He often felt being unshaven added to his mystique, his manliness, much like it did for celebrities. He transferred his notes to a murder book, which he titled, simply, Geoff. He wrote a note to himself to contact Philip Nickerson, and added,

relationship?

What was he doing at the Jenkins' for two hours or more?

Is Nickerson Lisa's friend or was he Geoff's friend, or both?

Where they in business together?
Was there any type of money exchange or loan?
Was Lisa having an affair with Nickerson?
Check on other friends and relatives.
Who wanted Jenkins dead, and why?
Who had motive?
Who had opportunity?

Rick looked up from his desk to find Stenson standing there.

"Hey, Rick. How goes the battle?" He smiled.

He never saw Stenson when he wasn't smiling. He believed

that Stenson had a perpetual smile that appeared to be cosmetically affixed to his mouth. He looked up at him and wondered if he ever frowned at home or in private, to offset his permanent grin that displayed his even, almost perfect teeth.

"The battle is just starting, but I'll soon have to turn up the juice."

"You okay?"

"Of course I'm okay, Stenson. Why wouldn't I be okay? Why do you ask?" Stenson shrugged. "What the hell do you want anyway?"

Stenson hovered above him, smiling, gloating, as though he knew something that Rick did not. Stenson stood straight, his shoulders back, but he gave the appearance of being totally relaxed; there was no rigidity in his demeanor. He always dressed in casual sport clothes. Today he wore a colorful but discreet shirt, tan slacks and a pair of Clark's brown, burnished leather loafers. Some people who knew him, and did not call him by his last name, referred to him as the "big easy" because of his resemblance to Ernie Ells, the professional golfer. Most people did not know that his first name was Edwin, nor did he make an effort to tell anyone. He carried his six-foot-three, 200-pound plus frame effortlessly, with a grace that was admired and often emulated. Because of his ease, he gave the impression that he was soft but, on the contrary, his body was hard and toned and, interestingly enough, non-threatening. In fact, his strength was often underestimated, and in some situations, people tried to take advantage of him because of that misconception, much to their chagrin. His fitness was closer to that of a 20-some year old man, although he had just turned 39. Stenson worked out with weights for strength, Pilates for balance and core strength, and Yoga for flexibility.

"Well, Rick, to tell you the truth, I heard that you were working a murder case."

"News travels fast. So?"

"So I thought you might want some help." Redmond just looked at him.

"Are you kidding me?"

"The truth of the matter is, Barnes assigned me to the case. He's under the impression that it's high profile, a priority and one that will be difficult and time-consuming."

"Sweet. I can use all the help I can get. You can start by going over my notes." He shoved the murder book in Stenson's direction. Stenson looked at the book on the desk, smiled, and then picked it up. "Anything you want to tell me about it?"

"Read it first and then we'll talk about it."

"Sweet." He said mocking him in a good-natured way. Stenson picked up the book and went to his desk. He went through the book from the first page, reading every word. He was so engrossed in the murder book that he didn't notice that Copp was standing at his desk.

"I hear you're going to be working on the case with us," she interrupted, swinging her hip and sliding onto the front corner of his desk.

"News travels fast, as Rick says." He said, smiling as usual, without looking up.

"I am glad you'll be working with us, Stenson," she said shifting her weight off his desk, with a glint in her eye. She always seemed to perk up when she was around Stenson. His gentle, unassuming, but gregarious personality drew people to him like a magnet.

"Same here," he said without enthusiasm, continuing to go through the book without looking up at her.

. . . . .

Jean Jenkins walked briskly from her house on Chestnut Street to the police station. The walk took her more than twenty minutes due largely to her stature. She usually walked whenever the distance was within forty-five minutes. Even rain did not deter her ambulatory activity; it afforded her the opportunity to appreciate the city's forest-like amenities. Although at this time, Jean could only reflect on her brother's death, and ventured directly ahead, staring into space, seemingly, without seeing anything but the direction in which she was heading. When she reached the station, she climbed the concrete stairs to the entrance doors, her heart pounding, but not from the physical exertion of the walk. She wanted revenge; she wanted to know who killed Geoff and she wanted to know what she could do about it. She felt hatred, anger and emptiness at the same time; could not fathom why anyone would want to kill her brother. But mostly, because of her loss, she felt empty … a void. Jean walked through the front door to the police station. "Detective Redmond, please," she said to the overweight officer on duty, sitting in a small reception room behind a sliding glass window. His face was ruddy and tiny veins were visible on his cheeks and bulbous nose, obviously from drinking too much, too often.

"Your name, please? And what is the nature of your visit?" he asked.

"My name is Jean Jenkins and my brother was murdered earlier today," she stated with a lack of emotion.

The officer looked up at her and then said with as much sensitivity as he could muster, "I'm sorry. I'll get him right away. Has this…murder been reported, Ms Jenkins?"

"It has." She responded.

"Please have a seat."

Jean turned her back to the window, looked at the chairs arranged against the wall across from the duty officer, but did not sit. She stood, stiffly, waiting for Detective Redmond to arrive, looking at the unadorned walls above the chairs. Although the wait seemed interminable, only a few minutes passed before Redmond opened the door, went to her, and introduced himself. He led Jean to a small room off the corridor. Inside the carpeted room was a small inexpensive conference table with four chairs. The ceiling light was dim, but it was complimented somewhat by the light coming off the corridor through a small smoke-tinted picture-styled window. Redmond gestured for her to take a seat, which she did, and he sat down in a chair opposite her. He didn't offer condolences to her, but instead waited to hear what she had to say. Jean wasted no time and got right to the point.

"You know why I am here, don't you?" He nodded. "Do you have any leads? Do you have any ideas who may have killed my brother?"

"We just started our investigation, Ms Jenkins. We are still in the process of looking for evidence and doing an autopsy. So in answer to your question we have no leads at this time, but you can be assured that we are doing everything possible to catch this person as quickly as we can." When she did not respond, Redmond added, "I am so sorry for your loss, Ms Jenkins."

"Yeah, sure. Sure you are." She barked at him. And when can I expect some results? Tomorrow? Next week? Next Year?"

Redmond replied patiently, "These things take time. I know you are frustrated, Ms Jenkins and I understand your need to have results as quickly as possible, but we have to examine everything we've found, so that when we apprehend whoever did this, he won't slip through the cracks. We're just starting to look at what we have. We have to build a solid case based on hard evidence. I'm sure you can appreciate that."

"And I can assure you that if I find out who murdered Geoff, you will not have to worry about him going to trial, Detective. That is one thing you can be sure of." She threatened.

"Do you know someone who might have wanted Geoff dead? If you know anyone who might have had a grudge against Geoff, or any kind of disagreement, it would be helpful if you told us." Richmond said, ignoring her threatening remark.

"I don't know anyone who would do this to Geoff. Everyone loved him." She said adjusting her hat, and patting the back of her hair. "Let me ask you something, Detective."

"Sure. Go ahead."

"Do you think I should get a gun?"

"What?"

"I said…"

"I know what you said," Redmond interrupted. "I have to warn you, Ms Jenkins, getting a gun would be the worst thing you can do. There's no reason for you to have one. Carrying a weapon can be very dangerous. And under the circumstances, you wouldn't be eligible to get a license anyway, so don't even think about it."

"What about getting one for my protection. Suppose whoever killed Geoff wants to kill me too. What am I supposed to do?"

"Did someone threaten you?" She turned away and did not respond. Redmond read her silence as a negative.

"There's no indication that you or anyone else is a target, Ms Jenkins. Until we have evidence to the contrary, you have nothing to worry about. We believe that your brother's death might just be an isolated incident. However, if you know something that will lead us to a different conclusion, then tell me now and we'll look into it."

Jean again adjusted her hat, cocked her head, and just stared at him. "If I knew something, I'd certainly tell you, Detective. It would be despicable and disrespectful to Geoff to hold back any knowledge of his…" Jean bowed her head in an attempt to control her emotions.

"Thank you Ms Jenkins, I appreciate that. Is there anything more that you need?"

"Do you know if he experienced any pain before he died, Detective? Was it a quick death?"

"I'm not sure, but we believe that it was very quick, and that he experienced surprise only, but certainly no pain."

Jean shook her head without looking at Redmond.

"I'm sorry that you had to come here, and that I didn't inform you beforehand." She looked at him without saying anything.

"Then if there is anything I can do... if you think of anything that would help us, please contact me," Redmond said, handing her his card. She took the card and looked at him as if to challenge his ability to make good on his promise to apprehend Geoff's killer.

Redmond knew the look having seen it many times before.

"And remember what I said about the gun. Let us do our job. Believe me, we know what we're doing." Redmond got up to help Jean to her feet; she pulled back, refusing his assistance. Redmond led her out of the room and to the front doors without saying another word to her. Jean left uncertain if she had accomplished anything by her visit other than making her presence and feelings known. There was nothing new in the way of information that eased her pain. As she walked down the stairs outside the police station, she drifted in and out of the reality that Geoff was dead, that he was murdered, still unable to come to terms that he was no longer alive. Although the afternoon sun was warm, Jean felt cold and shivered. She started her return walk in a daze. On the way to her house, she considered the possibilities of the killer being caught and the efficacy of Redmond's investigation. She had no faith that the police would accomplish anything, at least, not quickly enough for her. Then she dwelled on where she might obtain a gun.

Chapter 6

Stenson poured over the murder book with the intensity of a Rhodes scholar cramming for a final exam. He was trying to make sense of Redmond's notes, checking continuity and searching for some little detail that might give him a lead as to where to proceed in the investigation. Donna Copp, Detective Martin and Constable Jim Slater had also added notes. They were all entered in chronological order. It was noted that the autopsy was underway and it took priority over all other forensic considerations. Stenson was aware that, under the current circumstances, the autopsy report would be completed by later in the evening or by early morning at the latest. He was meticulous in pursuit of a motive for the murder. At the moment, he was baffled. Whenever he was puzzled by a case, especially in the early stages, he would type up the entire murder book on his desktop computer. Sometimes, by typing it, it gave him a different perspective. He was a superior typist, having completed the elective course in high school; he maintained a typing speed of 80-words per minute. It took less than a half hour for him to finish the job. However this time, there were no answers; he was just as baffled as when he started. He downloaded the finished version from his desktop computer to a two-inch long, 8- gigabyte flash drive, which had a cord lanyard long enough to place around his neck. He hung it around his neck, and then tucked the drive under the open neck of his shirt. He could later upload the entire book to his laptop at home to study it further. At this point, there was no evidence or indication in the book as to why Jenkins was killed. There was no murder weapon found, no footprints in the soft grass of the fairway, or at the water hazard, nothing at all that seemed to belong to the killer, and no witnesses. The only thing found in the vicinity was a white wooden tee with no fingerprints. If it belonged to the victim, it would have had his prints on it. Odd, he thought. No one saw anyone or anything suspicious. How did the perp leave the area? Did he leave? If he…or she didn't leave, then the perp might have been right under our thumb all the time. Hmm. Maybe it was someone who is working at the golf course, a staff member perhaps? Did Jenkins insult or offend someone on the staff? Did he have an altercation with another golfer? If he did, who would have known about it? Stenson thought it might be worth a visit with Karen Kelder, the club manager.

. . . . .

Donna Copp threw a report on Stenson's desk, on top of the murder book. Stenson looked up without flinching. His hand was draped over his pursed lips. Removing his hand from his mouth, he smiled at Donna and picked up the report without reading it. "What do we have here?"
"Preliminary autopsy report, forensics, and canvassing report." She said.
"Why are you giving this to me; why not Rick?" Stenson

asked.

"He wasn't at his desk. I think he's downstairs talking to the victim's sister. From what I understand, she is quite a piece of work."

"Whom have you been talking to?"

"I have my sources." She said and then added. "The clerk on duty."

Stenson stood up. "Well I think Rick should see it first." Contrary to what he said, Stenson opened the report and quickly scanned it, making mental notes.

Redmond came into view, walking towards his desk.

"Speak of the devil and he appears." Stenson lifted his attention from the report.

Redmond ambled over to them. "What's up?"

"You look terrible. What hit you?" Donna asked.

Redmond laughed. "Geoff Jenkins sister, that's what hit me."

"What did she want?" she asked.

"To take matters into her own hands is my guess. It doesn't matter. What do you have? Actually let's go to the meeting room rather then discuss this out here." Donna picked up the report and carried it with her.

Once inside the meeting room, Redmond poured three cups of stale day-old coffee, giving one to each of them before he filled them in on his encounter with Jean Jenkins. Taking a drink of his coffee, Redmond sputtered, "Whoa! This shit is worse than any rotgut I've ever tasted. One of these days they'll give us real coffee."

"Sure." Donna shot back cynically. "They'll go to Java Blend

Coffee on North and pay fifteen dollars a pound for us. Who are you kidding?"

"That ain't gonna ever happen." Stenson said stating the obvious.

"Let's get down to business, guys." Rick said impatiently. "What have you got?"

Donna handed the report to Rick and said. "Looks like the Vic was hammered with a golf club. There are some line indentations on his forehead, just above his eye. Not sure if the lines are complete because his eye was crushed in and some of the lines there were lost. Not positive yet if that's what killed him, but we should know definitely by tomorrow morning. If we can come up with the murder weapon, the lines on the club might conform to the lines on the Vic's forehead. However, it doesn't look like much of anything else there. At least that's a start."

"Okay. What about Jenkin's club?"

"According to forensics, his club was clean."

"What about the golf course? Did the Forensic Unit come up with anything? Rick asked. Donna shrugged and looked to Stenson for help. Stenson spoke up quickly, remembering the info that he got from the report.

"Well it seems as though very little was found in the vicinity; some cigarette butts, beers cans, tons of golf balls, and a few candy wrappers, none of which was considered to be useful, except for a wooden tee found next to the body, no prints." Redmond interrupted, "Is it possible that the tee was left by the perp while he was waiting for the Vic?"

"Anything's possible, but it's not too likely that the perp was waiting by the pond for the Vic in plain sight. It doesn't make sense. And since there were no prints on the tee, it definitely didn't belong to the Vic, or another player that might have accidently dropped it."

"Let's hang on to the thought that it could be a signature." Redmond said.

"I've heard of worse things." Donna said.

Stenson continued. "The dogs found nothing. They covered a 500-yard radius from the murder site. The houses that are on the property were canvassed and no one saw anything that seemed suspicious; saw no one walking, but did see a few cars, all nondescript, coming and going, but nothing unusual that drew their attention."

Donna added, "It is possible that the perp went to the club in his car, killed Jenkins and left right away without anyone seeing him"

"And if he did," Redmond replied, "what does that tell us?"

"Not much. Maybe he's a regular?" He obviously had knowledge of the area. Stenson answered. "One thing did occur to me, though."

"What's that?" Redmond inquired.

"What if the perp never left? What if he is part of the course environment?"

"Hmm. You mean that he is either one of the golfers we saw, or possibly on staff?" Rick asked.

"I think we need to visit the golf club again, and find out the names of everyone who was at the course, staff included."

Donna said.

"I want you and Donna go out to the club first thing in the morning." He told Stenson, who nodded in agreement. Stenson took a drink of coffee without thinking and almost gagged, spitting it out. *God, that's awful." He spurted.

Donna laughed at Stenson. "Time to bring our own coffee."

"I have to talk to um … um … oh yeah, Philip Nickerson." Redmond stammered.

"And he is?" Donna asked.

"Lisa Jenkins friend. He was apparently with her when Geoff was killed. I need to know a bit more about him. I have a feeling he just may have had something to do with it. We'll convene here at 11:00 a.m. tomorrow." Redmond decided. Stenson ripped off a paper towel from the roll on the counter and wiped up the coffee he spit out. "Time to get out of here."

"Lets get a real cup of coffee, shall we?" Donna suggested.

"Sure, why not?" He agreed.

"Shall we meet at the Wired Monk? Or do you want to go someplace else?" She smiled.

"The Wired Monk is fine." Returning her smile. "Meet you there in ten."

Chapter 7

Driver sat down at his computer and after booting up opened the *List* file. He perused the list of the five remaining names, and considered changing the order. He reconsidered and thought, *'why bother?'* The existing order was perfect. He wiped his face with his hands, with emphasis on his tired eyes. Stress was unkind to him, especially stress caused by the displeasure of a task at hand. He wondered how easy it would be to connect him to Geoff and the others on his list. That worried him most. He obviously wanted to prevent that … but how? *Maybe I should unload the club.* He thought. *That's the only evidence even though it can't be linked to me. No, I think I can still make use of that club, no sense in tossing it. Still, what if I created a distraction; something to lead them in another direction? That's the ticket. The question is what, how and where?* Hmm. He smiled at the prospect of what he intended to do next. *Driver* drifted away imagining his new strategy, but was startled momentarily by the roar of a moving van that drove past his house. *I've got to get control of the situation, take action. The only thing worse than losing control is putting control in someone else's hands. In any case, it won't be long; it is only a matter of time before it's all over.* He took a breath, moved the cursor to the top of the list, and typed in a question mark.

. . . . .

Driver laid out a pair of old jeans on his bed; took a worn faded golf shirt from the wardrobe and arranged it on top of the jeans. He searched for a pair of shoes that had smooth soles, ones that would not leave a decipherable print of any kind, one that could be easily traced, and put them with the jeans and shirt, and, oh yes, his golf club. Driver went downstairs to the hall closet where he kept his full set of clubs. The driver was sitting outside and next to the bag. He picked it up, examined the head and stood it up in the corner of the hall near the front door. He took a ball cap from the tree in the hall and hooked it on top of the golf club. He locked the front door as a precaution. Driver would implement his line of attack the first thing tomorrow morning.

Chapter 8

Jean was practically comatose when she arrived home from the police station. She sat almost lifeless before deciding that she would not sit idly by. Giving herself a boot in the ass, she became angry; decided not to bury her head in the sand. She owed it to Geoff. It was time to take action. She began pacing through the living room and hall, her arms flailing and muttering to herself. The pacing gave back an impetus that had previously abandoned her. Jean felt a burning need for a weapon. If she were to take steps to find Geoff's killer, she would definitely have to obtain a gun, just in case. She hastily considered other options; she hated guns; she knew they were deadly. There were other ways to deal with the situation; she could seek a more intelligent approach; one that was weaponless. *A lota good that would do*, she thought. Just as quickly, she dismissed all other options. Yes, a gun, but where, and from whom? Jean knew that she had no knowledge of guns. *I'm not even sure what they are called, guns, pistols, revolvers? What a strange position to be in,* she thought. The most logical place to look for a weapon would be on the Internet. Perhaps there she would find the information she needed. So she sat at the computer, started it up and googled guns, Halifax, Nova Scotia. Among the results that came up were the Army Navy Store on Agricola Street, not good, and Nova Scotia business listings for second hand dealers and another, and the most important one; *Nova Scotia Business Listings for Guns*. Jean clicked on it and scrolled down the list, interested only in those gun shops located in Halifax. She scrolled past the firearms repair shop. It was Freedom Ventures on Kempt road that caught her interest. She clicked on the name, expecting to go to a website, but instead, the link only took her to another listing with the same information, address and phone. Jean called the phone number only to find that the store was closed for two weeks. The recorded voice offered a website address to go to for contact and email information. Jean immediately punched in the address and went to the site, which contained a number of logo links to various weapons. The first one she clicked on, firearms from STI International delivered her to another site that consisted of a catalogue and several specific handguns. Jean clicked on a GP6 logo that took her to a page with specifications for the 9-mm luger. The luger was an ideal lightweight weapon for civilian use. The GP6 weighed only 26 ounces. *How heavy is that* she wondered*? Almost two pounds,* she answered herself. *Is that a good size for a woman?* The GP6 came with two magazines and a magazine release that was user friendly for either left or right hand. Although she had no idea how much guns cost, Jean thought the price of $750 was reasonable. *God! What am I doing?* The description stated that long term durability testing had fired the weapon more than 110,000 times without any change in internal geometry. Jean doubted that that would be a factor. She checked one more pistol, the Rogue. It too was a 9-mm gun that measured six and a half inches in overall length and weighed only 21 oz. *That's a better weight.* It was touted as being the lightest pistol that the company sold. Although the price was almost double the GP6, the Rogue appealed to her the most. It seemed to be more suited to a woman than the GP6 and it came with all the necessary accouterments. Tomorrow she would call and find out what the necessary requirements were to buy a gun.

. . . . .

Donna parked her nine-year old Toyota Tercel in the parking lot behind the Jazz East offices on Hollis Street, just one building up from the Wired Monk café. She had been there once or twice and liked the spot. She walked to the main entrance from the parking lot, looked in to see if Stenson had gotten there yet. She didn't see him; she looked around, checking both sides of the street to see if he was parked nearby. He was not. Donna went in and found the coffee aroma to be irresistible. A young woman, casually dressed, sat at a two-seater table directly across from the counter. A student, she wondered? She was working at her laptop and drinking what looked like a latte. Perhaps she is writing a school paper or making an entry on *Facebook*. She wondered if anyone could tell that she was a police detective. *What does a policewoman look like anyway?* Donna immediately placed an order at the counter for a large Costa Rican coffee and almond biscotti, and retreated to a table in the back where it offered more privacy. The back area held two tables and several well-used easy chairs that you might find in a family room. Behind her on the wall was a painting of a jazz saxophonist. She sat and waited for Stenson to arrive. Her order was brought to the table only a minute prior to Stenson walking through the door. He stopped inside to see where Copp was sitting, saw her and went directly to the table. He sat down across from Donna.

"You brought your work with you, did ya?" She asked, referring to the flash drive dangling on the end of the cord outside his shirt.

"Yeeup. You know me well. Have to prepare for tomorrow."

"And I thought we were done work for the day."

"Shows how little you know." He said smiling. "I've been thinking."

"Not again." She said and laughed.

"The way I figure it the perp did not remain at the golf course. That would be too chancy. If you just killed someone, Donna, and there weren't many people around, and no one saw you, would you risk staying at the scene? I don't think so. I know I wouldn't."

"You got a point, Stenson. It is hard to imagine anyone staying there. If he did, he would have to be one cool son-of-a-bitch."

"True enough. However, we might just learn something new by talking to the manager. I have a feeling that she knows more than she is letting on."

"Are you going to order something, Stenson, or are you going to let me eat alone?" Stenson smiled, motioned to the waitress and when she found her way to the table, he ordered a green tea. "Are you still seeing Burke, Donna?" he said getting personal.

"Well, no...umm sorta, you might say. We haven't seen each other in at least a month."

"Donna, what's happening? I thought you guys were hot and heavy. At least you gave me that impression."

"I don't know. I don't think it's going to work." She said bringing her half closed hand to her mouth and tapping her lips with her fingertips. "I guess the ball is in his court. I called him the last time to get together. I figure if he is interested, it's his turn to contact me."

The waitress arrived with Stenson's tea, and the conversation stopped momentarily. Stenson poured the hot water over the tea bag in his cup.

"What do you think, Stenson? Am I wrong? Should I just go after him?"

"You're the only one that can answer that. If you like each other, does it really matter who initiates the hunt?" He raised his eyebrows and smiled.

"Jesus, when you put it that way, you make it sound like we're a couple of brainless animals just out for a hot fuck."

"Well?" Stenson said laughing. "And, by the way, with that mouth, you're beginning to sound a lot like Redmond."

"You asshole!" She said. Her laughter blended with his, but was hollow. She then added somewhat resigned, "Anyway, I got a feeling that he's seeing someone else."

Chapter 9

The predawn air was cool coming off the ocean, and the daylight on the horizon was barely perceptible. A single car passing the house slid by unnoticed; only its lights, like a bolt of lightning, flashed and dissipated. Driver paid no heed to the fleeting light. He busied himself with the work necessary to continue with his strategy. He wanted to be at the Indian Lake Golf Course before the sun rose. He dressed in the clothes, old golf attire he laid out the night before. He made his bed, brushed his hair and teeth and went downstairs. He looked in the cabinet under the sink and found a box of clear latex gloves that he bought at a medical supply store on Ilsley Avenue. He took a pair, put them on, and said silently, 'they fit like a glove,' at which he laughed out loud like a fool. Driver went to the hall to get his club, stopped and realized that he should also bring a pair of golf gloves, a right and left hand glove. He thought about eating first, but realized he had no time. He opened the front door, carrying the club, looked both ways to make sure no one was on the street. Then Driver looked at the houses across the street to be sure there were no lights on. Only when he was reasonably assured that he could leave the house without being seen he did so. He got into his car, putting the club on the floor of the passenger's side, started the car, turned the lights on, and started out to Indian Lake. Driver drove along Henry Street and once he turned left onto Coburg Road, he knew he was just another early morning driver on the street. Driver took a right on Oxford driving at the 50-km speed limit. He was just one of the few on the road driving to work. Then he headed down Quinpool Road toward the newly constructed Armdale roundabout. It was clear at this time of the morning, and Driver turned onto the Bay Road, gradually picking up speed. He knew that it was almost dawn, and he needed to get to the golf course before light, so as to be unseen. He was only five minutes away now. He turned onto Route 333 and began to exceed the speed limit, knowing that the old highway would not be patrolled at this time of the day. He drove past Exhibition Park and knew he was getting close to his destination. When he arrived at the course turn off, he stopped the car. There was no other traffic. He got out, taking the club and hid it in the bushes. Driver got back into the car and drove along 333 for about two minutes, saw Moosehorn Auto on the left, pulled his car into the unpaved lot and parked it among the other cars. Then, without being seen, walked back to the entrance to the golf course. The trek took about eight minutes. He retrieved his club, walked on the grass along the gravel road leading to the golf course so as to make the least noise possible. Moving cautiously, he paused at each house along the road to make certain there was no outdoor movement from any of the residents. Once past the houses, he approached the club parking lot. He saw no one; there was no activity, but he still stayed close to the right edge of the lot so as to be less conspicuous in case a staff member drove in. In no time, Driver was at the edge of the woods by the second hole. He moved into the woods holding his club at his side drifting out of sight and disappeared in the dark of the trees and heavy brush.

. . . . .

Jean Jenkins awoke at her customary time, which was at the first hint of daylight. She never set an alarm, yet seven days a week she woke and got out of bed without the slightest feeling of sleepiness, regardless as to what time she went to bed. However, her bedtime normally allowed her eight hours of sleep. This morning was no exception. Even though Jean bathed the night before, she took a shower, then dressed, and had breakfast that consisted of a half of a grapefruit, and one slice of toast with butter and marmalade. She also took several vitamins and supplements with a small glass of mango juice. Within an hour after she got up, Jean was on her computer to search for gun ownership requirements. To the left of her desk, on a small shelf was a photograph of her and Geoff, taken thirty years ago on a warm summer day. Jean remembered that on that day the family was on a picnic at Point Pleasant Park. She and Geoff had been throwing a Frisbee around and the game later turned into a wrestling match. As she reminisced, Jean let out a sigh that became a soft whimper. She returned to her undertaking at the computer. Jean googled gun ownership requirements and on the first page of results she saw and clicked on Gun Control laws in Canada. She read down the first page; the Canadian

Firearms Act required one to obtain a possession and acquisition license. In addition, Canadians who own or are buying handguns are required to take and complete the Firearms Safety Course, as well as having a present or past spouse, or common-law partner sign the application. More importantly, handgun ownership is restricted to collectors, target shooters and those who demonstrate a need of a gun to protect their lives. *I suppose I could qualify under the target shooting category*, Jean thought optimistically. As an afterthought, she realized that it would take forever to go through the process, even if she qualified, which was not likely. *I'll have to take another route. Friggin' gun control,* she thought, her eyes welling with tears. Jean dialed Lisa who picked up after the third ring. "Lisa, have you started preparations for Geoff's funeral yet?" Getting right to the point.

"Yes, I have, Jean," she said crying softly. "But I need to wait until his body is released. My mom is helping. Actually, she is doing most of it."

"Do you have a gun, Lisa?" Jean asked without hesitation.

"A gun?"

"Yes, a gun."

"No. No, Jean, I don't. Why do you ask?"

"Did Geoff have one, do you know?" Jean wanted to know, ignoring Lisa's question.

"If he did, I've never seen it. I just can't imagine him having had one."

"Nor can I, Lisa, but I just thought...well, it was a long shot."

63

Why do you want to know, Jean?"

Jean ignored her question again and asked, "Will you let me know if there is anything I can do, Lisa? Please let me know, okay? You know how much Geoff meant to me. We are...we were very close." She said holding back tears.

"I know, Jean. I know."

. . . . .

Rick went to the station earlier than usual. It was quiet; he was the only one there. He found the murder book on his desk where Stenson had left it the night before, and searched through it quickly. He found Philip Nickerson's home phone number, work number and address, and scratched it down in his note pad, then looked at the time. *Should call him now; maybe I'll catch him before he goes to work.* Redmond dialed Nickerson's number. He picked up, and said "Philip here."

"Philip Nickerson?"

"Yes, it is. Who wants to know?"

"Mr. Nickerson, this is Detective Redmond, the Halifax Police."

"What? Are you kidding me? What's this about?"

"Not kidding you at all Mr. Nickerson. I'm calling because someone you know had been killed and I need to talk to you about it." Redmond informed him.

"Oh my god! Who was killed? And how?"

"I have to meet with you, Mr. Nickerson. Is it possible to do that now?"

"What did you say your name was, Detective?

"It's Detective Redmond. And it is important that we talk as soon as possible."

"Well, Detective, I was about to leave for work, but I suppose we can get together now. Where do you want to meet?"

"I would prefer meeting at your place, if that's possible. I can be there in ten minutes."

"That will be fine Detective … a … Redmond. Do you know where I live?"

"Yes. I have your address. You're on Wellington, right?"

That's right Detective. I'll wait for you. I hope it won't take too long."

"I'll see you in about fifteen minutes, Mr. Nickerson. And it shouldn't take too long." He said and hung up. Redmond noticed that Martin had come in while he was on the phone.

"Hey, Dave." He called out to him. "Did you see Donna and Stenson?"

"Yeah. I saw them about a half hour ago. We came in about the same time, but I went back out for a coffee. I think they said something about going out to the golf course to talk to someone there."

"Okay. Thanks. If you see them before I get back, tell them to wait here for me. I need to talk to them both."

"You got it, Rick. Will do. Is there anything you want me to do in the meantime?"

"Yeah, Dave, call Lisa Jenkins and see what you can find out about her husbands friends. We need to know who they are, where they work, what kind of relationship they had with the

Vic."

"Consider it done, Rick." He shouted to Redmond as he left the office.

. . . . .

Donna and Stènson left early for the Indian Lake Golf Course, so as to avoid the early morning rush hour. En route, Donna called ahead to the club manager, Karen Kelder, to tell her that they were on the way to talk to her. After a short mild protest, Karen agreed to meet with them. Stenson pulled the car into the parking spot closest to the entry gate. Two other cars were sitting in the newly expanded lot. A man, who was landscaping the area of ground that was an extension of the gate, stood up and stretched to relieve the stress on his back. The area he was working on looked like a narrow seawall with stones on either side of the rich soil enriched by flowering bushes. "Good morning," he said to the detectives. "Good morning," Donna replied, Stenson nodding. "We're looking for Ms Kelder." Stenson added. "Oh. I'm her husband, Mitch. You don't look like you're going to play a round." He said smiling. "Are you the detectives who wanted to talk to her about Geoff's death?" He directed his question to Stenson.

"Yes, we are, Mr. Kelder." Stenson replied.

Mitch smiled. "That's Mitchell, 'Mitch', Kline. Karen kept her maiden name when we got married."

"Oh, sorry." Stenson said. "I shouldn't have assumed.

"That's okay. It's a common mistake. It happens both ways. Let me take you there. Karen is working the desk in the clubhouse. She's the social one. I'll fill in so you can talk to her." Mitch said, wiping his dirty hands on the back of his pants and as he headed toward the clubhouse.

"Thanks, Mr. Kline." Donna said as they followed him. Both Donna and Stenson recognized Karen from the first time they saw her. She was standing behind he counter busy with the daily setup. "Karen, these are the detectives that wanted to talk to you. I'll take over for you so you can talk in the office."

"Ms Kelder, I'm Detective Stenson, and this is Detective Copp."

"Yes, hi. I remember you," she said and turned to her husband. "No need to cover for me, Mitch. Liz is here. She can handle it. You have your own work to do."

"Good," Mitch said with a sense of relief. "You know that I would much rather be working outside." Grinning. "See ya later." Mitch left to return to his landscaping.

"Liz. "Karen called into the kitchen.

"Yes?" Liz answered as she went to the doorway between the kitchen and the counter reception area. Liz is a pretty girl in her late teens with a plump rosy-cheeked face, her auburn colored hair was pulled back neatly in a ponytail. She wore a white apron and was obviously preparing food for the day. "Can you look after the desk for a bit? I have a short meeting to attend to." She said gesturing towards the detectives. "I won't be long. If you need anything, we'll be in the office."

"Sure thing, Karen." Liz said warmly, undoing her apron and tossing it in the kitchen on a counter. Karen led Donna and Stenson through the kitchen to a small office in which was a desk and two chairs. She closed the door behind them. The desk was neat, with two piles of papers, a laptop computer, an electronic calculator and an accounting book. On a small table next to the desk was a printer-copier. Various forms and other papers were spread out on a shelf. Karen sat on the edge of the desk and offered seats to Donna and Stenson. Donna sat; Stenson did not. "Now, how can I help you?" Karen asked.

"There are a few things we need to know, Ms Kelder." Donna started. "We need the names of everyone on staff, especially those who were working when Mr. Jenkins was killed."

"That's easy." Karen reached behind her and took a sheet of paper from the desk. "This is a list of everyone who works here and the work schedule for the week." She handed the schedule to Donna to peruse. Stenson looked at the schedule over Donna's shoulder. "As you can see, there were only three of us working at the time of Mr. Jenkins murder; Mitch and I, and Buddy. Buddy works full time, does the grooming, and watering of the fairways and greens. He was here, but he doing maintenance on the machines in the shed just below the clubhouse. It was also his job to wipe down the carts before he brought them out. Liz wasn't in yet. She was scheduled to come in at ten. I hope that helps a bit."

"That's very helpful. Now, does the FT and PT after the names refer to full time and part time?"

"Exactly." She replied.

"What about the other employees?" Donna asked. "Is it possible that any of them were here, on a casual basis?"

"I don't understand what you are talking about. What do you mean by a 'casual basis'?"

"What I mean is," Donna explained, "were any of your employees, who were not scheduled to work, here for any reason, possibly hanging around?"

"It's possible, I suppose. Jim is on vacation. He said he was going to see family in Ontario, so obviously he wasn't here. Barb and Nick have classes at Dalhousie just about every day. You'll have to check with them to see if they were at class or not. I certainly didn't see them. Their phone numbers are on the schedule, by the way." She said, pointing to the copy that Donna held.

"Do you know if any of them had any contact with Mr. Jenkins: perhaps a run in or a confrontation of some sort?" Stenson inquired.

"Not to my knowledge. If anyone of them had a disagreement with Mr. Jenkins, I never heard about it. You'll just have to find out from them, I suppose." She said with some irritability.

Donna asked if they could keep the schedule or have a copy of it, and Karen told her to keep it, that she has it on the computer and would print another copy out for herself.

"Thank you so much for your help, Mrs. Kelder. You've been most helpful." Stenson smiled broadly. "Oh, by the way, where was Mr. Kline that morning?"

"Pardon me? Are you telling me that you suspect that Mitch

had something do with the murder? He's the most gentle man I ever met." Karen said defensively.

"No, I don't think he had anything to do with it, but we do have to ask; just to eliminate him as a suspect. Perhaps he saw something that might be helpful." Stenson offered.

"Well, detective, I find that quite offensive. However, Mitch was here in the office, calling gardening centers, Halifax Seed and Atlantic Gardens I think, to have some bushes delivered. You may have seen him planting them when you came in." She said folding her arms tightly.

Donna cut in. "We're sorry if that offended you, Mrs. Kelder. We had to ask. We wouldn't be doing our job if we didn't. Besides, as Stenson said, it is possible that he saw something that could be helpful. Thanks again for your time and trouble." Stenson as an afterthought added, "Do you have any idea who Mr. Jenkins played golf with? Or did he usually golf by himself?"

After giving it some thought, Karen said, "Most of the time Mr. Jenkins played with two or three other men. In fact, the only time I recall seeing the others is when they came with Mr. Jenkins. On the rare occasion Mr. Jenkins played a round by himself, like yesterday."

"Do you know the names of the other men, Mrs. Kelder?" Donna asked.

"Umm, let me see." Thinking. "Mr. Jenkins usually booked the times, but every once in a while a...a Mr. Devion or something like that, booked the times. I don't remember the names of the others."

"Mr. Devion." Donna wrote.

"If you remember or if you have the names down anywhere, please let us know as soon as possible, or if you think of anything else that may be of interest to us, please call. Anything at all, okay?" Stenson requested. "And thanks again, Mrs. Kelder."

"You're welcome; and yes I'll let you know when I find the names of the others. I am sure it's in my accounting somewhere. And I'll call you if I think of anything else." Karen quickly led them out to the front reception counter and then Donna and Stenson left the clubhouse.

. . . . .

At the third hole, Driver sat out of sight in the woods with his club at his side about 150 yards or so from the tee box. Mosquitoes were buzzing around his head as he sat still. The pests were starting to annoy him. He already had several bites on the back of his neck. He hoped for the wind to pick up and blow them away. It never happened. Driver took a small bottle of insect repellant out of his pants pocket, took the golf glove and the latex glove off his right hand, opened the bottle and poured some of the contents into it. He rubbed the repellant liberally on his ears, neck, face, and in his hairline. He repeated the process on his arms up to and under the short sleeves of the shirt. He felt immediate relief. The buzzing continued around his head but did not bother him at all, now that the mosquitoes were no longer landing on the exposed areas of skin. He was growing impatient waiting for the right moment. Several groups of golfers had already played the hole and moved on. He did not want to spend the entire day waiting; he deplored waiting. Waiting was enigmatic and could only set in motion a series of unwelcomed mistakes, he thought. Driver pulled several used golf balls out of his pocket an examined them. Each one was a different brand; all were the most popular commercial ones. Driver heard some lively talking on the fairway. He stood up, knowing he could not be seen, and peered from around a tree to see a group of three women playing the hole. He experienced mixed feelings about the group; too much chatter, too slow a pace. If anyone were playing behind them, they would be, more than likely, very close by. That was not good. In fact, it could be disastrous. Driver sat down again and waited. The women were laughing and noisy. None of them hit the ball any great distance, but when they hit it, it was very accurate, which did not help. Their banter aggravated him and he feared that he would not be successful today. He found that coming back again would be unpleasant and risky. The less time he spent in the woods, the better. He was pleased when the women finished the hole even though he could hear them chatting on the way to the next hole. Driver stood up to see if there was any more traffic. He saw a man and, what he believed to be, a boy at the tee box. The boy teed off first and drove his shot about a hundred yards down the left side of the fairway in the first cut of the rough, which was about seventy yards short of where Driver was waiting. The man followed with his drive and the ball was a high slice going into the woods and landing about ten feet from where Driver was sitting. He was in luck, which didn't say much for the man who hit the ball. They walked after their balls, and Driver heard the man say, "You might as well look for your ball and play through while I go ahead and see if I can find my ball." The boy said he would catch up to him after he took his next shot. Driver took the balls out of his pocket and strategically placed each one either under a log or bush, or in a hole. He then started walking around as though he were searching for his own lost ball. The boy arrived in the area where he hit his ball, but did not find it immediately. The man walked along the right side of the fairway, pulling his cart and bag behind him until he reached the spot where he believed his ball had entered the woods. He took a wedge from the bag, left his clubs in the fairway, and climbed over a small drain ditch, and found a worn path that he followed into the dense wooded area. He began looking for his ball after taking about ten paces into the woods. He kicked at new growth bushes, pushing the small branches aside with his club. He stopped and surveyed the entire are, looking at clear open areas with expectations of spotting his ball. At that point, Driver walked into view and said, "Hi. I think your ball is over here. I didn't see it, but I heard it rustling through the trees and heard the thud of it landing."

"Thanks," the man said, starting in Driver's direction.

"You're not playing this hole are you? I didn't see your golf bag."

Driver said, "No, I hit my ball from the fairway on the other side; a disastrous shot, I must admit." Driver pointed in the direction of where he planted one of the balls. "There's a ball. Is that yours?" The man checked the ball. "Nope. That's not it. I was playing a Top Flite XL, number three. Well, I think I'll just play another ball…the found one." Driver walks over to where he placed the other ball in a hole and said, "Hey, wait a minute, this may be yours." Pointing to the ball. The man bent over to pick the ball up, and Driver, moving in behind him, brought his club back, high over his head and swung down as hard as he could, striking the man square in the temple. Driver felt the skull collapsing under the force of the blow. Blood poured out of the open wound. The man fell to the ground and did not move. After taking a moment to watch the man, Driver reached down to check for a pulse in the man's neck. There was none. It was quick and simple. Driver wiped his bloody club first in the soil and then on the pants of the downed golfer. Then he checked to make sure that no blood spurted on his clothes. He found no specks of blood. Driver was startled by the voice of the boy who had been accompanying the man. He called out. "Dad, did you find your ball? You should have seen my shot. I got it on the green in two; first time ever. This is a great course; glad we came here." Driver did not have time to leave or obscure himself from the boys view. "Oh," The boy said. "Did you see my dad?"

Driver responded quickly. "Gee, son, I think your dad is injured. He may have fallen or something. I saw him lying on the ground and I was going to go for help. He's over there.

I'll show you." Driver lead the boy to the area and the boy ran to his father's body and bent over him to help. "Dad! Dad!" He cried. Driver was behind the boy and without hesitation calmly and deliberately lifted the club and brought it down swiftly and with brute force upon the boy's head. The boy's skull bore the brunt of the blow and he fell listless, his body coming to rest on top of his father's body. Again, Driver brought the club high behind him and level with his shoulders as though he was going to tee off and smashed it hard into the boy's skull, driving it home. He struck the boy several times more to ensure that the he would never awaken to identify him. He then took a white wooden tee out of his pocket and dropped it next to the bodies. When driver left, the boy's body was lying on top of his father's body in a loving embrace. The blood from the dead boy's head wound saturated the man's shirt.

Chapter 10

Redmond pulled into the driveway at Philip Nickerson's house on Wellington Street. There was no other car parked in the driveway. The small two-story modern, nondescript house, painted beige over cedar shingles, blended in easily with the other houses on the block. Rick walked up to the front door that Nickerson had opened and was anxiously waiting for him dressed in a grey pinstripe suit with a three-button jacket. "Detective Redmond." Rick said mounting the steps to the door. "Mr. Nickerson?" " Yes. Come in, Detective, come in." Nickerson said, bringing Redmond inside quickly, harboring a feeling of paranoia about being visited by the police. Nickerson preceded Rick into the living room, sat and offered him a chair. Rick sat in an armchair that was covered in a rich wine-colored fabric. The room was not large but comfortable without feeling confined.

"I don't have a lot of time. I have to get to work."

"I'll be as brief as I can, Mr. Nickerson." He said as he took a note pad from the inside pocket of his sport coat, exposing his gun and holster. He sat. Nickerson shuddered at the sight of the weapon and the violence that it symbolized. "You were friends with Geoff Jenkins, Mr. Nickerson, were you not?" Rick started.

"Yes, yes. Yes, I was. It was horrible what happened to him. Do you have any idea who did it?" He asked, his eyes shined with a glossiness that verged on tears.

"How'd you find out what happened to him?" Redmond wanted to know.

"Lisa, that is, Mrs. Jenkins, Geoff's wife, told me … she phoned me to let me know. It's so horrible, so sad." Nickerson said repeating himself.

"Where were you when Mr. Jenkins was killed?"

"What? You know very well where I was, Detective. I was with Lisa. She told me that she informed you that I was with her." He added quickly. Redmond looked up from his note pad at Nickerson, said nothing, then returned to the pad and jotted down another note.

"I suppose you know that Lisa and I were having an affair." He continued nervously. "I might as well be up front about it."

Without looking up from his notes, Redmond responded casually. "Oh, is that right?"

"Yes, that's right, Detective." He said, sliding his suit jacket and shirtsleeve up to check the time. "I'm sure you were aware of that." Redmond did not respond. "Didn't she tell you?"

"Why do you think I should know that?" Philip looked at Redmond without saying anything. "What time did you get to Mrs. Jenkins' house, and what time did you leave?"

"To answer your first question, I think it was about nine fifteen when I got there and, the second question, I probably left elevenish. I'm not positive that the times are exact … they are approximate, and reasonably accurate."

"Did anyone see you at the house, coming or going ... besides Mrs. Jenkins?"

"No, of course not. We ... that is, I didn't want anyone to see me there."

"And why is that, Mr. Nickerson?" Redmond inquired, knowing the answer.

"Jesus Christ! That's obvious, isn't it?" Nickerson snarled.

"Perhaps." Rick calmly replied. "But why don't you just tell me anyway."

"I told you we were having an affair, Detective, that's why. Geoff didn't know about it. He probably would have killed me if he knew. And besides, if anyone saw me at the house and told Geoff, he might have put two and two together." Redmond just looked at Nickerson and patiently waited for him to continue. He learned early on to be silent sometimes, to let the suspect wait, and when he felt uncomfortable enough, he would start talking again, and you never know what might come out of his mouth. "I ... I ... was supposed to join him at Indian Lake for a round of golf. I called him to cancel as soon as I found out he booked us in ... so I could see Lisa." Nickerson dropped his head into his hands, his elbows resting on his knees. "Oh man, if I were with him, this would never have happened." Redmond watched Philip's reaction wondering if he was faking. "So you feel bad that Geoff was killed, that you might be at fault, for not being with him?"

"Of course I do. What do you think? He was my friend."

"Really? Redmond feigned surprise. "Do you have affairs with all your friends' wives, Mr. Nickerson? What kind of friend is that?"

"No, not at all. You don't understand."

"Then fill me in so I will understand."

"I love Lisa. It's not just a simple affair." He divulged.

"So it was a complex affair, was it?"

"You make it sound trivial."

"Does she love you? Was she going to leave Geoff for you?"

"I think she loves me. Maybe. I don't know. No, she would not leave Geoff."

"Then she wouldn't want Geoff to know about you?" Redmond persisted.

"Oh no, she didn't want that. She definitely did not want Geoff to find out."

"I suppose that would be a good reason to get him out of the way. Did you kill him, Nickerson? I suppose it would be handy to get rid of him so you could have Lisa to yourself, especially since she wouldn't leave him ... and I wonder," Rick pushed, "would she lie for you?"

"No, I would never do that, never kill another human being. I couldn't do that. I was with Lisa ... I was with Lisa when Geoff was killed. You don't really think I could do that, do you?" Philip said, tormented.

"On the contrary. I think you could. I think any man is capable of murder, given the right motive..."

Redmond's cell phone rang interrupting the interview.

"Excuse me." He said to Nickerson. "Detective Redmond here." He said into the phone and listened quietly. "Oh? Oh boy, here we go. Okay. I'll leave right away. I was just about to wrap things up here." He closed his flip phone and put it into his outside jacket pocket.

"Are we through here?" Nickerson asked.

"We are for now. If you killed your friend, Nickerson, I'm going to get you for it. You'll slip up and I'll get you. I hope you're not planning on taking a vacation or leaving Halifax in the near future, Nickerson? I wouldn't, if I were you, "

. . . . .

Redmond turned on the flashing red and blue light that was mounted just inside the grill and used the siren as he sped through the city on route to the Indian Lake Golf Course. He donned his dark glasses to ward off the glare of the mid-morning sun, which, although it was high in the sky, was strong enough to inhibit his vision. When he arrived, the front entrance gate to the clubhouse had been cordoned off. Several would be golfers milled about somberly in the parking lot. An ambulance, an Identification Unit van and several blue and whites were parked haphazardly in the lot. A few of the grounds staff was standing in front of the clubhouse, tense and talked quietly among themselves. The policemen recognized Redmond and allowed him to pass through the gate without having to flash his badge. Inside the clubhouse, Mitch Kline was consoling Karen Kelder, his wife, who was sitting on a stool behind the reception counter. The color had been drained entirely from her face causing her to look deathly. Liz stood near the door to the kitchen, leaning against the frame.

She was biting her fingernails and looked devastated.

"Are Copp and Stenson here?" Redmond asked, directing his question to Karen Kelder.

"And you are...?" Mitch asked.

"I am Detective Redmond, sir, Chief of Operations." He replied flashing his badge. "And who might you be?

"I'm Mitch Kline. I own the club. Karen is my wife. She is very upset, as you can see. The Detectives are talking to witnesses in the other room, the dining area." He said, pointing to the doorway.

"Thanks." Redmond started toward the dining area and stopped. "Are you okay, Mrs. Kelder?" he asked.

Karen nodded, and Mitch said, "I think she'll be okay; I hope so. I can't believe it, twice in as many days."

Redmond walked into the small dining area to look for Copp and Stenson, and found them immediately talking to four men. Detective Martin and Officer Slater were with a group of about 30 people who had been at various holes on the course. Redmond addressed the four men. "Are you the party that found the bodies?" The men nodded somberly; one man looked like he had been or was going to be sick. He, the ill-looking man, spoke up. "I hit my ball into the woods and went in to find it when I ran across the two bodies. God! It was awful. I never saw anything like it in my life. The poor boy was just lying on top of the man; pools of blood around the bodies." The man was getting greener as he spoke.

"Excuse me," he said, covering his mouth and running to the washroom.

81

"Do we know who they are?" Redmond asked turning to Stenson, whose face was grave and his normal smile absent.

"Yes, we do. He and his son are…" he corrected himself, "*were* from New Brunswick. They were visiting his brother in Clayton Park. The man's name is John Harris. He had played here a few times before with his brother. This is the first time he brought his son with him… unfortunately. This was brutal, Rick. Absolutely brutal."

"And the bodies?" Rick asked taking Stenson and Donna aside.

"They are still out there, in the woods at the third hole." He said solemnly. "The FIS Unit and dogs are there; they're all out there; as well as the paramedics…to no avail. If there is anything to be found at the site, Rick, we'll find it."

"Is it too early, or can you tell if there is a connection between Jenkins and these two?"

Donna reluctantly added. "It is too early to tell, but there are some similarities. It looks like both the boy and his father were struck in the head by a blunt instrument. It could be a golf club, but we don't know for sure, and we won't know until the autopsy is completed. It sure seems like one helluva coincidence though. Oh yes, we found a white wooden tee next to the bodies, nothing unusual about it, one of a million. It looks to be similar to the one we found with Jenkins body."

"Do we have the names and phone numbers of everyone here, staff included?"

"Yes, we do. The group with Martin and Slater all claim they saw nothing. None of them had gone into the woods at the third hole, and saw nothing unusual. These four guys were in one of the last groups out. The foursome after that… well they never got to the second hole. Everyone was called in off the course."

"Do we have any idea when they were murdered?"

"There was about an hour time difference between the starting times of the victims and the group that found them. So we figure they were killed sometime between 45 minutes to an hour prior to the time that the party that found them left, making it in the vicinity of 10:30 a.m. or thereabouts." Stenson calculated.

While they spoke inside, another ambulance pulled up to the clubhouse lot. The attendants went inside to tend to Karen Kelder who had collapsed. Kline went to ask Redmond if it was okay for him to go to the hospital with his wife. Redmond, concerned about her health, told Kline that he could go to the hospital with her.

"Let's check the list of those here today with the one when Jenkins was murdered. And make sure you include the staff. I want to know if any of the golfers were here during both murders, and I want to know where all of these people were at the time of the death of the man and his son."

"I can take care of that, Rick." Stenson said. Redmond turned to Copp. "Donna, I want you to look into Jenkins' an Harris' background; see if you can find anything that may link them together. I want to find out if they knew each other, and if so, how. Did they have any business together? Find out what you can. I can't imagine both murders just being a coincidence."

Redmond called to Martin who had remained with the large group who had witnessed nothing. "Dave?" Martin walked over to Redmond. "Yeah?"

"I need you to canvass the same houses we did when Jenkins was killed, and then after you submit your report, I want you to check to see how Mrs. Kelder is. She was taken to the QEII a few minutes ago. And if she is going to be in the hospital for any length of time, see that she gets some flowers from the department. Also, tell Slater to close the club down for the rest of the week. I want every inch of this place covered. I want to know how the perp got in and out. We have got to come up with something. If we have a mad man on the loose, I want to find him before he kills someone else."

"Okay, Rick. I'll take care of it." He said walking back to join Slater who continued talking to the group. Redmond turned his attention back to Donna and Stenson. "We'll meet tomorrow morning at eight sharp. Make sure everyone is there. I hope and pray we don't have a serial killer on our hands. Now let's get to work."

. . . . .

Earlier Driver had walked back to his car, which was parked in front of Moosehorn Auto. The lot was filled, as often was the case, with cars that had been repaired or were in need of maintenance. Although, the shop was open, no one was outside, so Driver felt safe. Even if he had been seen, he most likely would not be connected to what took place at Indian

Lake. Especially since there were several other auto-related businesses side by side in the industrial strip mall. He could easily have been doing business with any one of them. Driver was pleased that he decided to hide his club in the woods and not carry it with him in the light; that would have been too conspicuous. He could not afford to be seen walking out of the woods with a single golf club. He drove back to his house staying within the speed limit. Now would not be the time to be stopped for speeding. On route, Driver thought about the boy that he killed. He wished that the boy did not come into the woods after his father. He didn't want to kill him, but still he felt no remorse. It was necessary. He saw me, knew what I looked like. He would have been far more unpleasant if the boy saw him, lived and later identified him as being in the immediate vicinity when his father was murdered. No, it had to be done, he reasoned. It had to be; I had no choice.

Driver pulled into the driveway, got out of the car and nonchalantly looked around before entering the house. He had taken off his golf gloves and carried them in his still latex-gloved hands. His head was buzzing, yet his mind was clear in spite of the circumstances. His astuteness was contradictory with the drone inside his head, yet a clear bright light seemed to prevail almost pushing him into a meditative state. He was acutely aware of everything around him, especially the condition of his clothes. He knew that the bottom of his pants were damp from the moisture on the weeds and bushes in the woods; he knew his shoes were muddy, he also knew that his pants and shirt were blood free, unlike one glove that was stained with he blood of the man, which was tainted when he checked to see if he was dead. Driver felt insuperable. Once inside Driver locked the door before he kicked off his shoes, leaving them in the hallway entry. Then he went down the stairs to the basement. Driver lifted the top of the washer, stripped naked, and put all of his clothes inside including his leather golf gloves. He added detergent, set the settings to hot, closed the lid and started the machine. Driver left the basement still naked, took off his latex gloves and put them in a small plastic bag that he tied and deposited in the large garbage bag. He picked up his shoes and took them into the kitchen where he found a stiff bristled bottlebrush underneath the sink. He held the brush under the hot water, added dish soap to it and slowly, but forcefully brushed his shoes; the soles, the tops, and in all of the crevices where there was stitching. Satisfied that no residue from the woods and the golf course remained, Driver rinsed the shoes and dried them with a dishtowel. He put his shoes at the bottom of the second floor stairs. Then he took the dishtowel to the basement and deposited it into the washer with the other clothes. There he remained, thinking, wondering if he overlooked anything. After a short period of time, Driver went upstairs to his bedroom, taking the shoes with him and putting them in the bottom of the closet where he kept all of his shoes. He calmly walked into the bathroom to take a shower. Upon completing his shower, Driver went back to the bedroom to dress. He put on a pair of jeans, a clean, short-sleeved polo shirt that he took from his dresser, and pulled on a pair of socks that he took out of the top drawer. He put on a pair of black soft-soled walking shoes and then went downstairs. He inspected the floor of the entryway to make certain it was free of any droppings from his shoes. It was. To conclude his plan, Driver went into his office, booted his computer, and brought up the *list* file. He looked at the last entry at the top of the page, the question mark. After it, he typed in *who?* and then hit the space bar and typed *two done*. He was about to close the file and shut down when he decided to highlight the entire line, which he did and clicked on delete.

Now only the names on the list remained. He closed the file. I hope I did the right thing, killing them both, he thought, without concern for the act, but more so for the possibility of avoiding detection, and perhaps of eliminating him from being directly linked to the murders. Remorse was never an issue. It was always about not getting caught.

He recalled the time in his childhood when he approached a boy who was going to church on the street. Driver was angry. He couldn't remember why, but he knew he was in a rage. As he was passing the boy, he struck him in the stomach with as much power as he could muster. The boy doubled over and fell to the sidewalk. The boy was crying and trembling on the ground. Driver had picked up a rock, bent over the boy, and said you had better not tell anyone about this and hit the boy in the head with the rock. The boy was laid up in the hospital for a week with a ruptured spleen and a concussion, but he never told anyone what happened or who attacked him. Driver never felt remorse. He remembered that it was all about not getting caught.

Driver, without closing down the computer, dialed his office and told his receptionist with an air of superiority that he had finished his meeting and would continue working from home for the rest of the day.

Chapter 11

Jean skimmed through her email addresses, hoping to find someone who might have or help her to obtain a handgun. She had decided against trying to acquire a permit and then purchasing a weapon. Submitting an application might only alert the authorities as to her intentions. Most of her friends were intellectual, concerned about the environment and pro gun control. She did not anticipate finding a likely candidate in the group of people who she held dear and with whom she had a great deal in common and who were her loyal friends, some of whom were members of Mensa. Jean sat high on a cushioned chair in front of the computer, pulled her hat down hard above her eyes in frustration. She thought less now about Geoff being dead, than she did about the person who killed him. She harbored hatred for the perpetrator, as the police called him, who killed Geoff and sought to avenge his death. When Jean made up her mind to undertake an issue, she would continue incessantly until she accomplished it. In this case, she would not rest until she attained retribution. Vengeance was all that she thought about from the onset. Her only inclination was to settle the score. Jean decided to send an email to everyone in her address book. It may cause her flack, she thought, but figured that if maybe only one person had a contact with someone who knew where she could find a gun, it would be worth it. What did she have to lose? She couldn't

lose more than she already had. If she did nothing, she knew
she would have to face her demons.

Jean sent the following email to everyone in her address book:

> *Dear friend,*
>
> *I need a handgun. Yes, a real one.*
> *A small, light one that is in good*
> *working order would be acceptable.*
> *Please don't ask any questions. If*
> *you have a gun and are willing to*
> *temporarily surrender it to me, no*
> *questions asked, let me know. If my*
> *request offends you, you will not*
> *offend me by not replying. If you do*
> *not have a gun, but know of a person*
> *who might, please pass the name of*
> *that person to me. Or, if the owner*
> *of a gun wishes to remain*
> *anonymous, give them my name and*
> *email address or phone number so*
> *they can contact me. I will return*
> *the gun sometime in the near future.*
> *I will use the gun for target practice*
> *and then hang on to it for a while.*
> *Rest assured that I don't plan on*
> *doing anything criminal or stupid*
> *like taking my own life. I am totally*
> *indebted to you as always.*
> *Yours in friendship,*

Jean

Jean waited until she received *message sent* and signed off from the email provider. She waited, looking at the email icon, expecting to have an immediate reply as ridiculous as it seemed. She sat in her chair on the cushion waiting for a half hour without moving, without taking her eyes off the notification icon and listening for the sound that alerted her to a new message in her inbox. She sat motionless, like a cat in hunt of its prey, waiting with a quiet intensity. A response did not come.

Her immobility proved fertile ground for memories of Geoff. The way he would smile so charmingly when she expressed her opinion about whatever they were discussing, whether it was literature, sports, which was seldom, politics, either provincial or federal, which was often, and even how long it would take for the Halifax harbor to be clean of the sewage that had been deposited there since the city was founded even with the three treatment plants that were now in operation. Geoff made Jean feel like a complete human being both emotionally and intellectually; for that alone, she would retain a perpetual memory and love for her brother. In her reverie, she could not help but wonder if she expressed her love for Geoff. Jean was a firm believer in telling someone how she felt about him or her each time she was in their presence, in the event that she never saw them again. It was her way of saying goodbye, never allowing her feelings for that person to go unspoken. At that moment, Jean was reconsidering her action to acquire a handgun, wondering if it was the right thing to do, an eye for an eye, in which case the entire world might go blind, when the message alert sounded. She calmly opened her email account and saw a message that said only, *Sorry, I cannot help you. I'm not sure it's appropriate to say it, but ... good luck.* It was signed, Ellen.

. . . . .

Redmond and Stenson hooked up outside of Stayner's, a popular jazz mainstay. They met for a drink and a break from the case. Redmond was overdressed in his grey suit and white shirt, but was tieless; while Stenson wore jeans and a casual purple cord jacket over a blue turtle neck shirt. Some nights Stayner's was so packed that it was difficult to get in. This night was no exception with Doris Mason, who hails from New Glasgow, performing at the piano and doing the vocals. However, with Stenson being a loyal supporter and member of Jazz East, and a permanent fixture at Stayner's since the no-smoking by-law went into effect, he was always allowed in, no matter how crowded. Doris Mason was hot, as usual, as was the crowd. Stenson and Redmond found a spot at the bar and squeezed in. The bar was noisy but Mason's voice and piano could be heard over the din. Stenson decided on Stayner's because it *was* noisy and consequently would be difficult to discuss the case with Redmond. Stenson waved to the bartender to let him know they were dry. When he finally moved up the bar to them, Redmond ordered double bourbon on the rocks and Stenson, who did not drink often or much, ordered a gin and tonic. Still, it was difficult for them to not think about the latest murders, Harris and his son. "What do you think about the two today, Rick?" Stenson asked reluctantly, close to Redmond's ear.

"There has got to be a connection. It's the same MO. There is no doubt that the same person committed both crimes."

"But why?" Stenson wanted to know. "It's senseless killing a young boy. He was only 14 years old. There is no way that he can be connected."

"The fucking perp has got to be crazy." Redmond steamed, hardly concealing his anger.

The bartender brought the drinks, and Stenson put a twenty-dollar bill on the bar.

"Well, we'll find out how they died first thing tomorrow, no doubt. The autopsies are being done as we speak."

"Yes," Redmond added, "I made it a priority."

"The chief's on our ass about it. He wants the bastard caught before we even know who he is." Stenson complained.

"You know, I kinda like Nickerson for it… at least for the time being."

"Why him, Rick? Wasn't he with Jenkins' wife when her husband got it?"

"Yeah, so he says; so she says. But they were having an affair and Jenkins didn't know about it, and my hit is that they wanted to keep it that way."

"That gives them motive, I guess, but weren't you with Nickerson when the other two were killed, assuming the same person killed all three?" Stenson pursued.

"True enough. I was with him, but that doesn't prove anything. Jenkins' wife may have been in on it too. If she was, that gives her opportunity to do the other Vics."

"That doesn't make sense to me, Rick. Why kill Harris, if she and Nickerson want to get rid of her husband?"

"That's a question we still have to answer... if they're good for it."

"Another thing that bothers me is why did the perp leave a tee? What the hell is he trying to tell us?"

"I don't have the answer to that either, Stenson."

"Yeah. Well, it is a bit of a conundrum."

The live music stopped and was replaced by recorded jazz as Doris Mason finished the set. A louder drone permeated the room as the previously quiet patrons started to jabber.

"I'm not sold on Nickerson... yet. And I can't see Lisa Jenkins killing anyone, especially a 14-year old boy." Stenson said, finishing his drink.

"You're entitled to your opinion, Stenson. Ready to go?" Rick asked. "If I stay any longer, I can kiss tomorrow's eight o'clock meeting goodbye." He drank the last of his bourbon, sucking the small remainder of ice into his mouth to suck on. Stenson picked up his change, leaving a tip behind, and they left the bar with the recorded sound of Oscar Peterson trio elapsing softly into the night.

Chapter 12

Donna Copp had an unrelenting ache in her head and was consumed by depression. She could not shake the image of the bloody dead boy on top of his father's body. It was senseless and cruel killing she thought and she was totally devastated by the flagitious act upon a helpless child. There was no doubt that the man was killed first... unless the bodies had been moved and posed. But that was unlikely. She wondered how the mother must feel, losing two men in her life, a husband and a son. What a horrific feeling it must be. She never wanted to be in that position. Perhaps a good reason to never have children she thought. What could motivate a person to kill a child anyway? Evidently, there would have to be a tremendous amount of rage. On the other hand, she thought, a person might have to be entirely void of any emotion whatsoever. This was the time when Donna began to question her career choice. There were so many other choices she could have made that would have prohibited exposure to the tragedy that she faced earlier in the day. Tonight Donna could not watch television or listen to music as she might have done on other nights so as to erase the day's activities from her head. Instead, she ate a light meal, a vegetable salad with French dressing. She tried thinking about her ex boy friend, with whom she shared an apartment for almost two years and was separated from about four months ago. Thoughts of him made her even more disheartened and would not chase the impression left by the sight of the bodies in the woods at the golf course. Donna fixed a drink. She was a Scotch aficionado. A taste she acquired during her days at the university. She half filled a glass with a 30-year aged Old Malt Cask single malt whiskey distilled at Clynelish distillery given to her on her 30th birthday. The fact that the scotch was a gift from her ex-boyfriend did not deter her enjoyment of it. She sipped the drink that she had poured over two ice cubes and thought about Stenson as she felt the whiskey warm her throat. She was interested in him; she liked his looks and his personality. More importantly, his positive attitude appealed to her. Nothing seemed to bother him. If the work did bother him, he never let on. She wondered about that, whether he hid his feelings, kept them to himself, and did not let other people in. If that were the case, it would perhaps be problematic in a relationship, if not now, then perhaps in the future. It could easily lead to explosive behavior. However, Stenson did not exude that impression. Perhaps it was a good thing to leave his work at the station. Donna took out her notepad, ran a hot bath, and looked over the notes she took earlier at the murder site as she soaked. She read and re-read her notes, changing nothing, and sipped her drink. She left the tub, looked at her naked body as she dried herself off, and thought how average it was. Then went to bed, her head no longer aching, but it was now reduced to a dull almost imperceptible throbbing, she hoped that sleep would come quickly and effortlessly.

Chapter 13

The office was humming with activity at 6:30 a.m.
Chief Barnes had called Detective Redmond into his office to
be prepped before holding a press conference. Rick brought
the murder books with him, which now included all the notes
taken by all of the officers, identification units at both sites
and the forensic reports. Redmond briefed the chief on all of
the details, including that they suspected that the same person
had most likely committed the three murders. The theory was
backed by the fact that the same weapon might have been used
on the three victims, even though the forensics was not yet
conclusive. "There is only one suspect, possibly two if we
consider the murders a conspiracy, but again there is no
definitive evidence supporting that theory." Redmond
reported.

The Chief sat back in his high-back leather chair, crossed his
arms, and told Redmond from across the large oak desk the
importance of wrapping up the murders quickly. "Did you see
this morning's headlines?" Barnes did not wait for a reply.
"It read, *Mad golfer strikes again.* The press is on my tail for
details and they're looking to call the murders serial killings.
The national press is already getting interested. We don't
need that kind of notoriety." He emphasized. "I don't need to

tell you the importance of this case. I'm under the gun, Redmond. I have already heard from several community groups looking for protection. Everybody seems to be on the edge and frightened that a mad man might possibly attack them. Both the mayor and the premier are on my ass. Soon the entire city will be on my ass. And if we don't solve these murders quickly, everybody in the country will want my ass." He said exasperated. "Don't we have anybody who looks good for it, Detective?"

"Well, Chief, as I said, we have one or two possible suspects, but, more importantly, we are trying to tie the murders to one weapon. We believe that all three people were murdered with a golf club and most likely by the same person. In the Jenkins' case, we can identify the club if we find it. The type of club used to kill Harris and his son has not been identified yet. Forensics are doing their best to take marks off the Vics head and we hope we will be able to match up the marks and put them with the same club that was used to kill Jenkins. We also found a wooden tee at both murder sights, neither of which had prints on them, which indicates that they do not belong to the victims. We don't know what the tees have to do with the murders, but we are looking at them as the perp's signature." Redmond said in an attempt to clarify his position.

"Jesus Christ, Redmond, get on it! I want answers, not supposition. The media is out there expecting me to give them answers. They would just love to publish that a serial killer is on the loose. That would scare the shit out of everyone in the province." He shouted at Redmond, flustered and frustrated.

"I can't give you any answers yet, Chief. We need more to go on and more time. The case is only a couple of days old." Rick said, trying to appease Chief Barnes. "We have most of the department and the RCMP team working on both cases."

"Good. Well, I'll have to give the press something. Yes, okay, we have a good idea about the weapon in the first killing, and we're looking to tie that weapon to the other murders. Can I tell them it was a golf club? And what about the tee?"

"Yes, Chief, you can tell them about the club. That would be a good idea. No doubt, they'll want to know what kind of weapon was used. I would hold off on the tee. We may need that information later."

"Okay, that's a start. I'll also let them know that we're looking at one or two people of interest in the case, and are considering others, but no one has been arrested yet. I will make it vague enough so that they won't have anything to grab onto and push me for more details." Barnes paused to catch his breath and stood up "That's good Detective Redmond. Your team is doing okay. Just keep it up; keep moving forward. No one can complain if we keep making headway."

"Thank you, Chief. I hope the information will help you."

"I'm sure it will, detective, we'll make it work." Barnes said, coming from around his desk, patting Redmond's shoulder. "Now get going, so I can think this through and put it on paper." Barnes went back behind his desk and sat down as Redmond left the office, closing the door behind him. Chief Barnes picked up a Mont Blanc pen and wrote *the investigation of the horrendous murders of three innocent people is well underway. Our heartfelt condolences go out to the families. We have a full team working hard around the clock. The murder weapon has been identified but we cannot release that information at this time for obvious reasons. I realize that you all have questions for me, but I can only tell you that when we have more information we will be happy to share it with you. Thank you for you cooperation and understanding. God willing we will have the perpetrator in custody in the very near future. No questions please.* Chief Barnes wrote a few more words, then got up, and put the paper in his pocket.

Chapter 14

On a board in the meeting room, Redmond had photos of Geoff Jenkins, Harris and his son. Below the photos, was an aerial view map of the golf course, with a red mark to indicate where the bodies were found. Next to the map, the names of Philip Nickerson, Lisa Jenkins, and Mitch Kline were listed. Stenson came into the room bringing half dozen coffees from Tim's. Stenson's hair was awry and he looked a bit disheveled from the wind that picked up coming in from the East. The others, Detectives Donna Copp, Dave Martin and several of the officers who were at the murder sites, including Jim Slater, wandered in after Stenson. Each of the officers took a coffee and prepared it with either sugar or milk, or both before grabbing a chair. Oddly enough, all of the detectives took their coffees black. Once everyone was settled down, Redmond started the meeting off. "The Chief is very pissed off. Not so much about our work, he thinks we're doing a good job, but he's pissed more about the pressure from outside. Everybody is on his ass, and he's on mine. And you know what that means?"

"Yeah." Donna piped up. "You're going to be on our ass." She said turning to look at the others and laughing.

"That's right, and if I clamp down on you, it won't be very happy. We are going to be putting in a lot more hours. Starting today, we'll be working a minimum of 12 hours a day… or until we drop… and that may only be half of it. So let's see what we've got. The autopsy reports are in and all the Vics were killed with what looks like a metal golf club. Forensics said that they found similar titanium particles on all of the Vics, and they believe it came from the same weapon, although that still needs to be confirmed. So, it looks like we are looking for a titanium golf club with a series of lines on the face of it. If we find the club, there is not doubt that we can match it with the metal left on the victims' skulls and the line marks on two of the victims. In each case, the skulls were crushed in and each victim died within minutes. The victims were struck once each, with the exception of the boy, who was pummeled several times in the side and back of the head. For the most part, we have ruled out robbery in both murders since nothing was missing. We found money, jewelry and wallets on the bodies of each Vic except for the boy. He didn't have a wallet on him. The uncle and the boy's mother confirmed that the boy wasn't carrying a wallet. Although it is pure conjecture at this time, we think that the boy's death was unintentional in that he came upon his father who was in all likelihood already dead or in the process of being murdered. And if he spotted and could identify the perp, then that may have been cause enough for the boy being killed. The autopsy puts both deaths too close to say which one died first, but since the boy's body was lying on top of his father's body, it seems clear who died first. Although it is not conclusive, we believe that the same person murdered all three victims. The reason we believe that is simple; the Vics were all killed in the same place, and it looks like they were killed the same way, the same MO. At each site, we found a wooden tee with no prints. We believe the perp left the tee, a signature perhaps. Now why the fuck he'd want to do that is beyond me. So far, we're unable to place any significance on it. Okay? Okay. Donna, what do you have?"

Donna Copp sipped her coffee, remained sitting and then said, "I've checked both Harris and Jenkins looking for some kinda connection. So far, I've had no luck. Matt Harris grew up and lived in Fredericton, New Brunswick, with his wife and only child." Donna paused to gain control of her emotions at the mention of the *only child*, and when she did she continued. "He was 54 years old, and worked at St Thomas University, a small liberal arts school. His brother William lives in Halifax and works with the Power Corporation. I could make no connection with Harris and Jenkins whatsoever. Neither of them bank at the same institution, attend the same church; one is Protestant, the other is Catholic. They aren't members of the same organizations or clubs. Other than his brother, Matt has no friends in Halifax, and no work connections, even with any of the universities here. Jenkins similarly has no friends or relatives anywhere in New Brunswick, and his consultation work, as far as we can tell, has been confined to this area. He, Jenkins, also has not done any work for any of the universities. It's frustrating." Donna stopped. "I thought for sure my research would turn up something. There doesn't seem to be a plausible explanation for the murders to be connected, and I find them too coincidental to be random. I still have to check

Jenkins' computer and go through his files, to look for a link there. The Fredericton police said they would do the same there both at Harris' home and office at the university. That's all I have... for now." Copp laid her notes in her lap and took another drink of coffee.

Slater stood up and without notes stated, "Detective Martin asked me to close the Indian Lake Golf Course down for a few days. I spoke with Mitch Kline, the owner and he said he would comply with our order. We cordoned off the gate entrance with police tape, and posted a notice just in case someone did not get the message. We also have a uniformed officer there 24 hours a day. The publicity they were getting has just about killed any possibility of anyone golfing there for the next little while anyway. At least until we catch this guy. I spoke with all the people who were playing a round at the course when Harris was murdered. None in the group knew anything about what happened; most were quite surprised and shocked that a murder had occurred while they were there. No one saw anyone on the course except for other golfers that were playing the course. No one spotted anything out of the ordinary either, not one of them saw a single suspicious looking person anywhere on the course. I believe that none from the group I interviewed had any knowledge of what took place or had anything to do with the incident. However, just in case, I have the list of names and phone numbers for future reference. Oh yes, one other thing. Out of all those that I spoke with, not one of them knew any of the victims." Slater sat down erect in his chair, satisfied with his succinct report.

"Dave, do you have anything to add to that? You were working with the same group as Slater was."

Detective Martin turned to Slater. "Nope, Not a thing. That was about all the information we got from the group, and I concur with Jimmy that none of the group had anything to do with the murders. I had about the same luck with canvassing the houses on the course grounds. There are about eight houses along the road in to the clubhouse. We checked each house and no one saw a thing. They, of course, heard traffic coming and going, which was normal, but nothing that they paid any attention to. So once again, we hit a dead end there. However, it did occur to me that if someone in one of those houses had a hassle with the course owners... a little conflict of some sort... I know it's only an outside chance, but if they had a grudge with Kline, and sought revenge... of course, nothing like that came across from any of the people that I spoke with." He stopped for a moment, and then said as an afterthought. "It's just a thought, pure speculation, but it may be worth considering. The murders would reduce traffic, cut back on use of the course, and hurt Kline and his wife financially. By the way, I checked on Karen Kelder at the hospital. She's all right. She had a stress attack and was going to be released this morning. So, no flowers for the lady." He smiled.

Stenson took the floor. "Speaking of Karen Kelder, when Donna and I interviewed her, we found her to be in control of herself, and somewhat stress free. The only time she seemed stressed was when we ask her the whereabouts of her husband.

And then she wasn't stressed as much as she was defensive. In fact, I thought she protested too much." He said looking to Donna who shrugged. "But that's just me. I can't help but wonder if her husband, Mitch Kline, had something to do with this. However, when you think about it, who in his right mind would destroy his business by killing people on his own property? It doesn't make much sense does it? Aside from him, the entire staff was accounted for during the time of the murder, so I think we can count them out, at least for the time being. One of the foursome that found Harris was in the woods for less than five minutes when he discovered the bodies. A minute or so after he went in the woods he was joined by another member of the group. It was actually the two of them that found the bodies. We know that the time of death was at least a half hour before that, so we can completely disregard that group. Also, they were quite upset, to say the least. All four were shaking like a leaf. It didn't seem like they were faking it." Stenson stopped talking for a moment to check his notes and then continued. "Oh yes, I checked with the dog team and it seems that the dogs picked up a scent in the woods that headed back in the direction of the tee box, a few yards from the murder site. The report stated that the dogs were focused around one area, perhaps the spot where the perp was waiting, but we don't know that for sure. We can't be totally sure about that because nothing was found in the area, no cigarettes, papers, cans, tracks, nothing. So far, it turned out to be somewhat of a dead end. According to the dog team, about a hundred yards away, closer to the tee box, the dogs started circling around and seemed confused, like maybe the perp stopped and waited there or something. That is where the dogs lost track of the scent. Nothing was found there, but I would sure like to take another look at that spot. Perhaps, Slater and Donna could go with me to see if we could come up with something." Looking at his notes, he concluded. "That's it for me, Rick."

Rick turned to the board, and added *wooded area – dogs,* then said with his back to the others. "Where does that leave us? What do we really have? Not fucking much, two possible suspects, maybe three, and all with collaborated alibis, two with a motive, and one possible suspect without any motive that we can see. That doesn't leave us with much." He turns back to the group. "Martin, I want you to follow up with the Fredericton police. See what they can give us on Harris. I don't know what it is, but I have a strange feeling about his and the boy's death. I also want you to look into both Harris' and Jenkins' finances. See what you can find; see if there is a business connection. I don't want to preclude the possibility that Harris is a copycat murder. Yet it seems too soon for a copycat to act. Donna would you take Slater for a visit to Jenkins' wife. We need to find out if there is anything on his computer. Something there could give us a clue as to why he was a killed."

Donna looked disappointed about the assignment or perhaps the choice of partner. Her preference was to visit Lisa Jenkins with Stenson. Rick picking up on her reaction added to clarify his decision, "The reason Slater is going with you is because he was trained in computer work. He will be able to access the system in the event that it's encrypted. And at the same time, you will be able to give him insight into what to search for."

"No problem, Rick." She responded positively, respecting his explanation.

"When you finish there, you will need to do the same at his office. I want every scrap of paper looked at. Our entire focus will shift to Jenkins until we have more to go on with the Harris case. Stenson and I will investigate the woods at Indian Lake." Looking at Stenson. "I think you may be on to something with the dogs. We should at least check it out. If anyone comes up with anything, I want to know about it immediately. I don't care what time of day or night it is or what you may think I'm doing, I will be contacted ASAP. Now let's get to it."

Donna paired up with Slater and Redmond grabbed Stenson as they emptied the meeting room.

Redmond called out to Donna. "Donna, see if you can get a list of Jenkins' friends, or anyone that he has been in contact with for the last five years.

"Yep, will do." She shouted back over her shoulder and muttered to Slater. "As if it didn't occur to me."

Donna went to her desk and sat as Slater followed her.

"Should we go see Mrs. Jenkins first?" he asked.

"I'll call first; she doesn't need any surprises." She said picking up the phone receiver. Looking at her notes she found the number for Lisa Jenkins and proceeded to press the numbers.

"Hello" Lisa said picking up after the third ring.

"Mrs. Jenkins, this is Detective Copp. I was wondering if you were going to be home for then next hour or so."

"I plan on being here for most of the day. What can I do for you?" She asked tentatively.

"I would like to stop by and look at Geoff's home office. I believe Detective Redmond mentioned to you that we needed to do that."

"He did mention it to me. Today is fine. Just stop by anytime, Detective."

"Thank you, we'll be there shortly." Donna hung up the receiver and said to Slater, "It's a go. But first let's make a list of what we want to look for."

Slater shrugged a 'sure, if that's what you want,' and asked her, "Does anyone ever ask you about your name, Copp... the coincidence of you having that name and being a cop?" He asked her smiling, almost snickering.

"Yeah, Slater, I get it all the time, more than you think. I'm just surprised that I'm getting it from you."

"I didn't mean to..."

"You didn't mean what?"

"I was just..."

"Forget it," she said cutting him off, knowing that if she were a man, the issue would never have arisen. Donna started preparing her list for the search at the Jenkins' house.

. . . . .

Outside the station, Redmond climbed into the passenger's side of Stenson's black Camry. He preferred to be driven, especially in a big comfortable sedan. Although the air had cooled a bit compared to the past few days, the major benefit was that it cleared away the persistent humidity. The conditions now typified what was considered to be a normal Maritime day.

"I don't get it, Stenson. Why do you think Kline is good for the murders? You sounded hard on him." Redmond said, shifting his weight in the seat trying to get comfortable.

As he pulled the car out of the police lot and without looking directly at him Stenson said, "I don't think Kline is good for the murders, Rick, even though it's possible. He seems too level headed for that"

"Then why the hell did you include him as a suspect?"

Stenson turned right on Rainie Drive and headed toward Quinpool Road. "You have to think outside the box, Rick. We don't want to go through the process with tunnel vision. Besides, I thought it would be good to look at him thoroughly, so that we don't dismiss anyone just because they *seem* innocent. As I see it, everybody's a suspect."

"Why didn't you just say that when you had the chance, Stenson?" Rick said, irritated with him.

Saying it straight out wouldn't have the same impact as including someone as a suspect, Rick. You name someone as a suspect that no one considers to be one, and you have our boys thinking." Stenson reflects on the comment and added,

"or girls thinking. What does he see that I don't see?
Meaning what do I see that they don't. Then they start to look
at the suspect in greater detail… try to find a weakness in their
story, or perhaps a motive."

"Hmm. Okay, I can see what you're getting at."

"It could get them thinking 'outside the box' as I said before,
maybe come up with a lead… something new… a motive.
Who knows, maybe even something that could put us on to the
perp."

Stenson drove along the end of Quinpool Road approaching
the Armdale roundabout. The water of the Arm, which
housed two yacht clubs, was calm. "Rick, may I ask you
something?"

"Sure. Fill your boots."

"Why did you team Slater up with Donna?"

"Why? Do ya have something against Slater, Stenson?"

"Jesus, Rick, give me a break, will you."

"Like I said before, Slater knows computers. He'll be helpful
in gaining access to Jenkins' system, in the event that it's
encrypted."

"You know, Rick, I think you're bull shitting me." Redmond
shook his head. "That's not the real reason, but even if it is, it
is not the only reason."

Redmond laughed. "Your instincts are right on, Stenson, as
usual. I think Slater will make detective within the next year
or two. At least that's what I'd like to see. He is a good man.
He goes by the book. Of course, in your mind that may not be
a good thing necessarily, going by the book, that is."

Prompting a look from Stenson. "In any case, I want him to work with us as closely as possible… to gain experience. Then we'll see if he has what it takes to make the grade."

"And that's it?"

"That's it."

"It's not because he's black, is it?"

"That too. We need to integrate the department."

"And why with Donna?"

"Simple. Donna is also still learning the ropes. She's fresh and she is not tainted in any way. She's easy going and will take the time to go over details with him. She's patient."

"And that's it?" Stenson persisted, watching the road as he drove.

"Jesus, Stenson. What do you want from me? Of course, that's it. Do you think I have a hidden agenda or something? You think I'm planning an interdepartmental conspiracy for god's sake?" Redmond barked, further annoyed with Stenson's line of questions.

They remained silent as they drove past Exhibition Park. Rick took a pack of cigarettes from his shirt pocket, tapped one out and put it in his mouth and started to light it.

"What are you doing?" Stenson asked, staring at him.

"I'm lighting up, that's what I'm doing." He answered.

"We don't smoke in this car, Rick." He stated, anticipating an argument from him.

Redmond looked at him for a moment before putting the cigarette back in the pack, but not without expressing his disagreement. Redmond did not respect Stenson's rule but he

113

tolerated it. He felt he had the right to smoke anywhere at anytime he wanted. He sat back in the seat and sulked. The two did not speak again until they reached the Indian Lake Golf Course.

Chapter 15

Detective Dave Martin was on the phone talking with his counterpart at the Fredericton Police station, when Donna and Slater left the station to meet with Lisa Jenkins.

"Look, Jason, I know you guys are busy, but this is a priority." He said and then listened. "Yes, that's right, a priority for *us*. I know that. But it is in your best interest if you can come up with some information that will help us in the investigation. The media is hitting the roof on this one." Listening. "Good. Chief Barnes will certainly appreciate everything you're doing. Then I expect you'll have something for me later today?" Listening. "Great, Jason. If there is anything I can do from this end, let me know." Listening. "Okay, excelente, señor." On the other end, Jason began to ramble on in Spanish. "Whoa. I didn't know you spoke Spanish, man." Listening. "No I don't. Those are the only two words I know." Laughing. "Good. I expect to hear from you later. Bye." Martin hung up the phone, with a little more hope than when he started, but with no great expectations.

. . . . .

Donna Copp and Jim Slater pulled up to the curb in front of Lisa Jenkins' house in Donna's Tercel.

"Nice house." He said as he stopped to admire the contemporary two-story house with the manicured grounds. He guessed that the house contained at least 3,000 square feet. "If you work really hard, you can have one just like it." Donna laughed.

"Sure, all I have to do is put in 24 hours a day, seven days a week at double overtime, and I'll be able to cover the down payment…in about six years." Both laughed at the absurdity of the conversation, as they walked to the front door. Donna pressed the doorbell and heard the muted chime that sounded inside. A moment later, Lisa opened the door wearing a pair of black, lightweight wool, fitted pants and a white long-sleeved blouse. "You must be Detective Copp." She said. "Please come in."

"Thank you." Donna said. "This is Officer Slater."

"Hello, Officer Slater." Lisa said as Slater nodded. "Come into the living room, please." Lisa walked ahead of them into the large room.

"How would you like to do this?" She asked, gesturing for them to sit, neither of which took up the offer. Lisa sat.

"If it's convenient, Mrs. Jenkins, we would like to look at Geoff's office first and then perhaps bedroom … if that's all right with you.

"It certainly is all right, Detective." She said getting up, feeling encouraged that some activity was proceeding in the investigation.

"Let me take you to his office first then." Lisa led them to a closed-door room just off the dining room. Geoff's office was medium sized, no larger than ten feet by ten feet. The walls were covered with a warm gray paint and held large framed photographs of desolate landscapes taken in what was, more than likely, an arid climate country. A small desk with an ergonomic chair behind it sat in a corner of the room and faced the door. A flat screen computer monitor sat on top of the desk, which was also piled with papers, pencils, pens and other administrative accessories. A second computer, a laptop was closed on the desk next to the monitor. A picture of Geoff and Lisa sitting on grass, with the ocean in the background, both smiling also rested on the desktop. Another door opened to the back yard. It looked new and was constructed, no doubt, to meet the tax requirements for a home office.

"Can I get you anything to drink? Coffee or tea?" Lisa offered.

Slater shook his head and Donna said, "No thank you, Mrs. Jenkins. We're good. By the way, did anyone else use this office?"

No. Only Geoff. He was particular about not having his computer or his office disturbed in any way. He always expected to find everything just as he left it."

"I can relate to that." Donna said.

Lisa said, "Then I'll leave you to it," and she left the room, closing the door behind her.

Slater started his work by booting up the IBM Notepad laptop, as Donna started rummaging through papers in the desk drawers.

. . . . .

Stenson and Rick walked along the third-hole fairway dressed in street clothes; Rick was in a suit and Stenson wore a sport coat. Both were thankful that the club was closed so that they did not have to deal with golfers. Along the way, Stenson found and picked up a stick about the length and size of a walking stick. As he walked, he occasionally swung the stick as though it were a golf club.

"Why don't you put that down, Stenson. You look silly." Rick told him feeling embarrassed.

Stenson just smiled and ignored his request. The detectives approached the area of the murder site. Stenson stopped, turned around to get a view of the fairway and the tee box, mentally calculating the distance. Then he turned back and they entered the woods. They walked to the familiar site where the boy and his father had been killed. Stenson tried to imagine the sequence of events; the victim meeting his killer, and having his skull hammered in. How could that have happened? Was the club swung like a baseball bat? He swung the stick trying to imagine the process. Was he standing up when he was struck? Maybe he was on his knees, looking for his ball. Did he see it coming? There was no sign of a struggle and no defensive wounds. The boy must have arrived just moments later, coming upon the perp. Stenson attempted to envisage what took place next. What did the boy see? Did he catch him in the act? Did he see his father struck, or afterwards when he was on the ground? It was difficult for him to imagine what happened to the boy because he could never imagine him being hurt, much less being killed. Still he tried to put himself in the killer's shoes. He walked around in circles allowing his mind to wander. Stenson sniffed the air and waited as if he expected a scent to send him a clue as to what took place and by whom.

Redmond squatted at the exact spot of ground where the tragedy had taken place, looking for something that may have been missed.

Stenson continued wandering, then stopped to look along the fairway. From his viewpoint, he could not see the fairway. He moved from spot to spot, brushing aside weeds and bushes with his legs until he found a place where he was reasonably well hidden, but could see the fairway through the thick of woods. This must be where he waited, Stenson thought.

"Rick." He called out.

Rick stood up. "What is it?" Rick said walking towards him.

"This must be the spot." He told him.

"What spot?" Rick asked.

"I think this is where he waited. The perp must have been here."

"You think?" Redmond asked.

"Yes, I do. Look. You can see the fairway almost all the way down to the tee box. Right through there." Stenson said pointing. "I'm almost positive he was waiting right at this very spot."

"Okay. Let's say this is where he waited." Rick said. "What

does that tell us? Any signs that he was exactly there?"

"No. No signs. But it gives me a sense of the perp. I can see him here. I can feel him here, Rick. Can I ever feel him here." Stenson stopped speaking for a moment. "Now if only I can think like him." He said, his eyes, looking, moving from side to side. "He waited here for a ball to be hit into the woods. Yes! That's what he did. Of course! He waited for someone to slice the ball into the woods. It's so obvious."

"And if he waited for just *any* ball to come into the woods…" Redmond added not finishing the sentence.

"Then he didn't select a specific person to kill. Fuck! The bastard killed Harris and his son at random, Rick. It was a random murder! It had to be." Stenson concluded exuberantly.

"Well I'll be god dammed." Redmond blurted. The whole Jenkins thing has nothing to do with Harris. No wonder we haven't been able to make a fucking connection."

"If the same person killed all three, then he must have used Harris as a diversion. He wanted us to think that all the murders were random." Stenson figured.

"This changes everything, Stenson. Now all we have to do is find out who had it in for Jenkins."

"Yeah, that's all we have to do." Stenson said sarcastically. "For the time being, let's see if we can find out what caused the dogs to be so stirred up."

"Do you know the area that we are looking for, Stenson?"

"The dog patrol took a co-ordinance using a GPS. It will be just like geocaching."

"What the hell is geo catching?" Rick asked.

Stenson laughed. "It's geocaching, Rick, g-e-o-c-a-c-h-i-n-g." spelling it for him. "It's sort of a hunt combined with hiking. Someone conceals a little box or tube that has been camouflaged somewhere in the woods, under a bridge, in the city, anywhere; they usually include some paper so the hunters who find it can write their names down to verify that they found the hidden object. Sometimes trinkets are left for the finder to take and perhaps replace with a different trinket of his or her own."

"And these hunters, geocachers, find these objects how?"

"By using one of these." He takes a small GPS unit out of his jacket pocket. The people who plant the object, which is often disguised with moss or whatever, take the co-ordinance of the spot where the cache was hidden. The co-ordinance is posted on an Internet site along with clues for the hunter. Then they search for the object using a GPS and follow the clues." He said, delighted to have explained the process to his technology deficient partner.

"So you have the co-ordinance from the dog patrol?" Redmond asked.

"Exactly, Rick."

"Well god damn it, why the fuck didn't you just say so?" Redmond asked impatiently.

Stenson continued. "So now all we do is turn the GPS on and follow the directions. I preset the co-ordinance in the unit before we left the station, and as we walk the unit will tell us when we are close, or when we arrive at the exact spot that the dogs were acting up. Except, if there is anything there, we'll have to discover our own clues to find the treasure."

"Hmm. Technology." They pressed on, walking through the woods reversing the direction in which they came. Stenson walked gingerly so as not to disturb anything along the way. Redmond's eye, glued to the ground in search of anything out of the ordinary, kicked at and brushed aside weeds, fallen branches and small bushes with his feet. During the walk, Rick found several golf balls that had been hit and lost in the woods. He picked them up and put them in a small plastic bag. Stenson stopped, distracted by the noise Redmond was making. He looked at the GPS to determine how close they were to the reported location. "According to the GPS we are about thirty or forty yards away now. Have you found anything?"

"Just a few golf balls. We'll take them back with us to check them out for prints, just in case."

Daylight was starting to fade and mosquitoes were plentiful and hungry. They buzzed around their faces, ears and necks occasionally drawing blood even at the expense of being crushed by a moving hand. But what do mosquitoes know? Their sole purpose was to draw blood. Stenson and Redmond strode through an expanse of dense underbrush. The bottoms of their pants caught on the bushes and tore somewhat as they pushed forward.

"Friggin' bugs." Redmond said slapping at his neck.

"They must like you, Rick. For some reason they're not bothering me." He laughed. "We're almost there." He said looking at his position on the GPS.

"Thank god." Rick grumbled.

"This is the place. This is where the dogs stopped and began circling."

"This is it?" Redmond echoed.

"This is it. We're within a five-foot radius…at least."

"We're losing the light. It's going to be dark any minute." Redmond looked up trying to see the sky through the heavily leave-laden trees.

"Let's take a quick look and then mark the area so it will be easy to find when we come back." Stenson unhurriedly looked around to find some indication as to what disturbed the dogs.

Rick walked toward the fairway. "We're pretty close to the fairway, Stenson. The woods are not as dense here, so we should just go straight out rather than retracing our steps."

"That makes sense," Stenson said. "Let's go. It's getting too dark now anyway. We can come back tomorrow."

"You think it's worth it?"

"I don't know if it is or not. But I have a feeling it may be. At least it's worth one more look in good light." They walked out to the fairway and Stenson placed two sticks in the ditch, marking the way back in. "X marks the spot." He said. The two retreated to the car to return to the city.

Chapter 16

After a break for green tea and lemon yogurt, Jean turned to her computer. She had several new messages. The first one she recognized as spam and immediately deleted it without looking at it. The second message was from her friend Annie. Annie told her in the text of the message in no uncertain terms that she had no business looking for a weapon. Wasn't she against violence? Aren't we all against violence and pro gun control? Even if she, Annie, had access to a weapon, which she did not, she would never in a million years offer Jean the use of the gun or the knowledge of where to find it. Annie's last line was, "I am so, so sorry about Geoff." Jean smiled. She expected as much from Annie, and for the most part, was in agreement with her. She moved the email message to her Annie folder. The last message was sent from zero at hotmail. Jean clicked on the subject, which read, *your request* to open it. The message said simply:

> *I have what you want.*
>
> *If you still need it, meet me at Local Jo Café at 7:30 tonight. Be sharp; they close at 8:00*

The message was signed zero.

Jean's heart pounded as though it was going to burst. She got up from the chair, did a turn as if to go somewhere, and then just as quickly, sat back down. She highlighted the text of the message, copied it, pasted it to a word document and printed it out. After a moment of consideration, Jean deleted the message without checking the email address. She again stood up, pulled her hat down over her forehead, and then retrieved the message from her printer. She folded it twice, in thirds, as though she was going to put the sheet into an envelope, and then she folded it in half and put the paper in her purse, which was on the floor next to her chair. She looked at her watch. Too early to go, she thought, much too early. She removed her hat and tossed it on to the desk and shook her hair out. 'I must go to the bank,' she muttered softly. 'Oh, I have no idea what this will cost. He or she should have told me how much it would cost. The gun in the catalogue was about $750 so one on the *black market* must cost at least $1,500. I better withdraw $2,000 just to be safe. Jean put her hat back on, straightened it on her head, and immediately left for the bank, which she knew was open for another hour.

. . . . .

Donna Copp and Jim Slater spent the better part of two hours going through Geoff Jenkins' belongings in his home office. Jenkins' computer was not encrypted and so required no deciphering for a password. Slater went through all the files systematically, changing the folders from icons to lists, putting them in alphabetical order. He then opened each one starting from A through Z, although the last folder was under Y and named *Youth Programs*. While Slater perused the electronic files, Donna searched the desk drawers and the three-drawer file cabinet.

"What are we looking for?" he asked.

"You'll know when you see it." She said. "Look for anything that doesn't fit, seems out of place, or is just plain odd. Sometimes the simpler the name of a file is, the better place it is in which to hide something. Also, if you haven't done it already, check the address book, and print out all the names…or better yet, let's take the laptop with us. With any luck, phone numbers and addresses as well as other information will be there."

"Sounds sensible…thanks." He said as he continued his search. "Here we go." At the top of the toolbar was an icon for Gmail. Slater clicked on the icon and it opened to the sign in page. He thought he would try his luck by double clicking on the username box and a pull down menu opened with three names, *Jenks*, *gjenks*, and *sparkle*. He clicked on *sparkle* first and the name appeared in the username box and an asterisked password with a checkmark in a small *remember me* box below. Slater put the cursor on the sign in box and a red message appeared saying that the username and or password do not match. Slater erased the information from both boxes and repeated the process using Jenks as the username. This time the email opened to the inbox. "Jackpot!" Slater announced vociferously.

"What do you have?" Donna said, stopping and looking up from the files.

I'm in his email. He has twenty-two new messages in the inbox and there is a humongous list of folders with messages in them, I would venture to guess. This is going to take time. I think you're right; we should take the computer with us and have a team help me go at it, go through each labeled folder and read every message. You think?"

"Sounds sensible." Donna replied, repeating his earlier response, tongue in cheek.

Lisa opened the door and stuck her head inside asking, "Is everything okay? I thought I heard some shouting.

"Yes, everything is fine. Officer Slater was a little exuberant when he accessed your husband's email account." Donna smiled. "By the way, Mrs. Jenkins, we will need to take the computer with us... and some of his papers. I hope you don't mind?"

"No, not at all. Please take whatever you need, if it will help you to come up with any leads in ...um ... yes, do take it."

"One other thing; where is Geoff's regular office?"

"His regular office? This is his only office. Geoff always worked at home. This was the only office he needed. He did all his work from here." Lisa said, sadness in her voice hung like a dark cloud, and she left the room.

"What did you find?" Jim asked after Lisa closed the door, referring to the papers that Donna wanted to take.

"I found a few applications that Mr. Jenkins had submitted for consultant work. Also, in the same file were rejections to proceed with two projects, and Jenkins' response to the rejections, which were not very amicable. The decision not to proceed on both projects didn't seem to be mutual. It also sounds a bit like Jenkins may have burnt some bridges. It may be worth a follow up. I also have some financial documents that we should probably look at. I didn't find a will. He may have one filed with his lawyer. I would like to know who the recipient of the estate is."

"I saw a will making program on the computer, but I didn't open it. There might be a copy of his will there. We'll find out more when we get this stuff back to the station." He said, happy to be able to contribute. "Shall we pack it up and call it a day?"

"Yes, let's bring this stuff back and call it at least a part of a day. We'll have to return to look throughout the rest of the house. We also have a lot more hours to put in before we're finished." Donna said decidedly. They carried the computer and papers to the car in two trips, said goodbye and extended their thanks to Lisa and drove back to the police station.

Chapter 17

Jean opened the family photo album, which contained photographs dating back to her childhood. Some of the photographs had been taken by and had belonged to her mother who died prematurely several years ago after a short bout with cancer. She treasured the pictures of her mother and father, Geoff and herself. She had only a partial memory of her father who was killed in an automobile accident when he was on a sales trip to Ontario. She was only twelve when her father died. Her memory of him was transitory since he traveled a great deal and when he was at home, they were always in a state of developing their relationship anew. As a result, she felt they seldom had anything to build on. She always thought of him as just a visitor. Her only recollection of what her father looked like was from old photographs, when he was younger. She could not picture what he looked like the last time she saw him. To her, he was eternally young.

Whenever Jean looked at the old photos, she was mostly reminded of her relationship with Geoff and often reminisced about the family picnics and the games they played at them. She loved chasing the Frisbee, or laughed hard whenever she and Geoff played catch. She would toss the ball as far away from him as she could to make him run for it. And when Geoff would attempt to leap and catch the ball, often falling down, Jean would laugh until tears rolled down her cheeks and she fell on the ground herself. The thought of never seeing or talking to Geoff again left an ache in her chest that she knew would persist forever.

Jean sipped her green tea as she walked her way through the pages of the album. She had eaten dinner earlier; it was soup, salad and a cheese roll. On the last page of the album was a picture of Geoff and some of his friends posing at the golf course. This particular photograph was taken at the Highland Links in Cape Breton. Geoff and his friends would stay at the Keltic Lodge for a golf weekend almost every summer. The picture taken two years ago looked old fashioned, with each of them kneeling on one knee, a golf club in their hands, maybe something out of the mid-1940s. All wore big smiles in addition to their golf attire. The photo made her smile every time she saw it. She closed the album, saddened by what the pictures represented to her.

Jean paused to question herself about the meeting with Zero. She found it a bit weird. She had no idea with whom she was meeting or even what he looked like, assuming it was a man. She found the idea of a clandestine meeting to buy a gun from someone she never met, and certainly one of questionable character quite frightening and possibly downright stupid. What if it was a scam? What if he knew she would have the money and decided to rob her? Perhaps I shouldn't go, she considered... and then reconsidered... and again reconsidered.

'God, I am so indecisive,' she said out loud. 'What if? What if? What if nothing!' She decided not to think about it. We all have to take risks sometimes. It was getting close to the time. Jean retreated to the bedroom to change. She wanted to wear something that made her look tough conceivably even dangerous, as if that was at all possible. She looked at a pair of black pants, but thought they were too sophisticated. She decided on a pair of black jeans that were thin cut, a pair of medium heeled black shoes and a plain long sleeve navy cotton blouse. She wished she had a pair of high black boots to wear, but she owned none and normally would not be caught dead in them, a woman at her age; even the thin-cut jeans were a bit over the top. She thought about donning a hat, but figured it was too ladylike. After dressing, she called a taxi and asked to be picked up at 7:15. Jean checked her purse to make sure the money was there, in the envelope where she put it. She was so anxious... she did not want to forget the money.

The taxi arrived and Jean got in. "Local Jo Café, on Oxford Street," she said and after a moment, "and step on it." She added harshly, surprised at her rude outburst, and indulging in her newfound persona. She thought her words and tone were out of a *Noir* movie.

The taxi dropped her off at the café with a few minutes to spare.

. . . . .

The golf balls collected by Redmond offered no vestige as to who the owners were and so they were disposed of in the nearest trash receptacle. Since no other bits of evidence were found, both Stenson and Rick directed their energy to their notes taken at the golf course, which were to be added to the murder book. Although it was well past seven, when normally the department was quiet, the team worked diligently at the information collected during the day. Dave Martin wrote up his notes that he received from the Fredericton Police Department regarding Matt Harris and his activities and relationships pertaining to Halifax. Thus far Martin was not able to find a single clue that led him to a connection with Geoff Jenkins; neither of the men had acquaintances in common, had attended any workshops together or extended study groups, had any financial ties in any respect, or, according to the report from Fredericton, knew any of the same people. Martin finished his write up. "I can't establish a single connection to the victims, Harris and his son, Rick." Martin said dropping his report on the desk in front of Redmond.

Redmond stopped writing and looked up at Martin. "I'm not surprised, Dave. We've pretty well concluded that the Harris and the boy's murders were a random act, and possibly committed by the same person solely to divert our attention from the Jenkins' crime. We figured the perp was waiting in the woods until someone drove a golf ball close to where he was, and it didn't matter who that person was… so, a random choice. Now we have to tie the two murders to the same perp.

It looks like the real target was Jenkins."

Martin stood silently for moment thinking. "Why the hell didn't you tell me that before I did all that work?"

"There was no sense in stopping you, Dave. You were well into it."

"Yeah. Thanks for nothing." Redmond just stared at Martin who retreated somewhat. "Is it possible, Rick, that Harris was the target and Jenkins was the decoy victim?"

"Whoa. Hmm. That puts a different perspective on the situation. Yes, it is plausible. I don't know why we precluded that possibility."

"Do you want me to follow up that lead? There may be an association of some sort with Harris and the Indian Lake Golf club that may account for something."

"Definitely, Dave, and come to think of it, what about his brother, William? He lives in Halifax. He might have had a beef with his brother. Look into that; see if there is anything to it. Let's find out if his brother had anything to gain by his death."

"Okay, Rick, I'm on it." Turning to go, Dave stops and turns back to Redmond. "There is nothing more I can do tonight though, Rick. Is it okay if I pick up on it tomorrow?"

"Sure. I'm certain your wife wouldn't mind spending some time with you tonight." Redmond said smiling. "See ya tomorrow. The meeting is at seven o'clock. "

"Thanks. See you then." Martin said and left, and Redmond returned to his notes.

Donna, who headed up the search team at Lisa Jenkins' house, had several officers, including Slater, picking apart the emails on Geoff's computer, looking for anything that could help, and compiling a list of names of anyone that seemed remotely possible to be considered as a suspect. The list included Geoff's close golfing friends. The more contact a person had with Geoff, the higher he was placed on the list. Donna expected that her team would work late into the night before she would have anything concrete to go on.

Stenson wandered to Redmond's desk, sat down and watched him writing his notes. "I don't want to close the books on these notes, Rick. At least until we go back to the club. Can we do that the first thing tomorrow?" he asked.

"Let's do that after our 7:00 a.m. session. Does that suit you?"

"That's perfect. I can't help thinking that there is still something out there; the dogs are savvy beasts, don't you think? Too bad they can't talk."

"You know, Stenson, we may be barking up the wrong tree, thinking that Jenkins was the target. Martin thought that maybe it was just the contrary, that Jenkins was the random killing and that Harris was the real target."

After giving the new idea some thought. "It's possible, but I don't think so, Rick."

"No? Why not?"

"Jenkins was approached and killed out in the open. There is not doubt he was chosen by the perp. Harris' murder was way too random. It could have been any one of thirty people who hit a ball into the woods. The spot where the perp was waiting was the right distance for a slice to occur. It could have been

Joe Blow who ended up in the woods."

"You have a point, Stenson. But what if Harris hit the ball there deliberately, to meet up with someone?"

"Get serious, Rick. Even if Harris were that good a golfer to control where he hit the ball, why the hell would he want to meet like that? Can you imagine me saying to you, 'Rick, hit the ball in the woods and we'll meet there to discuss our little arrangement'? No, man, that is highly unlikely. In my opinion, the meeting between Harris and the perp was serendipitous. And in my estimation, the murder was definitely a random act.

Chapter 18

In an attempt to hide her fear, Jean over compensated by walking in an unnaturally casual manner into the Local Jo Café. Even the most insensitive person could detect her affected manner and attribute it to apprehension, and the man sitting in a chair waiting for her was not insensitive. The man, sporting a three-day beard, wore a heavy knit grey sweater and a pair of stonewashed jeans. He had an Indiana Jones style fedora on his head, pulled low on his forehead just above his tired brown eyes. The chair he was sitting in was next to the rail on the upper platform in the back of the café. He watched Jean as she came in. He recognized her from the description that he had been given, sized her up, and relaxed. Jean stopped just inside the door to look around for the person with whom she was to meet. She was uncertain if the one she was meeting with was a man or a woman. She noted several couples sitting and talking, and dismissed them immediately as possibilities. She saw a woman sitting alone and the man in the hat, also sitting alone. The man, she noted, was maybe 40 years old or so. She was not good at determining one's age. The woman, probably in her 30s, wore a sweater and a multicolored scarf around her neck and was engrossed in a paperback book. The man's stare caught her eyes and she shivered. He touched the brim of his hat and nodded. Jean walked up the two steps to his table on the upper platform and stood there. The man looked up at her and said, "Jean?"

"Yes." She replied. "Are you Zero?"

"Sit down please." He ordered, ignoring her question.

Jean sat down across from him and said. "You have the advantage. I don't know your name but you know mine."

The man in the hat weighted her reference to wanting to know his name. "Yes. I do have that advantage and it will remain that way." After a pause, he continued. "You contacted a mutual friend recently." He said, looking around to ascertain that the people at the other tables were not listening to them. He looked back at Jean. "You requested a particular item?"

Jean answered in a normal but nervous voice with no concern of being overheard. "That is correct. I…"

The man raised his hand in a small gesture and scrunched his face interrupting her. He cocked his head slightly, shifting his eyes in the direction of the other people to warn her to talk quietly.

Jean took the hint and lowered her voice. "Yes, I am looking for a specific item."

"Have something first. A coffee, or something to eat?" He suggested.

"I'm not hungry, nor am I thirsty." She replied.

"Have something." He quietly demanded.

"Excuse me." She said unable to refuse. "I will get a cup of tea." She got up and went to the counter to order an herbal tea. She was told that the tea would be brought to her table.

137

Jean returned to the table and sat, saying nothing.

"I pride myself on surviving with the minimal amount of attention." The man in the hat started.

Jean nodded as if she knew what he was talking about.

"Do you know me?" He asked her.

Jean shook her head and again said nothing.

"We have never met. We are not meeting now, and we will never meet in the future."

Jean again nodded in agreement.

"I don't know, nor do I care how you put the item to use."

"You can be assured that…" She started but the man in the hat interrupted her and continued talking as if she said nothing.

"The item is lightweight, easy to use for a woman, and it's almost new, hardly used. It has been maintained and in perfect working order. I tested and maintained it myself."

"Does the item come with accessories?" She asked cryptically tilting her head forward.

"It has two…" he paused to look around, and satisfied that no one was listening continued quietly. "It has two fully operational magazines and is ready to go." He said softly. "I have included instructions on how to use this specific item, which is ideally suited to women."

The woman from the counter brought the tea to the table and set in front of Jean, who immediately placed two dollars on the table. They waited until the she left and was out of earshot.

"Is this item hot? Do I have to worry about it?" she asked. The question caused the man in the hat to chuckle inwardly.

"The item is completely unidentifiable. It cannot be linked to any other activity or person, and it has no numbers with which it can be traced. So you are protected in every respect."

"Is it illegal to carry it with me?" She wanted to know.

"You are not a child, Mrs. Jenkins." He said turning his eyes upward and then looking directly into her eyes. "You *know* what you can and cannot do with it." The use of her last name by the man shocked her momentarily. The man in the hat stopped talking. They sat looking at each other.

"What now?" Jean asked.

"What now?" He repeated. "I am satisfied that you are who I was led to believe you are; and now we can do the transaction."

"Here?" Jean questioned.

For the first time the man in the hat smiled. "I wouldn't take such a chance and bring the item with me. Where is your car parked?"

"I didn't bring my car. I came in a taxi."

"Then," he said, I will leave first and in five minutes you will leave, take a right on London street and keep walking, and I will be behind you. I will follow and catch up to you."

"How much does this item cost?" She asked tentatively.

"It will cost you twelve." He answered.

"Hundred?"

The man in the hat smiled again and nodded. He rose from his seat, went to the counter to pay his bill and left.

Jean remained sitting, checked the time, and opened her purse to count the money without taking it out. She took the remaining bills out of the purse, keeping them folded in her hand and concealed, and slid them into the front pocket of her jeans. She waited for the allotted time to pass, and left the café. Outside, Jean looked both ways on Oxford before she went to London, where she took a right and walked as if she were on an evening stroll, holding tightly to her handbag. A moment later, the man in the hat, with an unlit cigarette in his mouth, approached her from behind and said, "Excuse me, Ms, do you have a light?"

"What?" The question surprised Jean.

"In your purse, perhaps? May I?" He wanted her to surrender the purse.

"A.. um yes." She said giving him her purse.

The man took the purse, opened it, took the money out, and looking around, put it in his pocket, took a small item out of his pocket, and placed it in the purse, closing the snap and handing it back to Jean. With the matches he had held concealed in his hand, he lit his cigarette. "Thank you." He said. "May I keep these?" He asked referring to the matches. "By all means." She said walking away. The man in the hat stroked his chin, thanked her again, and turned and walked in the opposite direction.

Chapter 19

He was eating a chicken wrap, drinking a cola and checking his emails. He always ate late, whether it was dinner or a snack only. His laptop sat on the dining room table along with a pile of opened mail, as well as a smaller pile of unopened mail, several credit card application forms and a book. It was obvious that he lived alone; a woman would never have put up with the clutter on the dining room table. Driver was satisfied with his accomplishments thus far, and wondered where they would lead him. He loved the luxury that accompanied his Machiavellian activity, and from the outset put the proceeds to good use. He had already bought a dark blue three-button Armani suit in Toronto. He also bought a half dozen shirts designed by Ermenegildo Zegna, several ties by Roberto Cavalli and Hugo Boss, 18-k gold Italian cuff links with a single solitaire diamond set off center, and a few pairs of Allen-Edmonds and Dolce & Gabbana shoes. That was hardly enough. It was just the beginning. Driver was looking at luxury cars and villas. He knew he could get away with wearing designer clothes without drawing attention to himself, but a car and a villa? Driver drooled over a BMW Z4; he already owned an older and lower priced BMW. But he could not live without the 2007 Bugatti Veyron, of which only

300 were produced and 50 sold. He saw it as a car that will never depreciate, one that can do 0-100 km/h in 2.5 seconds and has a top speed of 407 km/h. The price of about $1.7 million was within Driver's reach provided he continued in the direction in which he was going. The price did not deter him from his goal, which would easily exceed his expensive taste in toys. It had been said about the car that *it is better than you can ever imagine*. That was good enough for Driver. He wanted nothing but the best and, of course, something that most people could never have or afford. Driver was no fool. He knew that he could not keep such an acquisition secret if the car was bought and kept in Halifax. Undoubtedly it would be the talk of the city. He obviously could not justify buying such a car without raising suspicions. But he knew he was clever enough to find a way. He was smart enough to get the money; nothing would stop him from getting the car. Perhaps he would start a rumor that he won a huge sum of money in a lottery in the United States or the Irish sweepstakes. Of course, he would have to find a way to bank the money as though it were coming from one of those sources. Not a smart idea. He knew in his heart that ultimately he would have to leave the country, start a new life. That would be easy and the most appropriate approach to newfound money. 'Enough of that for now, there are more important issues,' he thought. Driver was fully aware of the attempts to stop him, to find him, to discover who he is. More precisely, he was cognizant of the threat that Jean Jenkins represented. He was fully aware of her recent activities. He did not consider her a

serious threat, but more like a gnat buzzing around in a chaotic manner, inefficient and unorganized for which he needed a repellant. However, he didn't want a loose canon causing a stir and accidentally nosing her way into anything that he might be involved in. 'Her inappropriate participation might not be good for him, but it was undoubtedly less good for her,' he thought. In spite of the fact that she was directionless, Driver saw Jean Jenkins as a liability. He decided that he could not take a chance that she might get lucky. He could no longer afford to have her actively searching with the potential to point a finger at him. Driver realized the necessity to take steps to prevent her from going any further. There was no doubt in his mind that she could become a real irritation, a thorn in his side, which he could ill afford. The question was what should he do about her, and how and when should he do it? Driver did not relish the idea of another murder so soon, especially taking the life of the victim's sister. That would be too close to home, put too much heat on him, and force the police into a relentless investigation mode in an attempt to identify him. He wouldn't be surprised if the police brought in outside help. No, he would have to wait and hope that he was not placed into a position of having to prematurely do away with Jean Jenkins. Nevertheless, Driver decided to add Jean Jenkins to his list, placing her at the top. Eventually she had to go.

Chapter 20

Copp and Slater worked late into the night with their team in search of names that might have been instrumental in Geoff Jenkins' homicide. They fed on black coffee and donuts, after having downed a large pizza with the works. It was not by chance that they came up with only four names that were of any significance. The team scanned more than 290 saved emails and about 40 some unread messages. There were no new names in the address book that weren't accounted for in the email messages. It was no surprise that Philip Nickerson was one of the notorious four names. It did not seem accidental that the other three, Aaron John Devoe, Dan Lee, and Mike Fisher, were all close friends of Jenkins. Dave Martin walked into the office at almost midnight.

"Look what the cat dragged in." Donna said. "I heard you were having a romantic night with your wife, Dave. Over so fast?" She teased.

"Now ain't you something". He retorted. " As a matter of fact I got a reprieve." He laughed. "Besides, I knew you couldn't do without me. I am allowed to give you two hours, no later then 2:00 a.m. Since I got Matt Harris' financial information from the Fredericton PD, I thought we might want to see how they match up with Jenkins'."

"Fill your boots." Donna said. Dave Martin pitched in on the computer and paper work, assisting Donna and her team, focusing on the financial aspect of the investigation. He meticulously went through all the papers that Donna took from Jenkins' home office files. He separated the bank statements, credit card statements, of which there were three different card companies, insurance and investments statements. Martin went back two years in the bank statements, looking for any anomaly in deposits and withdrawals. Jenkins had accounts at two different banks, the TD Canada Trust and HSBC. The main and most active account was the TD. Jenkins used the TD account primarily for deposits from his consultant work, which at times, was quite substantial. Martin commented to Donna. "Christ! We're in the wrong business. This guy was making a fortune. "

Donna perked up. "Really? What're we talking about?"

"Each deposit he made was about the same amount we earn in a year." He declared.

"Speak for yourself, big guy. I make a helluva lot more than you do." She said laughing. Her sarcasm was not lost on him.

"Okay. Then more than *I* make in a year." He said, his face reddening.

"How many deposits are you talking about?"

"Let's see." He said counting. "At least 18… no… 21 in one year. Wow! That's a million dollars a year - or more."

"What about the withdrawals?" She asked.

"Only about half as much. He has a nice balance though."

"Had, you mean. A lot of good it's going to do him where

he's at." She said.

"Well, I wouldn't mind having that kind a balance in my account. Martin added wistfully.

"Yeah? It's definitely not enough to retire on." Donna said returning to her work.

"You think he would invest the money rather than just let it sit there." He said.

"Maybe he does invest it, maybe once a year. What was the previous year's balance, Dave?"

Martin put the current year's statements aside and looked at the previous year. "Well the previous year-end balance is very low by comparison." Laughing. "Actually, it is almost nonexistent."

"And the deposits?" She asked.

"Let me look." He said shuffling through the statements.

"Yep, yep, yep…just about the same in deposits give or take a few thousand dollars. And… the only difference is that there were four huge checks written totaling approximately three quarters of a million. Two checks were written to him and two totaling more than a half million went into investments. There you go. So he does invest."

"Good." Donna said. "Now we have something to go on. See if you can find out where those checks he wrote to himself went. Go through everything you have. I'd like to know how much money he has, just how much he is really worth. Check his insurance. See who his beneficiary is. I sure would like to know who's going to get his money."

The team continued looking over the files, both computer and paper, until midnight at which point Donna had combined the notes into one book and took them home with her to go over. The others left the office leaving a single light burning.

Chapter 21

Jean Jenkins arrived home from the Local Jo Café in a
taxi. When she paid the driver the fare, her hands were
shaking so badly that the driver asked her if she was okay.
"I am fine," she said, "thanks for asking." Pulling herself
together, she went into her house and turned on the lights. She
locked the front door, immediately went to the rear door, saw
that it was locked and then checked the patio doors, which she
locked. Jean hurried to her office and laid her purse down on
the desk without opening it. She nervously stood by looking
at her purse as though it were an imposing threat, a poisonous
snake about to strike. She brought her fingers to her mouth,
dropped them, and brought her other hand up to her cheek.
Jean sat down and just as quickly rose up from the chair. She
closed the blinds on the only window in the room, went back
to the chair and once again sat. She put her elbows on the
desk and lifted her hands, one clasped over the other, to her
chin and mouth. She looked at her purse, silently
acknowledging the conundrum she was facing and in which
she was entangled. Jean sat for what seemed like an hour,
pondering whether she would open her purse and examine the
item that she purchased. She never saw a gun before except
those carried by police officers, much less have one in her

possession. Soon, she thought, she would have one in her hand. She imagined standing boldly holding a handgun in her right hand with her left hand used to steady it, like she had seen on television and in the movies. She wondered if that was how policemen really held guns or if it was only done for the sake of dramatization. She felt more relaxed, less nervous. She questioned why she balked at taking the gun out of her purse. She knew why. It was a weapon of violence. And, after all, didn't she abhor violence? At least, she thought, it is almost new, so it probably was not used in any kind of brutal attack whatsoever. Still how could she hold a weapon in her hand that had the potential to kill another human being? Did she have the propensity to point a loaded weapon at someone, with her finger on the trigger? Time would tell.

Jean reached down to undo the clasp on her purse. She undid the clasp without lifting the purse, and it fell open, exposing the plastic package within. It was a small package. She reached inside purse and lifted it out, laying it on the desk. It felt light to her. She pulled off the tape that held the plastic pouch closed and took the gun, two magazines holding bullets and a piece of folded paper out. She was surprised that such a small *item* yielded so much power. She laid the gun on the desk, unfolded the paper, and read the instructions that were titled Kahr PM9. The description referred to the weapon as a lightweight ad small size gun, weighing a mere 15.9 ounces with an empty magazine. It is just 5.3 inches long and 4 inches high, with a very thin flat profile; the slide is 0.9 inches across, and the magazine that is the same length as the grip is a six plus one. Jean smiled when she read that the PM9 gun *was born to be carried.* As she read each line of instructions, Jean looked down at the weapon to identify the part that was referred to. On the back of the paper was the following operating and safety list:

> 1. Always keep the gun pointed in a safe direction
>
> 2. Always keep your finger off the trigger until ready to shoot
>
> 3. Always keep the gun unloaded until ready to use
>
> 4. Always keep guns out of sight and reach of children
>
> 5. Know your target and what is beyond.
>
> 6. Think first - Shoot second
>
> 7. Use only the correct ammunition for your gun
>
> 8. Wear eye and ear protection as appropriate.
>
> 9. Always handle a gun as if it were loaded.

Jean thought the instructions were sensible, and just plain common sense, but for the most part did not pertain to most people, considering why they owned such a weapon, and how they planned on using it. She thought, how ironic that she, who detested the ownership of guns, found that the list applied more to her than to most gun owners.

When she felt confident that she understood what to do, she picked up the gun, checked that the safety was on, and took a magazine and snapped it into the slot in the handle. The gun was loaded.   She held the loaded gun with both hands. It felt balanced. It felt comfortable. That was easy, she thought, forgetting about the last half hour of tentative approach to the weapon. Now, I must learn how to shoot the damn thing, she said silently, handling the handgun with an unforeseen confidence. *'Now let the reprobate fuck with me and he will never see the sun shine again.'*

As she often did, Jean resorted to her reliable computer on which to carry out research. She googled *handgun target practice in Nova Scotia.* Too long a title, no luck. She tried *shooting range in Nova Scotia.* Luck. She hit on Nova Scotia Department of Natural Resources, which gave her a list and location of shooting ranges throughout the province, including two within the Halifax Regional Municipality. The HRM she grumbled. What the hell happened to the cities, Halifax, Dartmouth and all the towns that were gobbled up by the HRM? The HRM, foolishness, she thought. That's enough of that nonsense.

Jean was particularly taken with one site called the National Firearms Association, which accommodated indoor and outdoor ranges for handguns, with links for a site called *Becoming an Outdoors Woman.* This would have appealed to her if she were or even pretended to be an outdoor person. She would try to find a shooting range that met her criteria, one that did not require proof of a license for her handgun. She figured, with some degree of logic, that such a range would not be a busy one nor would it be a high-end establishment. In fact, one could reasonably assume that it would be loosely run. "Now that's my kinda place." She said aloud. "All I have to do is find such a range, and hope that the

regulations, whatever they may be, are not followed to the T."
Before Jean went to bed, she put the loaded gun and the extra
magazine in the drawer of her night table at only an arms
length away. She felt safe; she felt confident, and she would
sleep easily, knowing that she had a loaded weapon within
reach. Yet it was the very fact that she had the loaded weapon
in the drawer that made her feel uneasy. She reminded herself
that she had locked all the doors in the house. Then she went
to sleep.

Chapter 22

Daylight in Halifax brought in the fog that had been hovering over the Atlantic for the entire summer season. The cool ocean air drove under the warm rising land air carrying the misty bank inland. The leaves on the city's trees, of which there were plenty, held the moisture until its weight bent them down allowing the wet drops to cover the city streets, at best an annoyance to most pedestrians.

Stenson, who never wore a hat, entered the office shaking the moisture out of his thick hair, much like a dog coming in out of the rain. He went to Donna's desk for a tissue to dry his face. Donna was the department's supplier of tissues and the dispensary. If you needed temporary relief of a headache, or were in need of a band-aid for a minor cut, Donna was the person to see. Stenson saw Redmond sitting at his desk, acknowledged him with a wave, and went to work at reviewing the previous day's notes.

Redmond was the first one to arrive in the office this morning. His early arrival allowed him the quiet he needed to concentrate on the details of the case. He had a predilection for working alone. It suited him. He had gone over the notes in the murder book several times, trying to piece together what seemed like a situation without a trace of evidence. It was too early to speculate who might have been responsible for the crimes at the Indian Lake Golf Course. Still he couldn't help but think that Nickerson was good for it. *I know he's hiding something, he thought. Yes, he admitted that he is sleeping with Jenkins' wife. He didn't deny that. He didn't lie about that, although Lisa Jenkins did not corroborate it. Yet. Nickerson seemed wishy-washy. Something is not right about him, but I can't put my finger on it.* Redmond checked his watch, fifteen minutes to meeting. He noticed that everyone was now in the office and the tension was starting to mount. Dave Martin and Slater were chatting with Donna at her desk while sipping bought coffee, combined with nibbling on sweet cinnamon rolls.

Stenson sat alone deep in thought. He philosophized, as he often did, about the significance of his work. He wondered if he really made a difference in the scheme of things. What if he wasn't here fighting crime? Would anything have changed? Would someone else be in his shoes? Obviously someone would be. If they were, would they be better or worse? And did it really matter? Stenson laughed out loud at his mental meanderings, prompting a glance from the others. He knew that the work he did was just a temporary solution, a stopgap if you will. The process he was going through at the moment reminded him of the same thought process he entertained as a kid, what if…?

"What's the joke, Stenson?" Donna asked tapping him on the shoulder and interrupting his reverie.

"Oh nothing." He said looking at his watch. "Is it time to go to the meeting?"

"It's time." Donna said.

"Get your ass in gear." Dave piped up. "Let's get this meeting over with so we can do some real work."

. . . . .

As usual, Redmond conducted the meeting. "I don't need to tell you that we don't have a helluva lot to go on right now. It is fucking unbelievably frustrating knowing that some son-of-a-bitch is out there killing people and we are about as close to catching him as we are to catching a greased pig in a muddy sty. We have never had anything like this case before in Halifax and I'm really worried that it is only the beginning. I'm starting to think we're getting to be like the hot spots in the U.S., like Detroit or some other high-crime city. I decided to live in Halifax because it is a small city, quiet and peaceful. Am I fucking wrong? Whoever this perp is, he is making me angry. He is giving us a bad name. And I don't like it. I want to see every one of you guys feeling the same way… Donna included. Fuck! Now what do we have?"

Donna uncrossed her legs and sat up straight in her chair. "We did a thorough search of Jenkins' computer and we came up with four names of consequence, one you already know, of course, and that's Philip Nickerson. The others are also close friends of the victim. The four of them hung out together, played golf together and on a few occasions played poker about once every two months or so, according to the emails. Apparently, it was only penny ante games; no large amounts were won or lost. There is no evidence of any animosity between them, no indication of deals, monetary or otherwise, had taken place, and no planned meetings, secret or otherwise were conducted, as far as we can tell. And that holds true for anyone else that Jenkins had contacted by email. We're planning to follow up by interviewing the friends today, with the exception of Nickerson, who was already interviewed by you, Rick. Dave, Jim and I will each interview one of the three, and then we will meet back here to compare notes."

"What about Jenkins' finances?" Rick inquired.

"I think I got that covered, Rick." Martin said. "First I would like to preface it by saying that we can find no financial connection between these rich guys, although Harris didn't seem to have *that* much money. So if there was any connection between the two, it wasn't financial. As far as Jenkins goes, the guy has a net worth of more than fifteen million dollars; it is not a huge amount, but people have killed for a helluva lot less though."

"Try fifty thousand." Someone piped up.

"Yeah right!" Dave continued contemptuously, with no love lost for the wealthy. "And I guess fifteen mil is enough for a couple or three of us to retire on." He said laughing. "His insurance has a payback of $6.5 million, most of which goes to Lisa Jenkins, his wife, with a much smaller portion going to his daughter by a previous marriage. I believe that the daughter will receive about a quarter of a million dollars. The value of the house is about $1.2 million, and if I am correct, there are savings of approximately $750,000, with the remainder in RRSPs and in investments. In conclusion, the probability of Jenkins being taken down for money is exceedingly possible and more than probable, and in my opinion, Lisa Jenkins and her friend Nickerson are the number one suspects." Martin wrapped up.

"Donna, are you of the same mind." Rick solicited.

"Well, it seems logical, but I wouldn't go that far; it may be is too obvious. I think we need to take a look at the others on the list. We shouldn't exclude the friends and the golf club staff as suspects. Of course, I am not precluding his wife from doing her husband." Her last remark provoked a burst of laughter.

"Okay let's keep it serious, guys." Redmond reprimanded. "Is that it, Donna?"

"After that what more can I say?" She said smiling.

Stenson who had been standing and listening carefully said, "at this point in the investigation, we can't exclude anyone. We must be resolute and diligent in our approach. Focus on as many suspects as possible and search for a sound motive. The process is painstaking, no doubt. It is fine to have expectations of quick results, but let's not be disappointed if that doesn't happen. We all know how long an investigation can take, and the smarter the perp, the longer the time to find him or her. And I think the person responsible for the crimes is very smart and systematic. Enough said. We are all professionals, and don't need a pep talk. As far as our progress goes, we ran out of light yesterday and Rick and I will follow up in the woods at Indian Lake Golf Course, and if necessary, we will again talk to some of the staff there." He nodded that he was finished.

"Thanks, Stenson. Thank you all for working so hard and putting in such long hours on this case. Please keep your focus and continue your good work, and you can rest assured that we will get a break soon. I know it's a fucking drag, but we'll have to keep up the long hours in order for our work to pay off, and I assure you it will. Once again, if you come up with anything new, contact me immediately, any time of day or night." Redmond closed his notepad, and the group broke up and exited the room.

. . . . .

Donna, Dave and Jim sat together to decide on who was to contact whom for an interview. Slater got AJ Devoe, Dave was given Dan Lee, and Donna settled for Mike Fisher.

Jim, who was the only uniformed policeman working the case, called Devoe who had been sound asleep and answered the phone on the fifth ring.

"AJ Devoe" He said into the mouthpiece.

Slater could hear the rustling of bedding as Devoe moved to sit up.

"Mr. Devoe, this is Constable Jim Slater of the HRM Police.

"Yes. Is this about Geoff?" He sat up higher in bed.

"It is about Geoff Jenkins, Mr. Devoe. He was murdered and I would like to talk to you to see if you can offer any insight as to what may have happened."

"God. I heard about it on the news and then called Lisa to find out if she was okay. I don't know how I can help, but I would be more than willing to meet with you." Devoe said.

"Is it convenient to meet in about a half hour or so at your place? Slater asked.

"Absolutely. No problem at all. Actually, can we make it in about an hour or an hour and a half from now? That would give me time to shower and eat." He requested.

"Sure. Let's make it in an hour and a half."

Devoe gave Slater his address and directions how to get there. The delay gave Slater time to review the emails received from and sent to Devoe to give him something to go on before their meeting, although there didn't seem to be anything incriminating.

Dave Martin put a call through to Dan Lee but was unsuccessful in reaching him. Martin knew that Lee owned an operated two coffee shops called *Grounds for Coffee*. One was located on Granville and the other on Spring Garden Road; both were business thoroughfares with high pedestrian traffic. Martin figured that the Spring Garden location would be the busiest, so he decided to go the other route by calling the Granville location. He got lucky and reached Lee at Granville. Lee agreed to meet him at the coffee shop at 9:30, before the mid-morning coffee break rush. During the brief conversation, Lee sounded quite upset about his friend's death. Dave could hear his voice was quavering; probably the best time to interview a potential suspect is when their guard is down, when they are vulnerable, he thought. The need to pressure them was less likely.

Donna had tried reaching Fisher. He was not at home. There was no phone number left on the recording indicating where he could be reached. Copp went back to work, sifting through Jenkins; financial papers, hoping to learn the name of the company in which Fisher worked. She carefully studied each document that she came across, checking for names of officers and directors of each company. She noticed that one document was signed M.A. Fisher, President and CEO. The name of the company was simply called *Investments and Securities*. Donna jotted down the name, address and phone number, and then continued looking through other documents. She was astonished by the amount of the investment, more than a half million dollars. She found two other documents, dated three months apart, from the same company. The amounts invested were all similar, and the signature at the end of the document was the same, M.A. Fisher. Donna found no other papers with Fisher's name on it.

Donna called Investments and Securities and asked for Michael Fisher. The receptionist said he was in a meeting and could he return the call. Donna gave the receptionist her name and cell phone number and told her it was urgent. She said she would have Mr. Fisher return her call as soon as possible. While waiting for the call, Donna took advantage of the break to look through the email files, examining the messages from Fisher. Most of them were insignificant. None seemed important or were cryptic; consequently, none contained any information that was remotely suspicious. Donna's phone rang, startling her. It was Fisher.

"Donna Copp," he asked.

"This is Detective Donna Copp. Is this Michael Fisher?"

"Oh?" Fisher seemed uneasy when he heard Donna introduce herself as detective. "I thought this was a private phone I was calling." He said.

"It is a private phone." Donna replied with no explanation.

"Then are you calling about an investment, Ms Copp, or rather Detective Copp?"

"No. Actually I am calling about Geoff Jenkins."

"Oh God. That was horrible what happened to Geoff. His wife called me to let me know. I couldn't believe it. Is there anything I can do to help?"

"Yes, there is. I would like to meet with you to see if you know anything about Geoff that might lead us to why he was murdered."

"I can't say that I would be happy to see you, considering the circumstances, detective, but I would definitely be open to meeting with you."

"Can you meet me here at the station?" She asked.

"Today?"

"Today would be good. If that's not good for you..."

"I am quite busy with meetings today, so it is not good for me, unless you can meet me at my office. I am free for the next 45 minutes and then I am expecting a client. How is that for you? I am at Purdy's Wharf, by the way."

Donna was quick to respond. "I will be there shortly. Thank you Mr. Fisher." She said and hung up. Donna was not exactly comfortable with business executives. She felt that most of them demanded unearned respect, and unconditional agreement. Since the window of opportunity was short, and parking limited, Donna had a blue and white drop her off at the Scotia Square Mall where she took the pedway directly to Purdy's Wharf.

Chapter 23

Even though the fog had dissipated over the city, it continued to hover over the property at the Indian Lake Golf Course; the woods were wet from the dense mist. The groundskeepers and the owners were the only ones at the clubhouse, but none were outside tending to the grounds. Inside the clubhouse, food was not being prepared, nor needed to be since the course was temporarily closed. Stenson alerted Mitch Kline that he and Redmond would be exploring the woods off the third hole. No surprises. The detectives arrived at the spot that Stenson had marked off with an X the day before. Stenson picked up one of the sticks and they entered the woods. Their shoes and pants cuffs quickly became soaked from the sodden underbrush as they hiked to the site of interest, which was no more than five minutes from the fairway. Stenson stood silently on the spot and Redmond walked aimlessly around the area or so it seemed. Rick mutter softly "What do I see?" He stopped to look around. "What is here? What the hell am I looking for?"
Stenson spoke to himself silently, *'what would I be doing here, if I were the perp? I am the perp. I just killed two people. Wouldn't I be in a hurry to leave the scene? What would make me stop, slow me down?'* Stenson looked out to the fairway. *'Did I see someone? Could I be seen? I can't see out, so they can't see me.'* He crouched looking around,

adrenalin flowing, anxious from the imagined kill. *'I've got to get out of here without being seen.'* He started to move forward and stopped. He found the stick to be an encumbrance. He dropped it and started to move on. Stopped. *'Can't do that. That's the murder weapon. Can't leave it. Have to take it with me.'* He picked it up. He started and stopped. *'Can't take it. Can't be seen with it.'* He dropped it again and this time left it. Stenson bent his knees, slowly dropping to the ground and crawled around on all fours like a dog. He dropped his head close to the wet ground. He did not sniff, but instead circled around with his nose still close to the ground. Then he sat up on his legs and looked around. Rick just stood there watching him in amazement as though Stenson had lost his mind, had flipped out. He started to walk towards the half sitting Stenson. Stenson held his hand up, palm facing Rick, to stop him. Stenson then rose to his feet, walked to the edge of the clearing, looking in the denser underbrush, slowly, methodically. He bent down and used his hands to push the covering aside, a step at a time, until he stopped and shouted. "Yes! Yes! Eureka!"

Rick ran over to him and Stenson pointed out his find, a golf club hidden under impenetrable ground cover. The club was fully intact, clearly not broken. Stenson put on a pair of clear vinyl gloves and picked up the club from the ground. Both detectives looked at the head of the club and saw what they thought might be a smear of dried blood. Stenson handed the club to Rick, who was astounded at the find and exclaimed, "I'll be a son-of-a-bitch."

Stenson resumed searching with renewed commitment, pushing bushes aside, hoping and expecting to find more evidence. After thoroughly exploring the surrounding undergrowth, he paused to reflect; subsequently he conceded that there was nothing more to be found. The two men began the short but jubilant trek back to the clubhouse. Before going inside the clubhouse, Stenson took the alleged weapon from Rick and carefully put it into the trunk of his car and locked it. He and Rick briefly discussed the need to either keep the course closed or to reopen it, and then went into the clubhouse.

Karen Kelder was working behind the reception counter, catching up on previously unfinished work and writing a newsletter by hand to the club membership informing them that the course would remain closed for a few more days. Karen was less stressed than the last time they had seen her. The break from the daily rush of golfers had resulted in Karen being far more relaxed. She managed a smile and brushed her hair away from her face as they approached the counter.

Rick said to her, "We're just about finished here, Mrs. Kelder, so we'll be leaving shortly."

"I hope it was a productive visit." She said, instead of asking, sensing their optimism.

Stenson, with his smile returning, said, "You and your husband have been very patient with us regarding the interruption of your business. And we appreciate your help. I hope you are feeling better after the last traumatic episode you encountered here."

"Traumatic is hardly the word for it, Detective Stenson. It was devastating, to say the least." She laughed. "I thought I was going to die." Laughing even harder. "But that's not funny. Yes thanks, I am feeling so much better. I think closing the course down for a few days was a godsend, and it gave me a chance to rest and also to catch up. By the way, do you have any idea when we can open up again?" She pleaded scrunching up her face.

Redmond responded to her plea. "We were just discussing that a moment ago, Mrs. Kelder. We think it's okay to reopen immediately, meaning tomorrow. But, we would like to keep someone posted here, just in case."

"Oh that's wonderful." She said. "I was in the process of writing a newsletter to send to the membership. Now we can let them know." The phone rang. "Excuse me." She picked up. "Indian Lake Golf Course." She listened. "Yes, we are. Would you like to book a time?" Listening again. "Yes, that's fine. And that will be for 18 holes? Good." She said booking the time on a sheet. "I'll see you then." She hung up. "Sorry about that."

"No prob." Rick said.

"I have one question for you though. This policeman you want to post here, is he necessary?" She asked tentatively. Stenson quickly reacted. "Very necessary. We think it is essential for the safety of everyone here. There is no saying that whoever is responsible for the murders won't hit again. It wouldn't be responsible to expose everyone here to that possibility without some kind of protection. However, we can make it less obvious by dressing him in casual clothes and give him a set of clubs to walk around with. How does that suit you?"

" Perfect. It is the best of both worlds. Will whoever you post here check in with me, so I know who he is?" Karen asked.

"We'll make sure of that, Mrs. Kelder." Redmond answered.

"It's just that I don't want someone strange playing golf or, wandering around the course if we can't account for him having paid … or whatever." She explained.

"I understand. That makes sense. We will also make sure you have his cell phone number, in the event that you need his help. Okay?" Rick offered.

"That'll be perfect."

"One other thing. Did anyone report losing a club during the last week or so? Rick inquired in an offhanded manner.

"What kind of club?"

"Say a driver."

"Not to my knowledge. But if they had, it would have been found and returned by now." Karen said, checking her lost and found notes. "One second. Nope. I don't see that any clubs were reported missing during the last two weeks."

"Okay. Good." Rick said.

We may need to talk to some of your people at a future date." Stenson added.

"Sure." Karen agreed. "I don't see that as a problem. Just let me know when. We've had enough surprises this week. I don't need anymore."

"It won't be right away, maybe in a few days."

Stenson and Redmond left unceremoniously, just as the counter phone rang.

Chapter 24

Donna Copp found Michael Fisher's office without difficulty. It was on the sixth floor, and on a brass plaque, mounted on the wall next to the solid wood door, was etched Investments and Securities. She tried the door, but it was locked. There was a lighted button off to the right of the door, with a small sign underneath, *Ring to Gain Entrance*. Donna pressed the button and a moment later a young, pretty woman dressed in a grey pencil skirt, a dark grey long sleeve blouse and black heeled shoes, opened the door, greeted her and asked her in. The receptionist tossed her dark brown, curled, shoulder length hair as she turned and returned to behind her L-shaped desk. She sat down before asking with a genuine smile. "May I help you?"

"Yes, you may." Donna said kindly. "My name is Donna Copp. I am here to see Michael Fisher."

The receptionist, whose small name plaque, which was sitting on the front of her desk, indicated that her name was Linda Belford, looked down at a pad, said. "Yes, Ms Copp, Mr. Fisher is expecting you. Have a seat please. He'll be with you momentarily."

Donna sat on one of two plush padded armchairs that were on either side of a small oak table that was stained a honey color with a smoked glass inset. Above her on the wall was a large original oil painting of the Halifax Harbor with McNabs Island in the background. The lighthouse on McNabs was seen through a heavy haze, with its light barely discernable through the mist. She picked a copy of the Financial Times from the table and opened it. The receptionist entered a number on her phone and pressed the intercom. She announced that Ms Donna Copp was here to see him, and then hung up. "Mr. Fisher will be with you in a second, Ms Copp." She said with polite professionalism.

"Thank you." Donna said without looking up from the paper. Donna expected to wait a few minutes, but was surprised by Michael Fisher's immediate appearance. He introduced himself and invited her to follow him to his office. He was a picture straight out of GQ. He was wearing an expensive tailored navy suit, a pale blue dress shirt, with a muted multi-colored tie that picked up the color of both his shirt and suit. Business must be good, Donna thought. The outfit must have cost him at least two months of her take home pay she figured. Fisher walked in front of her. His gait was smooth with a slight swagger. He was five inches taller than Copp, probably just short of six feet, and was powerfully built at approximately 200 to 210 pounds, she estimated, with the agile movement of a confident athlete. His well-groomed hair was sandy, the color of someone who spends a great deal of time outdoors.

Fisher stopped to allow Copp to pass first into his office, which was lit by natural light coming through the wall of windows facing the outer harbor. The view was not too dissimilar to the painting in the reception area, but not quite from the same perspective. Not only was McNabs in plain view, but also Georges Island. The walls of his office were painted a satin pearl color and held several original oil paintings that looked like the same artist may have produced them. The desk was simple; it was entirely finished with a white stain and it contained two small drawers. A single flat-screen monitor that sat on the desk was turned off. The computer was neatly concealed, nowhere to be seen. A small three-shelf bookcase with the same finish as the desk was to Fisher's left and behind the desk; it held several volumes of books. A round glass top table with four chairs that were similar to those in the reception area had mauve fabric cushioned seats, and was centered in the front of the windows. Fisher offered Donna a seat at the table. "May I get you something to drink?" He asked her.

Donna took advantage of the offer. "A glass of water would be fine."

Fisher called his receptionist using the speaker. "Linda, bring us two glasses of water, please." He cut off the intercom before she could respond. Fisher sat in a chair at the table opposite Donna. "Now, Detective Copp... by the way, that is an interesting name for a policeman, or a cop." He said smiling. "But I am sure you hear that all the time."

"All the time." She said not amused.

"I won't waste your time. What is it you need from me?" He asked coolly.

"I'll be as brief as I can and to the point." She said. "How well did you know Geoff Jenkins?"

171

"I knew him very well. We were very close friends."

"And you socialized together?" She continued.

"Of course we did. That's what friend do." He forced a smile.

"Played golf together?"

Fisher hesitated. "When we could. Geoff took a lot of time off. I couldn't do that, obviously, as much as much as I would have liked to."

"Why was that, Mr. Fisher?"

"Why was I not able to take more time off, you ask?"

"Yes. Why was that not possible for you? It looks like you are your own boss."

He smiled arrogantly. "Not just my own boss, detective, I own the business. When you are an entrepreneur of sorts, you end up putting in more time than if you were to work for someone else."

"Of course, how stupid of me. I should have known that." She said in an artificial attempt to gain his approval.

"Not at all, detective, there is no way for you to know that, is there? After all, you don't work for yourself, do you?" He said in a condescending tone.

Copp ignored his intended disparaging remark. "But you had gone golfing on some occasions with Mr. Jenkins?"

"Yes, that's true." He said offering a minimal amount of information.

"Who else would have gone with you, Mr. Fisher?" She asked knowing the answer.

"Usually, it was myself, Geoff, Nickerson, Phil Nickerson,

and AJ. AJ is Aaron Devoe. That would have been our regular foursome. When one of the regulars were unable to play, Dan Lee would fill in sometimes, although that wasn't very often."

"Why didn't he play often?"

"For one reason, he put in more work hours than most of us did combined. He too has his own business, you know."

"I see." Donna said writing a note in her pad.

"I must admit, even though I felt pressured to be here, at work, I really enjoyed myself when I went with the boys. We had great fun golfing. It was sort of like the old boys club. All of us have known each other since university." He said easing up.

"That must have been an enjoyable and relaxing experience." She said feeling as though she were gaining his confidence. "Do you know if any of Mr. Jenkins' friends had any disagreements with him? Any disputes or misunderstandings?"

"You know, detective, I never met anybody who hadn't had quarrels with their friends. No matter how good your friends are there's going to be arguments at some point. It's only natural. In fact, I think you, you in general that is, would probably argue less with someone who is *not* your friend." He emphasized and waited for her response. With no response coming, he added. "But I think you know that, detective."

"That's quite true, Mr. Fisher. Perhaps I didn't express myself very well. I was thinking more in the lines of an intense disagreement; maybe someone who held a grudge against him and might want to seek revenge." She explained and added. "Maybe someone who might want him dead."

"Ah. I see your point. That certainly is different. No, I don't know anyone who would have wanted Geoff dead, detective. It is unthinkable to even consider that one of his friends would do that. We were all so close. I am surprised, or perhaps shocked would be a better word, that you would ask such a question."

"I am sure many of my questions would shock you, Mr. Fisher. Do you think either of your friends had anything to do with Mr. Jenkins' death?"

"Absolutely not! Impossible! I believe that in my heart and soul and without exception." Fisher said with authority.

"And what about yourself, Mr. Fisher? Did you have any reason to kill Geoff Jenkins?"

"You surprise me, Detective Copp. I find your questions to be hurtful and insensitive. Geoff was my friend for as long as I can remember. I would never hurt him or anyone else in the worst of circumstances. How could you have the audacity to possibly ask me that?"

"It is my job to ask these questions, Mr. Fisher. I'm sorry if I offended you. The questions would be less offensive if you thought about the reason why I asked them, namely to find the truth about who is behind Geoff's death."

"I understand, detective. I'm the one who should be sorry. It's just that I am still saddened and quite upset by what happened to Geoff, as much as I try to hide it. I'm not one to wear my emotions on my sleeve." Fisher attempted to elucidate.

"Just a few more questions, Mr. Fisher. I know you have a meeting soon, so I'll try to be as brief as I can. Did you or your friends have any business dealings with Jenkins?"

"I really don't know about the others. I am pretty sure that AJ didn't have any business dealings with him whatsoever; he is pretty selective with his money, and most likely wouldn't have used Geoff's consulting services at all. As you might know, Geoff has used my services to invest some money, and in the past, he benefited substantially, making a considerable return on his money. I'm sure you can check that out. Lately the market turndown has not been kind to any of my investors, but that did not dissuade Geoff from continuing to invest. As far as Dan Lee goes, you will have to check with him, but I don't think Geoff was very interested in investing in his coffee shops. If I am not mistaken, Dan took out small business loans through the banks. And if I am correct in my assessment of his financial situation, Dan is well above water. That's about all the information I really have, Detective. I am sorry if I seemed a bit defensive. Geoff's death has caused all of us a lot of a grief, and there is no comfort in being considered a suspect."

"Perfectly understandable considering the circumstances." Donna said as the intercom rang and Fisher got up, excused himself to answer it. He left the speaker on. Linda said, "Your next appointment is here, Mr. Fisher."

"I'll only be a moment longer, Linda." He disconnected the intercom, and returned to the table.

175

Donna stood up and handed Fisher her card and said. "If you think of anything else, please contact me, Mr. Fisher. I would appreciate it."

"I certainly will, Detective Copp. I want to see whoever did this to Geoff caught and put in prison.

"Oh, by the way, where were you when Geoff was killed, Mr. Fisher?" Catching him off guard.

Fisher replied without flinching. "I was here in the office. I usually come in early."

How did you know that that was the time Geoff was killed?"

"I didn't know. I knew what time he was going to play golf though; he always sends me an email to see if I'm free to join him. But I had to be in the office early that day."

"Was anyone here with you?"

"Linda usually gets in about nine, so yes, she can verify that I was here." Fisher smiled ingratiatingly. "You'll have to forgive me, but I do have someone waiting to see me.

"Thank you for your time." She said as Fisher showed her out. Donna waited in the reception area, as Linda escorted the next appointment into Fisher's office. When she returned, Donna asked her what time she saw Fisher the morning Geoff was murdered. She said that although she arrived in the office just before nine but didn't see him until about 9:30 or so. He was in his office and asked her to bring in a coffee to him about that time. "So he was here before you came in to work?"

"He is here almost every morning before I get in. Sometimes he is in at seven or earlier."

"How do you know what time he gets in?"

"The sign in sheet." She motions to the sign-in sheet at her desk. "We always use that so that if someone calls, I'll know if he is in or not."

"It is a small office. Is it so hard to keep track of each other?" Donna smiled.

"It may be small but if I am filing, or photo copying, or away from my desk in a different office, I may not have any other way of knowing if Mr. Fisher had come in or gone out."

"I see. Thank you." Donna said giving her card to the receptionist before leaving the office.

Chapter 25

Dave Martin parked in a loading zone in front of *Grounds for Coffee*. As he went inside, the sweet coffee aroma that overwhelmed his senses and brought a smile to his lips greeted him. He thought he died and went to heaven. The counter and cash was directly in front of him. Several large ornate silver coffee urns with brass plaques indicating the type of coffee sat on the counter. A glass case next to the urns contained a variety of oversized decadent sweet rolls. There were several round tables both to the left and right of the door. There was an odd number, three, of chairs to each table. Martin walked up to the counter; he was wearing an inexpensive, but well-manicured suit and could easily have been an employee on a coffee break from a nearby office.

"May I help you?" A young woman with rosy cheeks and her hair pulled back asked him. She was wearing a full white apron over an orange long sleeve shirt and black pants.

"You certainly may help me. I'm looking for Dan Lee." He said smiling, deliberately flirting with her.

"Dan went out for a minute; he should be back soon. Can I get you something while you wait?" She asked with a bright warm smile.

"I'm sure you can." He said smiling back. She laughed. "Do you have a special blend?"

"We do. Would you like a regular or large?"

"How strong is it?" Martin asked.

"Strong." She said. But I doubt it will take the coating off your tongue."

"I'll have a large then, dark and strong." He stood waiting.

"Have a seat and I'll bring it to your table." And added as an afterthought. "When Dan comes in, I'll let him know you're here."

"Thanks, sweetie." He smiled, continuing his flirtation. He took a table in the corner, sitting with his back to the wall so he could see the door. Shortly after he sat down, a partially balding, grey-haired man wearing jeans and a white wrinkled shirt came through the door and went behind the counter. The rosy-cheeked girl said something to him and he looked in Dave's direction. The man tied a white half apron around his waist. The girl brought the large coffee to Martin's table, trailed by the man in the apron.

"I brought two things at once for you, your coffee and Dan." She said with a gregarious smile. "Dan, this is the gentleman that's waiting for you."

"Dan Lee," he said extending his open hand.

"Thanks for you help." Martin said to the girl, who turned and went back to the counter. "Detective Dave Martin." He said shaking hands with Lee.

Dan Lee sat down and said, "I suppose you want to talk to me about Geoff Jenkins." His eyes started to well up with tears, which he quickly brushed away.

"Yes, I do, Mr. Lee."

"Please call me Dan, everyone does. I've hardly been able to think straight since I heard about what happened to Geoff. We have been friends since forever."

"When was the last time you saw Geoff, Dan?" He stirred the coffee after adding sugar to it.

"The last time I saw him was the day before he died. We had coffee together at my Spring Garden shop location. I haven't been able to go there since then." He lamented.

"I am really sorry for your loss, Dan." Martin said uneasy using the cliché, trying to make it new and fresh.

"Thank you. I want you to know that I am willing to do whatever I can to help. Geoff was so vibrant, so full of life…and way too young to die." Lee said shaking his head sadly.

"Do you have any idea who might have killed Geoff?"

"Let's see." He pondered. "It may sound strange, but I don't know a soul who disliked him." He said still shaking his head in disbelief. "He was so even keeled, and genuinely accommodating. How could anyone be so heartless to take his life?"

"It certainly happens, Mr. Lee…"

"Dan, please." He interrupted.

"There are some very bad people in this world, Dan, with no regard for other human beings." Martin sipped his coffee.

"Is there anything I can do?"

"I have to ask where you were the morning Geoff was killed."

"I understand." He ran his hand through the remaining grey hair and patted his bald spot, expecting the gesture to temper his feelings regarding his friend's death. "I am not sure the exact time he was killed, but I was at the Spring Garden Road shop at seven a.m., and when it was up and running I came here to open this one, which is usually about seven thirty or thereabouts. Then about eight, I picked up some fresh bagels and cinnamon rolls for both places."

And someone was with you at those times?"

"Oh yes, at both shops."

"Can you give me the names of those who can verify the times?

"I will have to check the schedules, but that's not a problem." Lee called to the girl at the counter. "Annie, please bring me the work schedule and a piece of paper." The girl brought the schedule and a pad to Lee. He looked at the schedule and wrote down the names.

"I could use the phone numbers as well." Martin said with little tact.

Lee looked up at him and then returned to the pad, and added the phone numbers next to the names. "There you are. I am sure this will relieve me from suspicion." He said without malice.

"Maybe I shouldn't say this, Dan, but personally I don't think you had anything to do with it. But just for the record, did you have any financial dealings of any kind with Geoff?"

"None whatsoever. Geoff wanted to invest in the two shops, but I didn't want any partners. I think he wanted to do it more as a favor than anything."

"A favor? Why do you think that?"

"He told me that if I couldn't get the start-up funds, that he would gladly help me out. I suppose it was a gesture of friendship."

"But you were able to get the start-up funds, Dan?"

"It was no problem getting a small bank loan. I have always been fortunate that way."

"What about Geoff's other friends, could they have done this?" Martin looked at his notes. "Like Philip Nickerson, AJ Devoe and Michael Fisher."

"I don't know about those guys. Phil is okay. I can't imagine him killing anyone. AJ is a bit lazy. He comes from money and doesn't do much. I just don't know."

"What about Michael Fisher?" Martin pressed.

"He's more of Geoff's friend than he is mine. We didn't pal around too much. Frankly, I am not very fond of him. He's a bit too egotistical for my liking. But that doesn't mean I think he was capable of killing Geoff. He and Geoff were very good friends, just as we all were."

Do you know of anyone that might have had a grudge with Geoff? Maybe someone with whom he did consulting work?"

"I have no idea whatsoever. Geoff never really talked much about his business. As a matter of fact, he rarely talked about himself; he was more interested in what others were doing."

They ended the conversation with Martin giving Lee his card in the event that he thought of something else that might have been important. Martin sat and savored his coffee before he left the *Grounds for Coffee* shop.

Chapter 26

Jean woke invigorated. Impregnated with thoughts of
the previous night, picking up where she left off, and
continuing the process without the previous night's anxiety,
she reached over to the table drawer that held the gun. She
took the gun out and having reached an accord handled it with
the ease of holding a cup of tea.

Jean got out of bed, and put on a white robe that reached down
almost to her ankles directly over her nightgown. She put the
gun in the robe pocket. The gun would now be her
companion, everywhere she went. It would accompany her
like a trusted friend, whether she went to the Oxford Theatre
to see a movie, a dinner party in the south end of the city, the
Neptune Theatre to watch a Canadian drama, or to the Cohen
for a performance of Symphony Nova Scotia. Her gun would
be her cc, constant companion; it would become a part of her
and known only to her.

Jean carried the gun with her to the breakfast nook, where she
opened the wood slatted blinds to let in the morning sun. She
felt it against her thigh as she prepared a poached egg and
toasted an English muffin that she coated lightly with butter.
After her breakfast, Jean showered; the gun remained in the
pocket of her robe that hung on the bathroom door hook.
Once she toweled dried, she put the robe back on, feeling the
weight of the gun. She went into the bedroom, put the gun on

the bed, and dressed in grey wool pants and a pale green cashmere sweater. She decided on a fanny pack to carry the gun, and then decided to the contrary, considering it as being too exposed and possibly subject to theft. She wanted to get use to her new friend, so the only option was to carry it concealed in her purse. The weapon, weighing only a pound, carried in her purse would surely go unnoticed even if she allowed someone to handle it, her purse.

Her *mission*, as she considered it, was to find a shooting range that would allow her to enter, to practice shooting with the least amount of questions asked and even fewer requirements. Jean called several shooting ranges while maintaining anonymity. After an hour of talking to proprietors and managers, she came across one that not only did not require any ID or proof of license, but also was small, out of the way, and, for a small fee, provided ammunition for her weapon. She made an appointment for early afternoon, to give her time to prepare and drive to the out-of-the-way shooting range.

Jean was concerned about Lisa. Jean called her to see if she needed help with Geoff's arrangement, only to discover the his body had not been released yet. All other arrangements had been made and were in order. Jean told her that she needed to spend the afternoon alone. It was understandable. They would talk later.

Jean felt uneasy about her email request to her friends and decided to cover her tracks somewhat by sending a follow-up email message to those she originally contacted. The content of the message was:

Dear friend,

*I must have been out of my mind to
ask for your help to acquire a
handgun. I have come to my senses
and ask you to forgive my ungodly
request. I hope you will not think ill
of me in my moment of madness
caused by the grief of my brother's
death.*

Yours in friendship,

Jean

Jean sent the message and hoped that it would soothe the savage beast.

Chapter 27

Aaron John Devoe was ravenous after he finished taking his shower. This day, he prepared bacon, two eggs and a toasted bagel, in addition to a large glass of orange juice. He wore a pair of designer jeans that fit tightly on his slim frame, and sand colored short-sleeved tee shirt with a subtle olive stripe. His feet were bare. AJ had spent a long night out lounge hopping, drinking and dancing from which he had yet to recover. He had traveled from The Dome to the Marquee Club, among others, and ended up at the Seahorse Tavern on Argyle Street. He was unsure if he had picked up a woman and brought her home; but if he did, she left before he had awakened. He might have still been in bed had he not received a phone call from the police. As he energetically attacked his breakfast, AJ felt a drip of water running down the back of his neck from his still wet dark brown hair. Although he was entering the *new* middle age, almost fifty, he maintained a full head of hair without any graying. He liked his bachelor life, preferring it to his previously disastrous marriage that left him a cool million dollars less in his coffers. However, he did feel fortunate in that it hardly made a dent in his assets. AJ was on his second cup of coffee when the doorbell rang. He went to the door and opened it to Jim Slater. "Mr. Slater, I presume?" He asked humorously, and smiled exposing his very white and perfectly even teeth.

"Yes, that's correct." Slater responded with a smile, appreciating his humor.

"Please come in, Mr. Slater. I just finished my breakfast. May I offer you a cup of coffee?

"I would love a cup of coffee. I need a good one; the station coffee is not even close to being drinkable." He said following Devoe into the kitchen.

AJ took a cup from a hook inside one of the cabinets, and poured a coffee from a stainless steel thermal carafe. Slater noticed that AJ's arms and face were tan, perhaps from a trip south in the sun.

"Sugar and cream?" AJ asked aware that Slater checked out his tan. "I recently returned from a trip to Costa Rica." He said raising and referring to his arm. "When I say recently, I mean in early spring. Of course, I have enhanced it a bit during the summer, playing golf, hiking and beaching."

"Black is fine, thanks. Sorry, I couldn't help noticing your tan." He added, sitting on a stool at the breakfast counter.

"I guess it goes with the territory, doesn't it?" AJ asked as he cleared his breakfast dishes, rinsing and putting them the dishwasher.

"And by that you mean...?" He asked taking a drink of coffee.

"What I mean is that you being a cop, you would notice things like that." AJ explained.

Slater nodded in acknowledgement of his explanation. "The reason I'm here is to ask you a few questions about Geoff Jenkins."

"As you undoubtedly know, Geoff and I were very good friends, very good friends." He repeated.

"I was under that impression, Mr. Devoe. Could you tell me where you were when Mr. Jenkins was killed?"

"My god, man! We were friends. Are you accusing me of murdering Geoff?"

"Absolutely not, Mr. Devoe. We need to know where everyone was at that time, so we can eliminate them as suspects, look at timeframes, and track Mr. Jenkins whereabouts, so that it gives us an overview and helps in the investigation of his death." Slater said trying to maintain a civil tone.

"Sorry. I am still quite upset about what happened to Geoff. I just can't accept that he's gone. I can't believe it. Perhaps if I had gotten out of bed earlier and joined him for a round of golf, he'd still be alive. I just wish there was something I could have done. I don't know. In any case, I was here, home, in bed. I had another late night."

"Did anyone see you, verify that you were here?" He questioned.

"Is that necessary? My word's not good enough?" Slater shrugged. "I *guess* there was someone who saw me; in fact, she spent the night here."

"And was she with you for how long in the morning?"

"I'd say she left about 7:30, or thereabouts. She had to be at work by 9:00.

"And could you tell me her name, Mr. Devoe?"

"Let's see…I only met her once." He said looking for and

finding a piece of paper on the breakfast counter next to the phone. "Here it is, her name and phone number. I asked her to write it down before she left."

Slater took the paper, wrote down the name and number in his notepad. "Only a first name? Do you have her last name?"

"Sorry, Mr. Slater. I only met her once, as I said. I figured that when I called her for a date, I could get her last name, if it worked out, you know what I mean?" He asked smiling.

"Yes, I know what you mean. I'll find out her name when I call her." AJ frowned. "That is not a problem for you, is it, that I call her?"

"No, not a problem at all."

"When did you last see Mr. Jenkins?" Slater continued with the questions.

"It was sometime last week. Geoff, Dan, Dan Lee, and I got together for lunch. That was the last time I saw him."

"And were you discussing business?" He pursued.

"No, not really." AJ said casually.

"What did you discuss, Mr. Devoe?"

"Not much. Just old friends stuff. Geoff was looking at a potential new client, and we talked about things in general, politics and religion, nothing too specific, as I recall."

"That's it?"

"Look Mr. Slater, it is difficult to remember conversations that were uneventful. After so many conversations, they all run together. You know what I mean?"

"No I don't know what you mean." Slater said contrarily.

"Did you and Mr. Jenkins have any business arrangements or

dealings?"

"Are you kidding? I have a policy of not doing business with any of my friends. It can lead to too many problems. As I see it, money and friends don't mix." He said adamantly, and added in a derogatory tone, one that was not to be misconstrued by Slater.

"Sounds like you might have had a bad business experience." Slater remarked. AJ just shrugged.

"Mike Fisher is the investor, not me. Talk to him about business dealings."

"Do you have a lot of money to invest, sir?"

AJ was at first annoyed by the question and then laughed. "I suppose if you wanted to find out about my finances, it would take you less than a day to discover that I have had a rather substantial inheritance and a trust fund early on that I have been living on quite comfortably for the last twenty years or more and expect to continue on in that vein for the rest of my life, with lots to spare; that's why so many women find me attractive, Mr. Slater. Money attracts women; it is a sign of power."

"So I can safely assume the you are quite well off."

"You would not be incorrect in making that assumption." AJ smiled. "Now if you will excuse me, unless you have further questions you wish to ask me."

"No, I have no other questions, Mr. Devoe." Slater said in a congenial manner. "Thank you for your time." He added giving AJ his card.

"You're welcome. And please, if you don't mind, show

yourself out, Detective." Slater smiled and nodded. He got up from the stool and left. AJ remained sitting on the stool, pondering the loss of his friend. He had mixed emotions; he felt emptiness, a void in his life, which he knew time would fill, and at the same time, he shrugged and thought c'est la vie. 'Goodbye, Geoff, old boy.'

Chapter 28

Driver had the urge to make a move. It was more of a need than an urge. There were several new potential targets, all of whom were interfering in his ultimate goal. However, he had to be calm and cautious. Being impulsive could turn out to be a grave error and lead the police investigation in his direction. He had to create a foolproof plan. He had started to prepare an outline, a strategy that would mislead the officials. His instincts told him that his diversion was not as successful as he would have expected; it was ill planned, and could have resulted in disaster. His aspirations, he thought, had better not be shattered because of his lack of foresight. He didn't think he was self-destructive. Driver felt that he was too smart to allow failure to materialize. Besides, he had gone too far to turn back now. He would change his MO. That would be easy. He disposed of the weapon he used at Indian Lake Golf Course. If it were found it could not be traced to him. It was not part of his set of clubs. He left no prints on the club, and no other signs that could link it to him or his house. Driver would modify his method. He owned a gun, a 38 caliber. That would be good choice... in some instances, he thought, as he followed the car that was four cars ahead of him on the MacDonnald Bridge. He was losing his concentration. More planning will have to come later; now I must act; must work on the list if my objective is to be met. The demise of each person on his list would make him wealthier, and after all wasn't that the purpose?

Driver knew that there were no video cams on the bridges to Dartmouth; that gave him one advantage in establishing an alibi, if one was needed. He could not be placed there if push came to shove. One thing that concerned Driver though was his MacPass. The MacPass would automatically record him as he went through the tollgate. Easy. I will go through the only lane that does not accept MacPass and pay in cash, he thought. Simple. As long as I don't lose her everything will be okay. For me, that is, not her, he smiled. The car he was following continued on through the easy exit. Driver slowed to pay his toll; two cars preceded him. Hurry up girls; he said to himself, referring to the two cars that were ahead of him, both driven by men. I have a date. Thoughts of his *date* swam through his head like water flowing out of a fire hose. By the time Driver paid his toll, he was unsure in which direction his target had gone. He continued driving straight towards Victoria Road, did not see her, so turned right into the Dartmouth Sportsplex parking lot where he turned around and headed directly to the bridge to return to Halifax. Driver was not disappointed. There is always time. Time was on his side. He did not want to force it; that's when mistakes are made. Jean continued driving, unaware that she had been followed, and also oblivious that she had lost her predator.

Driver returned home and called the office. He said that his meeting had just ended and that he was going continue his work from his home office, should anyone wish to contact him.

. . . . .

Before Jean was to leave for her first target shooting practice, she checked her email messages. Besides the usual spam, which she immediately deleted, there was one message from an unknown source. The message read: *You're welcome*, and it was unsigned. She wondered if it came from Zero, from whom she acquired the handgun, or from one of her friends, one who might have put her in contact with Zero. In any case, it had to be from someone who knew she had the gun. Jean found the message somewhat disturbing. Obviously, whoever it was, he or she did not want to be connected with the transaction of the item. Fair enough. Since she had plenty of time, Jean took the long route, via Dartmouth, to the shooting range. Jean thought it was peculiar that the other ranges weren't open to target practice without having either a membership or presenting a license and ID. Maybe it was a good thing to control who comes and goes. Following the directions she was given, Jean drove for about 40 minutes in the comfort of her red Lexus when she pulled off the main road, down an unpaved road, along what looked like good farmland on both sides. About a half mile down the road that twisted to the right sat a long, unpainted shed-like building on the edge of a dense forest. It was a good location, far away from houses; and the trees would muffle most of the sound that might escape from inside. A single, simple wooden sign hanging next to the door said, *Shooting Range*. Jean picked up her purse that had been on the passenger side seat, slipped the strap over her shoulder so that the purse rested against her thigh, and went inside. The entrance area was quite small, housing a single open window, with a small ledge, and to the far right a single door that presumably led to the shooting range. A man wearing an old worn, but clean, denim shirt appeared at the window. He poked his head out of the window to see who came in. "Hello", he said brushing his dirty blonde and slightly long hair back.

"Hi," Jean said approaching the window. "I have an appointment to take target practice." She said still nervous about not having any documentation for the handgun.

"Your name, please?"

"Jean. Jean Jenkins."

"Do you have your gun with you?" He asked.

"Yes, I do. It is here." She said taking the gun out of her purse.

"Nice little gun. Brand new, too. Is that a K9, or the PM9?" He sounded interested.

"It's a PM9." She said sounding knowledgeable.

"The price is $55 for the hour and I will supply and charge you for the ammunition that you use. You are required to use our ammo." He explained. "I will give you a box and deduct the amount that you don't use. Otherwise, the entire box is $35." "What if I only want to practice or a half hour?" Jean asked.

"It'll still cost you $55. You pay for the entire hour whether you use it or not."

"Fair enough." She answered, careful not to ask to many questions.

"The only rules you have to follow are that you don't load the gun until you are in your designated area, you use earplugs, and you unload the gun before you leave. There are three buttons that you should know about. One is to retrieve the target in order for you to see where your shots landed, the second is to have the target changed, and the third, the red one, will get my attention when you push it. You push it and I will be there in a shake. They are marked with signage so you won't confuse which one is which. Okay?"

"That's clear. I understand it completely."

"If you need any instructions, it will cost extra, and I will send someone with you when you go to your slot."

"That's fine." Jean responded. "I won't need any assistance at this time, thanks."

"Good. You must pay before you go in. Once ya come back a few times and I get to know ya, you won't have to pay in advance. When you're finished, unload the gun and come back here with the remaining ammunition, if any, and I will make the necessary exchange." He reached below the window and put a box of ammunition on the ledge for her to take. "Slot six."

Jean handed him a $100 bill as a deposit and asked, "Is this the door I take?"

"Yes, go inside and keep walking straight ahead until you see your slot, number six. The doors are all numbered."

Jean could hear shooting through the closed door. She was quite anxious to start practicing and felt a bit awkward, even though the manager was not disparaging towards her in any way, and consequently made her feel a little bit more at ease. Jean was unsure of what to do and was equally uncertain as to what the gun would do. She went through the door walked along the back of the shooting range, and found her slot. Each spot had a door that would lock. Jean went into her small booth, about four feet wide by about five feet long. Directly opposite the entrance door was a half door that hinged downward and faced the target range. Jean locked the door behind her, loaded her gun and opened the hinged door. She looked down the range at her target of a torso and head. She put on her earplugs and with some trepidation aimed at the target holding the gun in both hands. The target looked so far away. She had read or heard from someone that you should squeeze the trigger rather than pull it back hard, which she did. The shot came as a surprise, driving her hands backwards only slightly. The sound of the shot was less than she expected and was underwhelming. After taking a few shots, she gained confidence, recalling that the instructions she read mentioned a stainless steel guide rod that helped dampen recoil. It was a wonder to her. There was not a big sound when she fired and very little recoil. She was amazed that such a little thing could cause so much damage to another human being. Periodically, she retrieved the target to determine how well she had done. Out of the first 10 rounds, she hit the target six times at a distance of 60 feet; none were even close to the center. After she had emptied the entire box at her target, with ever increasing accuracy, she felt confident that her shots could be reasonably true at a much closer range; and god help the person that she was shooting at who was within that range. Jean returned the empty box, asked for no change from her deposit, said she would call to make another appointment at a later date, and left with her two loaded magazines and her PM9 in her purse. Once in her car, she loaded one of the magazines into the gun. Maybe it is not so bad to own and carry a weapon, she thought.

Chapter 29

Redmond and Stenson were ecstatic with their find. They returned to the station with their prize as quickly as they could without causing any consternation to other drivers along the way. Stenson took the club to the RCMP forensic lab to have it checked for possible identification as the murder weapon and, with any luck, to determine its ownership. While Stenson was looking over the shoulder of the forensic investigator, Rick reported the discovery to Chief Barnes. It was the first real break through for the department. He told Barnes that the club was reasonably new and clean, save for what looked like dried blood stains and a few scuffmarks on the clubface. But in regards to the stains, forensics would soon be able to give them more detailed information. The club itself was a Titleist Pro Titanium 975L-FE with 10.5 degrees of loft, and had a graphite shaft. Redmond promised the Chief that he would put a push on to find out, if at all possible, where the club was bought and by whom. Stenson called Redmond to report that forensics were quick to determine that the dried stain on the head of the club was blood, and were in the process of seeing if it matched up with Jenkins and Harris' blood.

"The lab is trying to connect the wounds on the heads of the victims with the line indentations on the club. I will get back to you as soon as I find out about the blood, Rick, and if the club has been identified as the murder weapon." Stenson stated with renewed excitement.

Redmond left Barnes office and went back to his desk to enter the information and times in the murder book. He met briefly with Donna, Dave and Jim to get their hits on what they learned from each of Jenkins' friends. So far, there was nothing conclusive. The three compared notes. The only information that was of any interest was that Fisher was not looked upon kindly. Donna concurred that she arrived at the same conclusion, that she found Fisher to be uncooperative, disagreeable, and just a little short of being egotistical, as did the others.

"In other words," she told them, "he was a bit of an asshole." All seemed to be in agreement that Jenkins' friends had alibis for the time of the murder. Yet, it was deemed that the alibis were not necessarily carved in stone; times and places of ones whereabouts can easily be fabricated.

Slater still had to reach the one-night stand woman who AJ Devoe had given to him as his alibi. Her roommate said she was out until late afternoon or early evening. He left a message for her to return his call.

. . . . .

At the lab, the forensic investigators gave their report to Stenson. He held on to it, recognizing the results as a major break in the case. He called the team working the case together and immediately and gave the report to Redmond so that he could disclose the contents to the others.

"We got a positive match on two things." Redmond said with reserved jubilation. "The stain on the club is blood and it matches the blood of Harris and his son."

"Yes!" Donna said pumping her fist in the air.

"More importantly," Redmond continued, "forensics was able to match the indented lines on the clubface with the marks on two of the victims. The marks on Jenkins' temple were consistent with those on the face of the club. The same holds true for the marks on Harris' skull."

"All right!" Donna shouted, and the others breathed sighs of relief.

"So we have the murder weapon, but no prints." Rick smiled weakly, perhaps exhibiting a small triumph. "Now all we have to do is find out who the fuck owned the club. As you know that may be a helluva lot more difficult."

"It's a whole lot more than we had before; before we had nada." Stenson said, turning to the group.

"It's a start." Redmond added. "Now we have a lot of hard work ahead of us. We have to canvass all the golf stores in the area, and if we come up with nothing, we will have to go to every shop that sells clubs in the province."

"That's going to be a lota work." Martin said in a negative tone.

"I'm ready." Donna said enthusiastically.

Redmond smiled at her fervor. "The first thing we will do is to cover all the shops in Halifax and Dartmouth, and if we get no results, we will then look at the south shore, and if no luck there, we will hit every friggin' place within 50 kilometers of every golf course, including the pro shops at the courses." Redmond paused to consider the impact of his statement. "Stenson, I want you to head up the hunt. You will report to me every hour on the hour. I want a systematic search and report. By the way, everyone, I know I don't have to tell you not to say anything to the press. Barnes has taken on that responsibility due to the nature of the case. It's too hot; it is no longer local. It is no longer even fucking national. We've had calls from the media in Europe and the states. I'll be the go-between with Barnes giving him a full account every step of the way. All of you will report to Stenson who will report directly to me. If there is a single leak, there will be hell to pay. I'm talking about serious repercussions."

There were the usual 'yeah, yeah, we know', before they broke to organize.

Stenson divided up the local retail outlets between himself and Copp, taking the Halifax and vicinity locations, with Copp getting the Dartmouth locations. Martin was given the Pro shops within a 50-kilometer radius. He resented his assignment, preferring to approach the local golf shops.

"One thing we can be sure of is that the perp more than likely used the club spontaneously. In which case, the club was probably bought for golfing not specifically for the murders, and may be easier to trace them previously thought." Stenson considered. "One other suggestion," He added, "we need to contact Jenkins's golfing friends and check to see if one of them is missing a driver."

"Shouldn't we do that first?" Donna asked. "In case we get lucky, it may save us a time-consuming search through the retailers."

"Good idea, Donna. I'll check it out with Rick. In the meantime let's not waste any time; let's get to work to find out who the murder weapon belongs to."

Chapter 30

While driving from the shooting range, Jean gave the cause of Geoff's death a great deal of consideration. She wondered what could possibly motivate someone to kill another human being. Money, relationship problems, and revenge in general were foremost in her mind, assuming the killer chose his or her victim and it was not simply a random act. She couldn't imagine anyone killing him out of revenge. Geoff was always upfront with everyone. So, someone holding a grudge against him powerful enough to want to kill him didn't make sense. Was he having relationship problems with Lisa? Was Geoff having an affair? That was a possibility, although not too probable. Maybe Lisa was having an affair. Who the hell would want her, she thought. Hmm that's a bit unfair. Which one of them having an affair would most likely result in Geoff being murdered? If Geoff was sleeping with someone, and she was married, then... but then, again, I doubt that he would sleep with a married woman. He would have told me if he was interested in another woman. I know he would have. He always told me about the women he was interested in, so that can't be it. If there was any sleeping around, it had to be Lisa. If she was having an affair, how would that have led to Geoff's death? I think she really loved him, but that wouldn't have stopped her from having a man on the side necessarily. What if the guy was in love with Lisa and decided to get rid of Geoff. That's a good possibility. What if he wanted Lisa with the sole purpose of getting at Geoff's money? Not sure about that. Chances are that if Lisa had a man, he would have had money of his own. Lisa is no fool. That doesn't make sense to me. Lisa was way too upset to have had anything to do with Geoff's... – oh shit! He really *is* gone.

Jean parked her Lexus in the circular driveway in front of her house and went inside, feeling the weight of the handgun, still inside her purse, against her thigh. She even thought she could still feel the heat from the gun being fired. She went into the small office that housed her computer, sat down, took off her hat, and then, changing her mind, put it back on again. Jean took the gun out of her purse, went back to lock the front door, and then returned to her office, took her coat off, and put the gun on her desk. She picked up the phone and hit the speed dial number for Lisa's phone. Lisa picked up on the second ring.

"Lisa, this is Jean. Were you having an affair?"

Chapter 31

Slater heard from Devoe's late-night date friend and reported to Stenson that the one-night stand established Devoe's alibi for the time Jenkins was killed. So the confirmation let Devoe off the hook. Stenson asked Slater to change into his civilian clothes and posted him to duty at the Indian Lake Golf Course. He was to check out each of the golfers without being too obvious and walk the course looking for anything suspicious. First and foremost, he was to spend time in the woods carrying a golf club under the pretense of looking for a lost ball, making sure no one was lurking there in hunt of another victim.

Slater was aware that there would be few if any black golfers on the course. He also knew that he would stand out like an onion in a flower patch. He decided to dress golf smart so as to not to be confused with a grounds worker, even though he was unsure that there were any blacks on staff at the club. He also decided to buy a pair of golf shoes and a used golf club. Slater changed into a golf shirt, of which he had plenty, and a pair of tan khakis. He attached a Galco *ankle lite* ankle holster with an adjustable neoprene band to his leg to hide and hold a Glock 26, *baby Glock* subcompact handgun that uses a 9 mm cartridge. The gun was loaded with a ten-round magazine, although any 9 mm Glock magazine was interchangeable, up to 33 rounds. It was perfect for an undercover job. Next he went to Winners, the brand name discount store, for a pair of black golf shoes that were tagged at less than 50% of the original price. He relented on buying a used golf club. He was now geared up for Indian Lake Golf Course duty. He was physically fit enough to walk the course several times within eight or ten hours without being fatigued. He was now starting to feel like a detective, or possibly understand what it would be like to be a detective, working under cover. His adrenalin was beginning to flow, and he was anxious to get started. Slater picked up an unmarked police issue, a black Honda Accord. He knew as well as the others in the department that an unmarked police car was almost as obvious as a blue and white interceptor; extra aerials were dead giveaways, as were the blue flashing lights hidden in the grill. However, he was not on a stake out, so his car parked in the golf course lot would be less conspicuous. He left immediately for the golf course. Once there he rented a set of clubs and a cart, and bought a package of golf balls.

. . . . .

Stenson met up with Rick after he returned from his meeting with Chief Barnes. Rick told Stenson that Barnes was ecstatic about the news of recovering and identifying the murder weapon. Barnes was reluctant to inform the press that the weapon had been found. It was the kind of information that, if kept private, was useful when interviewing suspects, although referring to the club as the murder weapon would not raise any alarms. Stenson, on the other hand, updated Rick on Donna's idea of checking out the golf club sets of each of Jenkins' friends to see if they were missing a driver, and if their clubs were the same brand as the murder weapon.

"It's a good fuckin' idea, Stenson. It may just turn up something and save us a lot of man-hours. You and Donna get that done ASAP, so we won't have to delay our search in retail shops in the event that her idea doesn't pan out."

"Should we concern ourselves about warrants?"

"The only time you'll have to fuckin' worry about that is if someone is not cooperative. In which case, we may have a lot stronger reason to go after that person. Although I doubt that we'd have grounds for a warrant at this point."

"Okay. Good, Rick. We'll get on it right away. Thanks."

"Oh. Stenson? I'll check Nickerson myself. I want to see that son-of-a-bitch sweat. You and Donna take care of the others."

"Gotcha," Stenson said walking away.

. . . . .

Redmond drove directly to Philip Nickerson's house. He parked in the driveway behind a red Lexus. As he approached the front door, Rick heard shouting from inside. Concerned about the ruckus that was taking place, Rick rushed through the front door without knocking or ringing the doorbell. The loud voice of a woman came from the living room, and he hurried in, flipping the snap on his shoulder

208

holster. "Nickerson? It's the Halifax police. What's going on here?"

Relieved by Redmond's presence, Nickerson said, "Thank god you're here." He was backed up against the side of the fabric-covered armchair. The diminutive Jean Jenkins stood confronting him, one hand on her hip, the other holding the gun inside her purse, her hat awry on her head. Nickerson's white shirt was partially pulled out of his dress pants and his tie pulled down from his neck and off to the side.

"She thinks I killed her brother, detective."

"You were sleeping with Geoff's wife. You were having an affair with my brother's wife, you weasel." She screeched at him.

"Okay, Ms Jenkins. That's enough. Back off." Rick said stepping between them.

Resisting the separation, Jean said, "I am sure this son-of-a-bitch killed Geoff." She kept her hand inside her purse, but released her grasp from the cold steel of the gun.

Holding onto the chair, Nickerson was terrified. "She said she was going to kill me. I never did anything to her brother. I swear I didn't."

"Now just a minute." Rick said forcefully, stepping between the two and moving Jean away from Nickerson. "If he is responsible for Geoff's murder, we'll find out. I told you not to interfere in this investigation, Ms Jenkins. I could charge you with obstruction and assault for this."

"He admitted he was having an affair with Lisa." She protested removing her empty hand from the purse.

"That may have nothing to do with Geoff's murder. Now if you leave immediately, you won't be charged. But I don't want this to happen again. Understand?"

"Yes, but ...?

Rick interrupted her. "No fuckin' buts. Just leave and that will be the end of it. At least until I see you when I've finished here."

Jean said nothing. She turned around with her purse bouncing against her thigh and advanced to the door, slamming it behind her as she left. A second later she returned. "You have to move your car, detective so I can get out."

"Oh, yes." To Nickerson he said, "I'll be right back. Stay right where you are." He said pointing at him. " Don't go anywhere." After he moved his car Rick returned.

"Detective, you've got to do something about that woman. She frightens me. I'm worried she's going to try to kill me. I am so glad you got here when you did."

"Don't worry about her, Nickerson. She's upset about her brother's death, but she's harmless. In any case I'll talk to her, but that's not why I'm here."

"Why are you here? Am I a suspect, detective?" He said timidly.

"I wouldn't go as far as that. However we consider everyone a possible suspect, and that is why I'm here. I'd like to see your golf clubs, Nickerson."

"My golf clubs? Why?"

"Never fuckin' mind why, Nickerson. Where are they? And I don't need any of your shit. Got it?" He said pointing at him again, his eyes squinting and his jaw jutting out.

Nickerson felt the brunt of his threat, and said apprehensively, "Don't you need a warrant for that?"

"Only if you're unwilling to cooperate. Perhaps you have something to hide. Make it easy on yourself, Nickerson. If you want to be a fuckin' asshole, I'll get a warrant, or maybe I'll find another way to persuade you." He said menacingly moving toward him.

"Okay, okay. You don't have to be so pushy. The clubs are in the hall closet." He said retreating, having been attacked first by Jean and now feeling mentally abused by Redmond.

Nickerson led the way to the closet in the hall. The closet held several sweaters and a windbreaker hanging neatly on the right side, and the clubs were in a golf bag leaning against the left corner of the closet. Nickerson reached in and lifted the bag out of the closet.

"When did you last use the clubs?"

Nickerson straightened a painting on the wall opposite the closet, and then stood back to see if it was straight.

"I said when was the last time you used the clubs?"

"I heard you, detective. I was just trying to remember."

"Surely, it can't be that fuckin' hard."

"No it can't. But I want to be precise; otherwise it may come back to haunt me. I know how you guys operate. If I screw up with the time, you'll say I lied."

"Quit the bullshitting, Nickerson. I'm losing my patience. Give me a fuckin' answer." He said grabbing Nickerson by the shirt with both hands and shoving him hard against the wall.

He tried to pull away from Redmond, "Okay, okay. Take it easy. I'll tell you. It was about six or eight weeks ago, okay? Christ! You don't have to be so rough."

"I'll give you rough, you little slime bag." Redmond said releasing his hold and pushing him away.

"You know I can have you charged with police brutality."

"Don't tempt me, Nickerson." He said staring at him. "I can't count the number of times suspects were beaten while resisting arrest." Rick then turned to examine the clubs wiping his hands on his pants as though touching Nickerson contaminated them. Rick pulled a club out of the bag and looked at the brand.

"Hmm, I see you have a set of Titlist."

"Yeah, so?"

Redmond feigned lunging at him; Nickerson flinched and raised his hands to protect himself.

"I will use any excuse to beat the shit out of you. Any excuse, you fucking asshole."

"What did I do? I didn't do anything. Don't take your frustration out on me, man." He said retreating.

Redmond's eyes narrowed and he looked at him with hatred.

"Someone killed three people, one of them a young boy. And I think that that someone might just be you, Nickerson."

Redmond returned the club to the bag and looked for but could not find the driver.

"Where's your driver? Or don't you use one?"

"It's there." He said looking in the bag. "Somewhere. It's

got to be here." Nickerson pushed the clubs around but couldn't find his driver. "It was here. I used it the last time I played." He became frantic. "Shit! It's not here. I hope I didn't leave it at the course."

Redmond looked at him unconvinced. "I think you better come with me, Nickerson. I may have found your club."

"How is that possible? I swear to god I had the club. It was here. In fact, I had the club when I was at Lisa's house, the day Geoff was killed. I put it back in the bag when I got back home. Ask Lisa, she'll tell you."

Chapter 32

Stenson and Donna sat in the reception area of
Investment Securities waiting for Mike Fisher. They had
arrived unannounced and without an appointment. The
receptionist, Linda Belford, recognized Donna immediately,
and addressed her by name. Linda was wearing a black skirt
with a long sleeve white blouse, same theme as before but
different colors. They were sitting for less then five minutes
when Belford's intercom rang. After she hung up, she got up
and took them to Fisher's office.

Once inside, Belford asked them if they wanted anything to
drink. Both declined.

"And what do I owe the honor of your presence?" Fisher
asked attempting to be charming.

"This is detective Stenson, Mr. Fisher."

"Detective. I presume this is official police business." He
said with a lot less charm.

Stenson smiled naturally, projecting his own charm. "I'll get
right to it. We would like to take a look at your golf clubs,
Mr. Fisher, if that is not a problem."

Fisher paused, taken aback. "Well, detective, I didn't know
you had an interest in the game." He said smiling.

"As a matter of fact, I don't, except from a purely
psychological point of view. I see it as a puerile game, an
investment in or an exploration of one's past." He smiled

again. "However, that's not why we're here. Where and when may we see your clubs?"

After a moment of pondering the question, Fisher responded with his own question as he tapped his pencil softly on his desk. "And is a warrant necessary for this search, detective?"

"First of all it is not a search, and a warrant is only necessary if you think it is."

"Since you put it so nicely, I certainly can accommodate you. I just happen to have my clubs with me, here at the office."

"Do you keep your clubs here all the time, Mr. Fisher?" Donna asked.

"No. No, of course not. At this time of the year, I bring my clubs in, only if the weather for the week looks good. Sometimes, if I don't have an appointment, I will play hooky like a ... a *puerile* schoolboy ... and take the day off to play a round of golf, you see."

"So," Stenson asked, the sarcasm not lost on him, "may we see your clubs?"

"Of course you may. I keep them in the closet near the reception area. Please follow me." Fisher rose from his plush, high-back chair and led the way to the office closet. The set of golf clubs was in a black golf bag that was fabricated to look like leather. The set of PING clubs was complete and intact. Fisher picked up the bag with one hand as though it were a small briefcase and handed it to Stenson. Stenson, in turn, took the bag with the same ease and set it down on the carpeted floor. "PING. Nice. Everything seems to be here." Stenson said.

"Yes, PING. I love expensive toys. Nothing but the best."
Fisher glowed with pride.

"Is this your only set of clubs?" Donna asked.

"Should I have more?"

Donna opted not to answer.

"Yes. I only have need for one set, Ms Copp. I can only use one set at a time." He said, emphasizing her name, toying with her.

"Well then," Stenson said with displeasure. "I think we're through here."

"You sound disappointed, detective. What did you expect?"

"Not disappointed at all. Perhaps envious."

"Envious?"

"Yes. If I played the game, I would be envious of the beauty of your clubs. And they are so clean, almost new."

"I do take care of my toys. You might say I am a neat freak."
Fisher said with pride.

"Thank you for your time. We appreciate your candor."
Donna said.

"My pleasure. Let me show you out."

. . . . .

Outside Purdy's Wharf, Donna and Stenson commented on the freshness of the air coming off the harbor from the south and debated walking along the waterfront. It was not something that they were in a habit of doing. They agreed to walk hoping it would clear their heads.

"What d'you think?" Donna asked him.

"He seems to be covered. Those clubs are not even close to the brand we found, and the driver is there. Unless he has another set kicking around, he's clean. He sure is a nasty guy though, an arrogant son-of-a-bitch."

"Yes he is. If he didn't have an alibi and those clubs, I'd make him for the perp."

Stenson was a little more cautious. "Let's not jump to conclusions. Just because he acts like an arrogant prick doesn't mean he is capable of murder."

"Acts like?" They both laughed. Stenson's cell phone rang. "Stenson here." He answered. "Hmm. Oh my." He listened. "Okay, we're on our way in." He flipped his phone closed and slid it into the leather holder on his belt. "Rick has Nickerson. He brought him into the station. Get this. Nickerson is missing a club from his set. The same brand that we have."

"Oh boy. Let's get back." Donna said grinning.

When they arrived at the station, Nickerson was sweating it out in an interview room. Redmond had retrieved the golf club found in the woods from the evidence room.

Donna and Stenson immediately connected with Redmond and Donna reported on the meeting with Fisher. "We got nothing from Fisher, Rick. He had his clubs in the office and not only was the set intact, but it was an entirely different brand. We had no chance to check out the other guys."

"No matter. It looks like Nickerson is our man. He is missing a driver and the brand matches up with the one we found. He

swears he had the club with him when he was seeing Jenkins'
wife on the morning of the murder."

"Where have I heard that before? And maybe, just maybe, he
did Jenkins at the golf course and *then* went to see his wife."
Stenson remarked.

Redmond told them about his meeting with Nickerson and that
he may have diverted a disaster with Jean Jenkins. "I want to
let Nickerson cool his heels for a bit. In the meantime, I need
to talk to Jenkins sister about her uninvited visit to
Nickerson."

"If only friggin' people would let us do our job. But that
would be too easy." Stenson added.

"I want you to come with me." Rick said to Stenson. "Donna,
keep an eye on Nickerson. If you feel inspired, talk to him,
but don't say anything about the club we found. I want him to
sweat."

"No sweat." She said laughing.

As they left, Rick brought Stenson up to snuff on Jean
Jenkins' visit, and Donna went to observe Nickerson through
the one-way mirror.

. . . . .

Rick drove along the Citadel to Brunswick Street,
then went south on Brunswick and took the scenic route west
on Spring Garden Road. Redmond called it the scenic route

because it was concentrated with shops, restaurants and was heavily trafficked by women in short skirts and tight tank tops, which gave him great pleasure during the summer months. They continued west along Spring Garden Road, which changed to Coburg Road, and was the beginning of the Dalhousie University campus. Several streets further on they passed Walnut Street, turned right on Chestnut, and continued on until they reached Jean's house. Redmond explained to Stenson that he had been tickled by Jenkins' behavior with Nickerson, and that Nickerson had been quite shaken by the way she went after him, like a pit bull attacking a miniature poodle. Redmond parked in front of Jean's house and went up to her front door. Jean was waiting for them. She opened the door, turned her back without looking at them, and walked into her living room.

"May we come in?" Redmond asked waiting tentatively at the entrance.

Jean waved them in and said, "I see you brought backup. Were you worried that you couldn't handle me?"

Stenson covered his mouth and muffled a laugh, and then closed the door behind him, as he followed Rick into the living room.

"Very amusing." Redmond said shaking his head. "This is Detective Stenson."

"And quite a big handsome backup." She added, cocking her head and raising her eyebrows, with her hat still on her head.

"Please sit down, Ms Jenkins." Rick asked firmly. Jean sat quietly but was, without a doubt, high on adrenalin.

"You know that I can arrest you for assault and for interfering in this investigation." Rick continued

"That bastard was having an affair with my late brother's wife." She blurted.

Stenson interjected. "We know all about that, Ms Jenkins. We also know how you feel. It is frustrating to sit back and do nothing, to feel helpless."

"Exactly." Jean responded, and Stenson knew that he hit the right spot.

"Now you must give us your word," Rick took up were Stenson left off. "You must promise that you will no longer take any action, and leave the investigation to us."

"I don't know if I can do that." She said rearranging her hat on her head. "Can I get you gentlemen a drink? Tea or coffee, or something?"

"No, we're fine, Ms Jenkins." Rick said, clearing his throat. "Look, you don't understand. If you don't agree to discontinue the search for your brother's killer, I will have to arrest you and charge you with interference. In which case, you may be kept in jail until we complete our investigation." Redmond threatened.

"You can't do that to me. I haven't done anything." Jean said angrily.

"Unfortunately, Ms Jenkins," Stenson added admonishing her, "not only can we do it, but we will do it, if only for your safety. And, by the way, you *have* done something. You've interfered with our investigation, and that is a serious offense."

"Also, we've arrested Philip Nickerson. He is at the police

station right now. Redmond said.

"I knew it! I knew that mealy mouthed bastard killed Geoff … all because of Lisa." Jean said, standing, and her voice rising. "I should have killed him while I had the chance."

"Whoa." Stenson quickly interposed. "We don't know for certain that he had anything to do with it. He may have or may not have killed your brother. We can't jump to conclusions. If you want the person who killed your brother brought to justice, you must give us your word, Ms Jenkins that you will stop meddling right now. Or else we *will* arrest you. You can count on that. If you wish, you can sit in a jail cell until this is over. If that happens, you can rest assured that you will be prosecuted." he emphasized.

Jean looked at Stenson, and then at Redmond, adjusted her hat with both hands, and sat down. She twisted her body and sat erect. "Well," she said after a pause, "I don't have a choice do I." Both nodded in agreement. "I agree not to interfere, … provided that you keep me informed of anything new that occurs." She negotiated.

Redmond said, "You will agree with no terms."

Jean looked away and raised her eyes. "You have my word."

"Thank you, Ms Jenkins." Stenson said.

After the detectives left, Jean went to her purse, retrieved the gun, made sure it was loaded, and put it back in her purse. She put on a lightweight dark colored jacked, took her purse and went to her car. She then drove off.

Chapter 33

Donna Copp observed Nickerson's behavior in the interview room for at least a half hour. He was indeed sweating it out. He got up from his chair, paced back and forth, sat down, and looked around expecting someone to come in and talk to him. He was nervous and looked at his watch impatiently every few minutes. When he sat, he looked at the one-way mirror, wondering if anyone was watching him. He was behaving exactly like someone who had committed a crime, so Donna thought. She had not interviewed a murder suspect for quite a while and considered this as good a time as any. No longer able to resist she went into the interview room.

"Well, it's about time." Nickerson stood up and said anxiously, and actually pleased to see her as Donna entered the room.

"Sit down, Mr. Nickerson." He did and she sat opposite him, giving him space, turned on the video to record the session, and said without looking at him, "I am detective Donna Copp; the time is thirteen hundred hours and I am interviewing Mr. Philip Nickerson." She looked at Nickerson without saying anything.

He started to fidget. "Why am I here? Why am I being interviewed?"

Copp read him his rights. "You are not under arrest Mr.

Nickerson. However, you have the right to retain and instruct counsel without delay. We will provide you with a toll-free telephone lawyer referral service, if you do not have your own lawyer. Anything you say can be used in court as evidence. Do you understand? Would you like to speak to a lawyer?"

"What? What is going on? Why am I here?" He repeated.

"No, I don't need a lawyer."

"Why do you think you are here?" She responded.

"Am I being charged with something?"

"Should you be charged, Mr. Nickerson?" She said, again answering a question with a question.

"Look, I didn't do anything. I don't even know why I am here."

"I think you know why you're here."

"Should I have a lawyer?" He asked.

"Do you think you need one?"

"I didn't do anything. I didn't break any laws." He said, extending his arms as though pleading with her.

"If you didn't do anything, why would you need a lawyer?"

He shifted in his chair. "Well … then I guess I don't need one."

"Where were you when Geoff Jenkins was killed?"

"You know were I was, detective. I already explained that." He said somewhat agitated. "Is that why I'm here?"

"Tell me again, just so I have it right."

"Do I have to answer that?"

"No, you don't. You don't have to answer anything I ask. However, it may look like you're hiding something by not answering my questions. So you decide."

"I'm not hiding anything, detective. You know I was with Geoff's wife. Lisa and I were having an affair."

"What time did you arrive at her house?"

"I don't know. I think it was about nine or so."

"And you stayed until when?"

"It must have been about eleven." He started to stand up.

"Sit down, Mr. Nickerson." She told him adamantly. He sat without hesitation.

"How long have you been seeing Lisa?"

"Seeing her?"

"Seeing her, as in a relationship. In other words, how long have you been sleeping with her?"

"Maybe six months or so. I'm not sure exactly."

"Are you in love with Ms. Jenkins?"

"That's none of your business, detective. I don't have to answer that."

"No, you don't, but it would clear things up a bit, give us a better picture. And it would make me feel better to know that you are not hiding anything, you know, so I could trust you, trust that what you are telling me is the truth."

"Yes, yes, I am in love with Lisa. I wouldn't sleep with her if I weren't." Donna raised her eyebrows. "That's just the way I am, okay."

"Is that why you killed Geoff, so you could have Lisa to yourself?"

"Now just a minute. I did not kill Geoff or anyone else, ever."

"No? I certainly understand if you did kill him. When you

love someone…"

Nickerson interrupted her. "What do I have to do to make you understand? I was with Lisa when Geoff was killed." He started to become undone. "I love Lisa but I would never kill my friend."

"Who would you kill then, Nickerson? Your enemy?"

"Oh god! You don't understand." He cried in frustration. Redmond opened the door and joined Donna in the room. Stenson took a spot in the viewing room behind the one-way mirror. Rick carried the golf club that he and Stenson had found in the woods, and a file folder with Nickerson's name on it and placed both on the table close to him as he sat. Nickerson looked at the club and at the large folder with his name on it, but did not touch the club, nor did he say anything. His heart pounded and he shuddered at the sight of his name on the folder. This is for real, he thought.

"Detective Rick Redmond joined us in the interview room." Donna said for the purpose of the videotaping. Redmond slid the club slowly toward Nickerson, who lowered his eyes to follow the motion without moving his head. Redmond watched him without saying anything. No one said anything. Again Redmond slid the club a little closer towards Nickerson, who made a move to take the club, but Redmond stopped him with, "Ehh ehh, don't touch." To Donna, "Did you read him his rights?"

"Yes." She replied. "Mr. Nickerson has been very cooperative."

"Where did you find it?" Nickerson asked, looking at the

club.

"Where you put it, Nickerson." Redmond said smiling. "It is yours, is it not?" He said pushing the club next to Nickerson. "I don't know. Maybe." He looked to Redmond for permission to touch the club. Redmond nodded and Nickerson picked it up and examined it. On the bottom of the club were several scratch marks in the metal. Nickerson recognized the marks and said, "Yes, it is definitely my club. I put those scratches on it, accidently. Where did you find it?" He asked again.

"Would you like to tell us what you did with *your* club, Nickerson?" Redmond asked moving to a chair to the end of the table and closer to Nickerson.

"What do you mean? I did nothing with it. What would I do with it? I use it to play golf." He said, stressed, his voice quivered.

Redmond tilted his head to the side, looked at Nickerson and said softly, "We have evidence that this club, *your* club, was used to kill Geoff Jenkins, Matt Harris and his son."

Nickerson was horrified and started to tremble at the news.

"What? That's impossible. How can that be?"

"You tell us how that can be. We have hard evidence. Now would you like to tell us how your club came to be the murder weapon?"

"Tell us how you did it, Mr. Nickerson. Did you kill Geoff first and then drive to his wife's house after to make love to her?" Donna prompted.

"No!" He protested. "I swear to god."

"You will feel better if you tell us the truth, Mr. Nickerson. I can understand killing a man because you love his wife; it is simply a crime of passion. No one would condemn you for that." She continued.

"I am telling you the truth. I swear I am."

"C'mon, Nickerson. You expect us to believe that." Redmond pressed.

"I...I..." he attempted, but was interrupted by Redmond.

"What do you take us for? Do you think you can kill a man, fuck his wife and get away with it? How many other wives have you fucked? Did you kill anyone else? Who are you, Nickerson, needle-dick the bug fucker? C'mon, Nickerson, own up."

Stenson smiled behind the one-mirror at Redmond's approach. He could see the sweat pouring off Nickerson's face. His shirt open at the neck was becoming soaked with perspiration.

Donna pampered Nickerson. "Would you like something to drink? Water, perhaps?"

"Yes, please. Water would be fine." Donna went to the door, opened it, said something to someone on the other side, and returned to sit down.

"Well, Nickerson, what's it going to be? Are you going to fess up?" Redmond pushed.

"To what? That I had an affair with a murdered man's wife; my friend's wife?"

"No, that's not what I want you to do. Own up to what you did, you fucking pervert. We know you killed Geoff Jenkins, Harris and the kid."

Nickerson sat in his chair in disbelief, shaking his head from side to side. The sweat dripped down his face and he wiped it on his shirtsleeve. He no longer felt obligated to respond to their questions. He thought that no matter what he said they would twist it around. He couldn't understand why, but suddenly he felt like a different person, not a submissive tool. He realized that no matter what he said, it wouldn't make any difference. He leaned back in the chair and felt relaxed; his breathing slowed, and he regained his composure. He felt as though he had nothing to lose. He couldn't account for what was happening to him, why he transformed. Maybe because he began to believe that he was innocent. Nickerson no longer felt claustrophobic by Redmond's closeness as he did at first. He was now overcome by an aura of tranquility, and he wasn't offended by Redmond's crude remarks; instead he said simply and with strength, "I can't own up to what I haven't done. No matter what you do or say won't make me think otherwise." Copp and Redmond looked at each other amazed by Nickerson's metamorphosis, and were no less astonished than Nickerson himself was.

"So, you are telling us that you had nothing to do with Jenkins' murder?" Donna asked.

Nickerson responded without hesitating. "That's what I'm saying, exactly what I am saying. I had nothing to do with it." Redmond did not accept his answer for a minute. "How can you sit there and tell us a bold-faced lie like that? We have proof that you did it. We have the weapon used in all three killings, and it belongs to you. How do you account for that,

Nickerson?"

"I can't." He said calmly. "But I am sure there has got to be some explanation."

"There sure is an explanation." Redmond said. "You planned to golf with Jenkins, setting him up; you went to the golf course to kill him, and after that you left to set up an alibi with his wife. The only thing I can't understand is why you killed Harris and his son. Was it because you wanted to mislead us, diverting our attention from Jenkins?" Without waiting for him to respond, Redmond continued. "You left something behind too, didn't you, at both murder sites? Why did you do that? Is that your signature?"

"What? What are you talking about? I wasn't even there. You guys are so pigheaded. Don't you understand...."?

Redmond jumped to his feet, pulled Nickerson out of the chair and pushed him against the wall, his face inches from Nickerson's. Nickerson cowered and raised his arms to protect himself from potential blows.

"Rick!" Donna blurted. "Stop! Stop it!" She pulled him off and away from Nickerson. Rick, breathing hard, held his ground.

"You can beat me if you want, but it won't change anything. I didn't kill anyone." He said to Redmond, visibly shaken.

"You are under arrest for the murder of Geoff Jenkins. Do you understand?"

"Yes, I understand, and I want a lawyer." He said, once again gaining his composure.

Redmond gestured to Donna that they leave.

"We are suspending this interview with Philip Nickerson."
Donna said and switched off the video recording. Both left the
room, leaving Nickerson sitting alone. They met with Stenson
in the viewing room.

"What the hell were you thinking, Rick?" Donna asked.

"What d'you think, Stenson?" Redmond asked, ignoring
Donna's question.

"Whew. I was a little worried there for a minute. You were
treading on dangerous ground, man."

"I wasn't worried. What do you think about *him*?"

That was quite a turn around. It's gotta make you wonder,
kind of puzzling, in fact."

"Well, I know he did it; I know that son-of-a-bitch did it. I
just know it in my gut." Redmond growled.

Donna added: "There is no question that it looks bad for him,
but you have to admit, he turned strange. Maybe he didn't do
it after all and maybe you went a bit too far, Rick."

. . . . .

Driver followed the woman in the car in front of him. The
timing was good. It was lunchtime; he was free for at least an
hour and a half. This time she will not be so lucky, he
thought. Each time it gets easier. I am starting to like it; he
smiled to himself, thinking that he could kill for a living.
However, he was uncertain about the demand of his time, and
what kind of revenue he could generate. But killing for a
living is not the same. You have to have a purpose otherwise

it is meaningless. Focus, he thought, focus on the task at hand; never mind the daydreaming. You have a job to do, he reminded himself. As he drove, he reached for and felt the butcher knife that was in the paper bag on the passenger's seat. He bought the rusty knife at the Salvation Army thrift store along with other eating utensils, all of which, he tossed in the garbage, with the exception of the knife.

The car he was following started over the bridge to Dartmouth. He would not lose her this time.

. . . . .

Stenson arranged for Nickerson to call a lawyer. He was not convinced that Nickerson committed the murders, nor was he convinced that he was innocent. However there was no doubt in anyone's mind that the evidence pointed towards Nickerson. The weapon that killed all three victims belonged to him. Stenson, Rick and Donna watched Nickerson while he waited for the lawyer.

Redmond was smiling, certain that they had the right man.

"We have him dead to rights."

"I don't know, Rick. Something doesn't seem right."

"What the hell are you talking about, Stenson? You think someone else killed these guys with Nickerson's golf club?"

"Well it is not outside the realm of possibility."

"Use your fuckin' head, Stenson. He admitted that he had the club with him when he was at Jenkins' house. How do you account for that?"

"You're right, Rick. This is one hell of a conundrum. If only we found prints on the club. That would have simplified it. I find it surprising that he would kill three people and leave the weapon that was easily traced to him behind."

Donna looked at both of them, still unsure that they had the right person.

"Well, if you figure it out, Stenson, let me know." Rick said agitated that Stenson didn't agree with him, not only didn't agree, but refused to see his point of view.

"Let's look at another possibility. What if someone took his club, killed Jenkins and then returned it before Nickerson went to see Lisa Jenkins."

"That's assuming a lot." Redmond said with an incredulous smirk.

"It's possible."

"But it's not very logical, Stenson. The timing is all wrong." Donna added. "Whoever did that, would have known that Nickerson wasn't going to meet Geoff to play a round of golf."

"Right!" Rick cried out.

Donna took little notice of Redmond's response and continued focusing on the thought. "Now we know that Nickerson didn't want anyone to know that he was having an affair. Right? So, who would have known what his plans were? He probably didn't know himself. It was more than likely a spur of the moment decision. We know that Geoff Jenkins sent an email to his friends about joining him for a round of golf five days before the scheduled day. It seems to me that those who received his email are the only ones that knew his whereabouts, and could be considered as suspects, assuming that the victim was a target."

Redmond responded quickly. "And those are the ones we interviewed, and they all have alibis. Except for our friend here." He said pointing at Nickerson. "I think it is high time we take him to task for the murder. That asshole thinks he is above the law. Well he isn't."

Within a half hour Nickerson was also charged with the murders of Matt Harris and his son. The lawyer, Eric Sampson, representing him arrived about an hour later. He apologized to Nickerson for taking so long to see him. He was finishing up with a case at the courthouse. Sampson understood that Nickerson was being charged with murder and cautioned him to say nothing further to the police. The first question he asked Nickerson was if he committed the murders that he was being charged with. Nickerson responded with a resounding no, a typical response for anyone being charged with committing a crime. Sampson then spent about an hour in determining what the circumstances were concerning the charges. After which, he spent the next half hour allaying Nickerson's fears about being found guilty, and then promised him that there was no way that the police would obtain a conviction considering the evidence that the police had, and the alibi that Nickerson had. Even if the murder weapon used had belonged to him, the police could not place him at the scene of the crime. In fact, he told Nickerson that the case would, most likely, never go to trial.

Stenson's cell phone rang. He answered it and turned his back to the others and spoke quietly. "Mom, I am busy right now." He listened. "Of course it's police business. Can I call you back?" After a pause, "Yes, mom, I did have my lunch. Is that all you wanted?" Once again he listened. "uh-huh, yes. Okay. Bye." Turning back to the group, hoping they heard none of the conversation, "Sorry about that." He said, visibly blushing.

Before anyone had time to respond, and before Sampson finished his private conversation with Nickerson, detective Martin entered the interview viewing room with news of another homicide.

"A new development, guys. A woman was just murdered in Dartmouth. She was found in her car at the Dartmouth Crossing shopping center.

"Yeah, so? Do you have the details?" Redmond asked.

"Apparently she hadn't been there long before she was found. Her throat was slit."

"Who found her?" Stenson wanted to know.

"A woman who had been shopping. Said she was gone no more than twenty minutes, and when she returned to her car, she saw the woman slumped over in the car next to hers, and she immediately call 911.

She was positive the dead woman was not there when she arrived in the parking lot."

"Did they find a weapon?" Donna queried.

"No. No weapon was found, but the area is being searched now. What was a bit curious though, they found a white wooden golf tee in her lap."

"What! Holy shit!" Redmond exclaimed.

"Yeah, exactly. I thought that might be of interest to you, Rick, considering this case." Martin said, gesturing with his head toward Nickerson in the interview room. "It looked like it was left deliberately. It had blood on it, possibly the victims blood, but we won't know that until later today or early tomorrow."

"Wait a minute. Just a minute." Stenson said with apprehension. "Did the police ID the woman?"

"Yeah," Martin said slowly, "they did ID her, Stenson. Is that important to you?" He said almost taunting him.

Stenson asked fearful of the response. "It wasn't Jean Jenkins, by any chance, was it?"

"No, it was not Jean Jenkins. It was a woman named Ellen McIntyre. I'll be looking into her background, to see if she is married, see if there are any unhappy boyfriends, or other men in her life, where she works, what the relationship is, if any, with Jenkins and Harris, and I'll also check her finances. If there is any connection, I'll come up with it. Is that thorough enough for you, Stenson?"

"What the hell's his problem?" Donna asked.

Stenson said, somewhat relieved, "Oh, for a minute I thought it was … oh never mind. Do you think it's the same perp who killed the other three, considering that a tee that was left behind?" He asked in general.

"What do you think, Stenson? That everybody who kills someone, drops a wooden tee? Jesus, give me a break."

Martin said with arrogance.

"It sure makes sense to me. Who else would have left a tee?" Donna said, not addressing Martin's pejorative comment.

Martin, frustrated by getting no response to his negativity retired to his desk to follow up on McIntyre's profile.

"Shit! Barnes is going to have a fucking conniption." Redmond spurted partially in disappointment and partially in frustration. "If it is the same perp, we have one helluva problem here. And it looks like we are wasting our time with this asshole." He said referring to Nickerson.

"Hmm where does that leave us?" Donna asked.

"We're back to square one." Rick said.

"Not really. Maybe we are a little bit closer." Stenson said.

"How do ya figure that? Rick asked doubtful.

"Well the way I see it, if it is the same perp who killed this woman in Dartmouth, then it eliminates Nickerson. That boils it down to three suspects, if we also eliminate Lisa Jenkins." Stenson addressed Donna. "You made a very good point when you said, the only people who knew what Geoff Jenkins was up to were his playing partners to whom he sent emails and his wife. I think we should concentrate on AJ Devoe, Dan Lee and Mike Fisher."

"Are you serious, Stenson?" Rick asked derisively.

"You think I make this shit up to amuse you? Stenson shot back.

"Dollars to donuts Nickerson is our man. No matter what was found the woman in Dartmouth has got to be an isolated incident."

"We can't ignore the fact that a white wooden tee was found at each of the murder sites. It can't be a coincidence, Rick."

"Shit! Shit! Shit!" Rick shouted, and then said as an afterthought, "Unless, of course, this asshole Nickerson has an accomplice."

Chapter 34

Jean Jenkins parked her car outside of Lisa's house. She picked up her purse with the gun inside, and hooked it over her shoulder. She never went anywhere without her handgun since she started target shooting. The last time she went to the range, she hired an instructor. She found that the instruction more than doubled her accuracy. The more she practiced, the more she hoped she would never have to use the gun, unless absolutely necessary. At her last practice session, Jean bought a stack of head and torso paper targets from the shooting range and decided to take her practice shooting to an isolated forest area in the future. She was aware that she was now hooked on possessing a handgun, and convinced that should the occasion arise, she not only could, but also would use the weapon. She also recognized the implications of using it, meaning that she would shoot to kill. She came so close to shooting Nickerson. She thought that if Redmond didn't interfere she might have just done that. What a mess that would have been she thought.

Jean wasn't sure why she was going to Lisa's house. She had no plan or reason to be there, but felt she had to talk to someone. Jean adjusted her hat and clunked in her thick low heels up to the front door and entered without ringing the bell, as she had always done.

Lisa alerted to the door opening, called out. "Who's there?" She started down the stairs to the main floor.

"It's me, Lisa." Jean answered quickly so as not to startle her, and walked into the living room.

Lisa went to Jean and hugged her. Jean stood stock still, not being fond of hugging. Under the circumstances Jean submitted to and welcomed the hug but did not respond. She held her arms stiffly at her side.

"I am so happy to see you Jean. This has been quite an ordeal."

Jean pulled back. "Did you have anything to do with Geoff's death?" She said bluntly with no consideration for Lisa's feelings.

"My god! How can you ask that?"

"Easy. How could you cheat on Geoff by sleeping with another man?" She said now realizing why she had come.

"Oh god, Jean, I...I don't know. It just happened. I just didn't think."

"That's crap, Lisa, and you know it. Nothing just happens. People make things happen. Geoff would never have done that to you."

"No, Geoff wouldn't have done that. I...I just needed the excitement, I guess. I don't know. I am paying for it now. You can't imagine how. I regret having cheated on him. I loved him so very much. I only wish I had him back."

"Lisa, you are a weak little slut. I could just kill you for what you've done." She said, her eyes blazing with anger. "You know they arrested your lover and charged him with Geoff's murder."

"What?"

"No, of course you didn't know."

"No that's impossible. He was here with me when Geoff was killed. He could never do that. He is too gentle to do that." Lisa protested.

"You mean he's too weak? I suppose you love him, do you? How could you, Lisa?"

"No, I don't love him. He was … he was just a…a… I don't know, but it's over. I will never see him again." She cried.

"It's a little late for that, don't you think?"

"Jean, do you really think he's responsible for Geoff's death?"

"I don't know, time will tell. It is all too much, first Geoff and now this. I don't know what to think." Jean looked into Lisa's eyes and threatened her. "If I find out that you had anything to do with this, Lisa, I swear to god that I will kill you. And don't think twice that I won't do it."

"Jean, you've got to believe me. I loved Geoff. How many times do I have to tell you?"

"Sure, Lisa, sure. Just remember what I said." Jean adjusted her hat, turned way from her and left.

. . . . .

Driver arrived home and ran into his house like a man possessed. After he sliced Ellen McIntyre's throat at Dartmouth Crossing, he ditched the gloves, knife, and the rag with which he wiped off the knife in a trashcan outside the

Best Buy store. He thought about the gloves possibly containing his DNA, but was too stressed out and rushed to retrieve them. It was on his way back to Halifax that he realized there was blood on his suit jacket, tie and shirt. He checked to see if there was any blood on his face, but found no specks. 'Fuck, I am getting so careless. There was no need for that. I should have been more meticulous,' he thought. Driver was now worried. He knew he was clear on the golf club he used to kill the others, but when they find the knife, they might just be able to trace it back to him, if they find his DNA in the gloves. Fortunately, his DNA is not in the system, and they have no grounds to get a sample from him. Why would they? He felt that he was covered, that he couldn't be placed at the scene. Inside, Driver went to the basement, stripped down to his skin and put all of his clothes in the washer save his suit and silk tie, which he put a grocery bag to take to the dry cleaner. He thought about his shoes, wondering if he picked up any dirt or gravel from Dartmouth Crossing. He cleaned the bottom of the shoes with a rag, which he tossed in the garbage, and then he washed the soles, just in case. He still had about forty minutes before his lunch break was over. He picked out a suit almost identical to the one he had been wearing, and found a tie close enough so that it wouldn't be noticed as being different from the one with which he started the day. No one really notices what tie you are or had been wearing. After he changed his clothes, he got into the car, dropped off his dirty suit and tie at the dry cleaner, drove to his designated rental spot in the underground parking lot and left his car. He still had about ten minutes remaining on his lunch break. Perfect. Now that he had completed his task, Driver felt a lot less anxious, and looking at him, one could hardly detect that he had murdered someone just minutes before. He smiled. His composure was back to normal.

. . . . .

Chief Barnes had his public relations officer, Constable Cindy Meyers, make a brief statement to the press regarding Ellen McIntyre's murder so as to avoid giving it importance. Meyers chose her words carefully. She did not disclose how McIntyre was murdered, only to say that she was murdered in her car in a parking lot at Dartmouth Crossing but she omitted that the killing might be linked to the homicides at the Indian Lake golf course. She said the investigation was being continued in the vicinity of the murder, and a forensic unit was searching the dead woman's impounded car for clues to identify the perpetrator. She would not release the woman's name until her relatives were notified and concluded that although they did not have a suspect in custody, they were getting closer to identifying him. Meyers declined to take questions from the press.

Moments after the press conference, Barnes called Redmond into his office. "I want to know what the fuck is going on here, Redmond, and what are you doing about it?"

Redmond stood uneasily attempting to respond to the question for which he had no answer. "We are doing our best, Chief. We might have eliminated one suspect and have several other possibilities. I believe we are getting closer, but we need more time."

"*Best*, Redmond? *Might* have eliminated? *Believe* you are getting closer? That's all bullshit and you know it. Now tell me, where the fuck are you with this investigation."

"Right now we have four strong suspects. We will be talking to each of them today and tomorrow. We have four detectives and more than ten officers working on the case. We are hoping to find some evidence at the Dartmouth site that will lead us to that person ... and we looking at one perp who may have committed all of the murders."

"I want to be kept informed every step of the way. The minute you come up with anything...and I mean anything, I want to know. You may contact me at any time of day or night. Just make sure it's relevant information, so you don't waste my time. I don't want to hear any excuses or any more bullshit. Understand?"

"I got you, Chief. I am hoping ... I am sure that something will break soon."

"Let's hope so, Redmond, for your sake." Barnes said threateningly.

Shortly after his meeting with Barnes, Redmond met with his staff in the meeting room. He now had pictures of each of the victims on the board including short biographies. Underneath was a list of suspects; Nickerson, who was charged with murder, AJ Devoe, Dan Lee and Mike Fisher, and at the bottom was Lisa Jenkins' name followed by a question mark. There were no arrests or records for any of the suspects, except for AJ Devoe who had been arrested several years ago on a DUI charge, for which he paid a fine and had had his license suspended for six months.

"We don't have a hell of a lot to go on, guys." Redmond said, including Donna in the guys. "Nickerson is now out on bail, but it is questionable whether we can make the murder charge against him stand up in court. What we have so far are three crime scenes, two on the Indian Lake golf course, and one at Dartmouth Crossing in Dartmouth. So far the victims have no connection with each other whatsoever. I don't get it. None of the Vics are associated with drugs, organized crime; we have no sheets on them; they are just regular citizens. They have nothing in common. Yet, as far as we can tell, the same perp killed them all. But for the life of me, we've been unable to turn up with a motive. He or she used the same weapon to kill three of them, and we have that weapon. We even know who the weapon belongs to, but we can't put Nickerson at the scene. Now the perp killed a woman at a different site, using a different weapon, but leaves his signature, a white wooden tee. All of the Vics had been killed in broad daylight."

"That takes a brazen and fearless sort of man." Stenson said.

"Yes, and might I add a bit slipshod. It sounds like he is begging to be caught." Donna said.

"There is one thing that the three murders have in common." Stenson considered. "All of the Vics were killed during the day. So what does that tell us about the perp?"

"He doesn't like to go out at night?" Donna offered laughing.
"That may not be as bizarre as you may think. Maybe he
works at night, or plays at night. For instance, Dan Lee works
late at night, doesn't he?"

"He also works early in the morning and practically all day
too." Redmond tossed in.

"Right. And AJ Devoe plays just about every night at clubs
and chasing women."

"True." Donna agreed. "But he sleeps most of the day, at
least most of the morning.

"So? Does their life style eliminate both of them? I don't
fuckin' think so." Redmond said. "Either one could have
found time. And what about Fisher?"

"He could have had the time, even though his receptionist
confirmed his alibi." Donna said. "Besides, we know he is an
arrogant bastard, but I think he's too greedy to even consider
cancelling a meeting to kill someone."

"Let's look at it from another angle. Suppose only one, or
possibly two of those who were killed were the targets."
Stenson surmised.

"Let's assume you are right, Stenson." Rick concurred.
"Who, then, is the target?"

"It might be easier to determine who wasn't the target."
Stenson said, removing his jacket and placing it over the back
of a chair.

"I don't think the perp targeted the Harris boy," Donna said,
"unless he didn't plan on the boy being with his father."
Stenson dismissed Harris as a target. "I think we can all agree

245

that Harris and his son was a random killing, committed to confuse us, at least temporarily."

Rick picked it up. "So that leaves us with Jenkins and McIntyre as possible targets. And to this point we don't have enough information on McIntyre to even guess if she was a real target or another random killing to throw us off the track."

"Right." Stenson said. "Without assuming too much, it appears that Jenkins is the only and mostly likely candidate for being the target.

. . . . .

Slater pulled the golf bag cart behind him, which occasionally tipped in one direction, then another, as the wheels dipped into ruts or ran over protruding rocks on the unleveled path. He was spending close to twelve hours a day on the course. He seldom hit a ball. But when he did it was because he felt that players behind him were observing him. Often he let the other golfers play through, in consideration of what would be his slow play. It gave him the opportunity to observe them, and also allowed him the liberty of spending a lot of time in the woods, looking for anyone lingering there. During the process, Slater found hundreds of lost balls. The largest compartment in his golf bag was almost filled to the top. He considered that he could augment his salary by selling the balls he found. That is what he thought as he chuckled to himself. Each day he spent a great deal of time in the woods at the murder site. The mosquitoes and black flies were worse in the early morning and late at night, especially if there was very little or no breeze. Slater wore a bug repellant all the time to ward off the offending gnats. He liked the duty patrolling the golf course. He particularly liked it for a number of reasons; one was that the weather was perfect, temperatures ranging between 20-27 degrees Celsius and sunny every day. The other reason was that he felt as though he was at a resort. Although he knew that he was no Tiger Woods, he could imagine playing golf for a living, not that he had proven himself to be anything but below the average amateur golfer. Yes, he could get use to this kind of duty. To this point he had not run into anyone that he knew and he didn't expect to. Not one of his friends played golf, nor did any of his colleagues at the station. To his delight, he found no one suspicious or threatening in any way. He found nothing new in the way of evidence at the murder sites. He went about his business of pretending to play a solo round or rather rounds, as was the case, and watching everyone he came in contact with.

Slater had married before he entered the force. He had graduated from the police academy. He had two children, a boy, eight years old and a girl, six. His wife worked as a medical assistant, and the family bought and lived in a house in central Halifax. They bought the house just before the surge in real estate prices. Since the purchase, the value of the house rose by about 45%. He loved central Halifax because the neighborhood was family oriented, and it was within walking distance to work and most of Halifax's shopping areas. Although the neighborhood was predominantly white, he and his family were accepted by the neighbors, but not necessarily invited into their homes. Slater's dream was to join the U.S. Marine Corps, but for a variety of reasons, namely that he did not want to leave his wife and children behind, opted for the next best career, in his mind, a police officer in the HRM. His movement up the ranks was a bit faster than average, mainly because of his neatness, and dedication to the force. The fact that he was more intelligent than the average cop also helped a great deal, as did the fact that he was black.

Today he wondered about the validity of policing the golf course, whether it was a waste of time. 'How often did the perp return to the scene of the crime,' he wondered out loud? Sometimes immediately after the crime a perp might appear to assess his handiwork, other than that he would normally shy away from the scene, answering his own question. During this duty, with no partner to share a word with, Slater often turned to discussing issues with himself. When he was younger, perhaps as a boy, he use to think it was okay to talk to yourself, ask yourself questions, but to answer them, well, that was a different story.

Jim Slater, his wife and family frequently attended the St Thomas Baptist Church in North Preston. Although he was not the most religious guy, he did believe in god, and felt that god was the only one you really had to answer to…except for his wife.

It was the second time around the course and Slater decided to tee off at the par-four third hole. It was a long and straight fairway. After planting the tee in the ground, and taking a few practice swings, he swung hard at the golf ball like he was swinging a baseball bat at a hard-thrown curve ball. The golf ball lifted high in the air, about 150 yards down the fairway and sliced far into the woods. Slater followed the path of the ball as it sailed between two tall birch trees into the wooded area.

"So much for a career in golf." He muttered to himself. "I'd better keep my day job." He put his driver in the bag, and pulling his cart behind him unceremoniously, trotted down the cart path to look for his ball that fell near the two birch trees. As he walked, he fantasized about being a detective. He had inkling that he was not far from submitting an application and having it accepted, at most a year or two.

Chapter 35

Word filtered down through the department that the knife, believed to be the murder weapon, and a bloody rag were found near the murder site at Dartmouth Crossing. Excitement built as Rick, Donna and Stenson awaited word confirming that it was the knife that killed McIntyre. They did not have to wait long. The report came quickly. The knife proved to be the one used in the killing and the blood on the rag matched McIntyre's blood. Unfortunately, there were no prints on the knife. A further search at the murder site resulted in the recovery of a pair of surgical gloves and they were being tested for DNA. There was a sense of hope and expectations of a break in the case. Nickerson was released on bail, considering that he had no past history with the police, and because he had a fairly ironclad alibi. Redmond called Slater to inform him of the Dartmouth murder, and to tell him to wrap it up for the day at the golf course. A forensic team was going over McIntyre's car with a fine-tooth comb for clues. Stenson and Copp joined Martin in the McIntyre paper chase hoping to find a connection to the other murders. The national radio and TV media took the story and ran with it; they linked the murders and suggested that a serial killer was at work in the Halifax area. Chief Barnes was indeed having a conniption. He contacted the newspapers, radio and TV reporters to set up a media conference to be held in two days, at which time he expected to have some positive results regarding the murders. The Halifax newspaper's front-page headline read: *Another murder – Serial killing?*

. . . . .

Nickerson called Lisa Jenkins immediately after he was released. "Lisa, it's Philip."

"Where are you? What happened? I heard you were arrested."

"I'm at home now. I was arrested, but I posted bail. I have to talk to you. I have to see you, Lisa."

"I don't know. I don't think that's a good idea."

"We have to talk. Another person - a woman, was killed while I was in custody. They think she was killed by the same one who killed Geoff."

"Oh my god!"

"When can we meet?"

"Not tonight. Tomorrow. I'll come see you tomorrow."

. . . . .

Redmond planned to leave the station with the sole purpose of getting something to eat. He then decided to call it a night and went home, taking the murder books with him to study. He found a week old steak in his fridge, prepared it with garlic, butter, and salt and pepper, and then put it in the oven to broil. While the steak was cooking, he poured a rum and coke and made a salad. After going through the murder books briefly, he began to see the murders as Stenson had. He relied heavily on Stenson's judgment and opinions. Although, he was unsure about McIntyre, he felt that Jenkins was the target, perhaps not the only target, but certainly the main one. However, he was a stickler when it came to Nickerson. He was convinced that Nickerson had killed Jenkins, but knew that he could not have killed McIntyre, since he was being held in custody at the time. If Nickerson was his man, he had to be working with someone else, and the only other possibility was that Jenkins' wife was involved. At least, that's what he thought. Rick fixed a second drink and ate his medium rare steak and salad dinner. He felt a second visit to Lisa Jenkins was in order. Perhaps he could trip her up. He checked his watch; too late to see her tonight. He decided to shave and shower before going to bed. Rick had two ways of shaving; he either shaved after he showered, which made his beard softer from the soaking and easier to remove, or he shaved before showering. Tonight he shaved before showering. Rick always had difficulty in getting the correct amount of shaving cream from the container. The amount he put in his hand always seemed to be too little, so he sprayed more cream and, as usual, it was too much. Not getting the amount right almost always led to a string of expletives. Tonight was no exception. After he finished swearing, shaving and showering, Rick fixed a third rum and coke, which he drank as he watched the national and local news. The murders' coverage was dreadful in that it would have frightened anyone in his or her right mind. The content was simply that a serial killer was on the loose, and that the police were baffled and had no real suspects, and all the citizens of the city should take caution. The broadcaster also said that no one should go out alone. Redmond turned the TV off and went to bed.

. . . . .

Martin, Stenson and Copp stayed late to mull over the paper on McIntyre. They came up with nothing that connected her with Jenkins, Harris, or any of Jenkins' friends. It was a dead end. They decided to call it a night. Martin left while Stenson and Donna were gathering up their notes.

"It's got to be one of Jenkins' friends. It just has to be, Stenson."

"I couldn't agree more. I think we are barking up the wrong tree with Nickerson though."

"Well, that's possible, unless Lisa Jenkins was involved."

"I've considered that, but you know, I kinda believe Nickerson. Somehow, I don't think he's lying."

"Look, why don't we continue this over a drink?" Donna suggested.

"That sounds good to me. Where would you like to go?"

"How about my place?" She said smiling.

"Hey, how can I refuse an offer like that? Nothing's better than free drinks." Stenson said as he put his notes in a manila folder, picked up his laptop, grabbed his jacket from the back of his chair, and put it on.

Stenson followed Donna's Tercel, which she kept in mint condition, and looked like it was brand new, even though it was at least nine years old.

Donna's one-bedroom apartment was small, clean and cozy. Though it had a feminine touch, it was not 'pretty' and 'dainty' feminine, but more middle of the road. Stenson felt quite comfortable there. Donna took Stenson's jacket and hung it on the coat tree just to the left of the entrance. Both unstrapped their holsters and put their weapons on a table. Donna, as an afterthought, locked the door. Stenson walked into the living room, which had three large windows that offered an unimpeded view of the Bedford Basin. The lights from Dartmouth sparkled on the calm basin water as if the surface had been covered with colored glitter.

"Nice view, Donna." Stenson said before sitting in a green fabric recliner, and laying his notes and laptop on a simple cherry wood table that sat lengthwise in front of a two-seat sofa that was backed by two plush pillows.

"Yes, I never tire of it. I find it peaceful, almost meditative." She smiled and added, "Can I get you something to drink?"

"What do ya have?"

"There is some beer, scotch, vodka, rum and gin, and mix to go with all of them."

"Gin and tonic?"

"No sooner said than done." She said, putting a CD on her Bose player, which was a remnant from her previous relationship. While Donna fixed the drinks, the dulcet tones of Jim Hall's guitar rendition of *You'd Be So Nice To Come Home To* spilled into the room through the speakers. The atmosphere was nice; it was good for a change to not think about the murders. Donna brought the drinks and asked, "What are you thinking?" She said sitting on the arm of his chair.

I was thinking that I'd love to *not* discuss the case, clear my mind, with one exception."

"And what might that be?" She asked lifting her eyebrows.

"I can't help feeling that we are missing something obvious." He took a sip of his drink. "Something that is right in front of us, so apparent that we are overlooking it."

"And we are to do what?"

"We need to go back. I want to go over everything that we found on Jenkins' computer. I want to review it. See if there is something there. I want to look at his insurance, and at every person with whom he had done consulting during the last year or two."

"You sure you don't want to discuss this tonight?" She teased.

"Oh Jesus." He laughed. "I'm sorry." He took another sip of his drink. "Who is that playing?"

"That? It's Jim Hall and some of his buddies."

"That's great. I thought I heard Paul Desmond on the sax."

"You are correct young man. You take the prize." She said swinging her body and spreading her arms out to the side.

"I didn't know you were a jazz aficionado."

"There are a lot of things you don't know about me, Stenson."

She said mysteriously, raising her eyebrows. "And by the way, speaking of not knowing things, was that your mother who called earlier, while we were at the meeting."

"Oh Jesus!" His face felt warm and starting to flush.

"Oh my, Stenson, your mother called you at work? Did you know she called the other day too? I took the call and she asked if 'Stenson' was there." She smiled and lifted her shoulders. She smiled with her entire body. "She didn't say Mr. Stemson, she called you by your last name; Stenson she said."

"Everybody calls me by my last name." He said, trying unsuccessfully not to be embarrassed. "Look, she always calls me Stenson, okay? Always has for as long as I can remember."

Donna laughed taunting him. "Did she want to know if you brought your rubber booties and umbrella to work?"

Stenson began to enjoy Donna's teasing. "Actually she wanted to know if I brought my lunch, and if I had time to eat it."

"That so sweet, Stenson. She must really care about you."

Stenson tilted his head, shrugging as he smiled.

Donna leaned closer, putting her hand on his arm. "How about another drink? Are you ready?"

"Ready? For what?" He said raising his eyebrows.

"You asshole. For a drink, of course." She stood up from the arm of the chair.

"Are you going to have one?" He said just a bit more seriously. She said nothing and after a moment of a searching look at each other, he felt self-conscious, got up from the chair and walked to the window to look at the water and without turning around said, "I'll definite have another drink." Donna went to the player and hit replay of the Jim Hall *Concierto* CD.

"I really like this CD." Stenson said.

"And did you notice the haunting horn of..."

"Chet Baker." They said in concert. Donna fixed two more drinks.

. . . . .

Earlier, the sun was setting in the west, the orange and red colors mixed with mauve and grey lifted up and drifted to the south giving the appearance of a raging fire. Slater took note of the splendid sunset, although the wooded area that he was about to enter to search for his ball blocked much of it. He received a call from Rick to inform him of the murder at Dartmouth Crossing, and told him to return to the office. He responded that he would wrap it up in a few minutes and then return. As he entered the dense section of the woods, which had darkened a bit, he looked for the two birch trees where his ball had fallen. It was deadly quiet now at the course; only a few foursomes remained. Slater saw the birch trees in question and headed toward them.

A man wearing a baseball cap and a scarf around his face stood in the shadow of a large tree. He held a machete loosely at his side. As Slater approached the two birch trees, the man loomed into the clearing, coming face to face with him. Slater, startled by the man's appearance, dropped to one knee. The man took a step forward, toward him, and Slater reached for the cuff of his pants, pulled it up giving him access to his gun. He pulled it out of the ankle holster and pointed it at the man. "Stop right there."

"Whoa, man, hang on." The man said, coming to an abrupt halt. "Just a second. There is no need for that."

"Stay where you are and drop the weapon." Slater demanded with authority.

"Sure, sure. But it's not a weapon. I'm just clearing some brush here, that's all." He clarified as he dropped the machete to the ground.

"You're working here?" Slater asked, with the gun still pointing at the man.

"Yes, yes sir, I am. There have been a lot of complaints that players can't find their balls with the heavy undercover, so I was given the job of clearing it a little better." The man explained.

"Why not use a trimmer, or a brush cutter? Why the machete?" Slater asked suspiciously, and rightfully so.

"You kidding? Too much noise. It disturbs the players. This is a much better option." He explained. "Do you mind not pointing that gun at me? It's making me feel a bit uncomfortable."

"Why do you have your face covered like that?" Slater dropped the gun to his side.

"Oh we all do that because of allergies, protection from little pieces of debris hitting you in the face, and to avoid poison ivy

258

from touching your face. All the usual stuff, I suppose." The man did not remove the scarf from his face. "By the way, your ball is right over there." He said, quickly changing the subject, and pointing just beyond those two birch trees. "You want me to show you where it is?"

Slater looked in the direction in which the man pointed and saw his ball exposed in the clearing. "No, that's okay, I see it." He turned to go to his ball and the man bent over and picked up the machete, gripping it tightly in his hand. He then followed Slater who walked through the short undergrowth to pick up his ball. The man was closing the distance between them; Jim bent down to pick up his ball.

"Fore!" A man on the fairway shouted. There was raucous laughter from a foursome that was approaching. Apparently, they saw Slater's golf bag and knew someone was in the vicinity. Slater and the man turned quickly in the direction of the shout. The man relaxed his grip on the machete. Slater stood up, with his ball in one hand, and the gun in the other. Both heard the ball rustling through the leaves in the trees and then a soft thump.

"Well, I've work to do." The man said, turning and slowly walking away mumbled to himself. "Soon it will be too dark to do anything."

"Yeah." Slater said, returning the gun to its holster. "I know what you mean."

Slater walked out of the wooded hazard to retrieve the cart containing his golf clubs. The foursome was upon him. All four were a bit tipsy, having had one drink too many, no doubt. They exchanged remarks with him and had a few laughs. All four men went into the woods to search for the errant golf ball. Slater, finished for the day, headed back to the clubhouse to return the clubs and cart.

Karen was closing the cash, when Slater came in.

"Any luck?" She asked.

"With the game or with my work?

"Both." She said laughing.

"Neither." He said smiling gently, exposing his perfectly white even teeth.

"That's partially a good thing then." She said.

"Had a little scare though." He said. "I ran into one of your ground workers in the woods; the one working with a machete."

"What? What are you talking about? The grounds crew left hours ago."

"You didn't have anyone clearing an area in the woods with a machete?" He said with concern.

"Machetes?" She laughed. "We don't use machetes to clear anything. It's too slow and inefficient. This isn't a third-world country, ya know."

"Oh my god!" Slater exclaimed. As he ran out of the clubhouse he heard Karen say, "What is it?"

He ran as hard as he could to the wooded area where he first saw the man with the machete. He was too late. The man had gone.

. . . . .

Driver was in a panic as he drove home. That was too close. What are the odds of running into someone with a gun? He thought. Was he a cop? Driver figured that the propinquity of the murders would send the police in a tizzy, drive them up the wall. I must admit it was exhilarating. I was so cool under pressure. I had him so fooled. I had all the answers. I love thinking on my feet like that. Shit! I'm just glad he wasn't trigger-happy. I can't deny how cool he was too. One never knows about those black dudes. I'm not too surprised that he was carrying though. He drove into the city faster than he should have, concerned about being stopped and searched. It wouldn't look good if the police found the machete in his trunk. He dropped his speed to just below the limit.

Now what, he thought? I think it is time to go after that bitch. She is way overdue for a visit from me.

Chapter 36

The morning light came fast. The sun flooded the room bouncing colors off the walls, creating a watercolor, diffused by the sheer curtains covering the windows. Stenson's cell phone, which rang to a jazz ring tone, woke him from a deep sleep. He realized where he was and got up from the living room couch wearing only his underwear. Donna, naked under the sheet on her bed, stirred as he answered it. "Yep." He said softly into the mouthpiece of the phone. "I'm definitely awake. Otherwise I wouldn't be talking to you, Rick, now would I?" He listened as Rick told him about Slater's episode at Indian Lake.

"What? When did that happen?" Donna sat up in bed when she heard the urgency in Stemson's voice. He listened to Rick's explanation of what took place. "Look, man, I'll be there as soon as I can, and I'll contact Donna to let her know. That will be one less call you'll have to make. See ya soon." He disconnected the call.

Donna rubbed the sleep from her eyes, put on a robe and went into the living room. "What was that about?"

"Slater had a little problem at the golf course. He thinks he may have encountered the perp we're looking for."

"Is he okay?"

"Aside from being a bit shook up, he's fine."

"Did you sleep okay on the couch?" She asked somewhat disappointed.

"Not as good as my own bed, but it did the trick. I had just a few too many drinks to drive. Thanks for the sofa."

Donna prepared French toast for the two of them. They left for the station soon after, Donna in her car and Stenson in his. All the members of the team were tired from having worked...or played relatively late the previous night and their movement and behavior exemplified exactly that. Stenson had picked up coffee at Starbucks for everyone. They sat slouched on the edges of desks or in chairs and sipped their coffee quietly, waiting for Redmond to bring them up to date. Slater stood nervously by in his civvies. His incident was the hot issue of the morning, even though Ellen McIntyre's death was not forgotten. An attempt on the life of one of their own was not taken lightly. Rick asked Slater to fill everyone in on the incident at Indian Lake with the presumed perp, which he did in a skillful and pithy manner. He ended his presentation of the event with, "I was so close. If only I had considered..."

Rick interrupted him and concluded: " It goes without saying that Jim found himself to be in a very dangerous situation, after the fact. It could have cost him his life. It was good that he had his gun with him. We will continue our surveillance at the golf course, but we'll partner Jim with Dave Martin. That way they will be able to watch each other's back."

"What did the guy look like, Jim?" Stenson probed.

"Like I said, he had a hat on and a scarf around his face, so I don't think I'd be able to recognize him if I ever saw him again. He was about my height, but bigger, that is, he weighed a lot more than I did. But he was not fat, could have been as much as maybe 200 pounds. Although it was difficult to tell because of his loose work clothes, he looked quite powerful. If only I had more experience…I…I should have nailed the bastard." His words trailed off.

"There is no way you could have known that he wasn't a groundkeeper, Jim." Donna said, consoling him. "You can't blame yourself for that. Fortunately, it was you rather than a golfer that hit his ball into the woods. We might have had another murder on our hands."

"Going back there was a big mistake on his part." Stenson figured. "And you know what? That son-of-a-bitch will make more mistakes, and we'll snag him. You can bet on that. We're getting close." The group quieted down, each member thinking about the incident.

"You know, Jim, you did good work." Stenson said. "Your description of him, his size, eliminates Dan Lee, who is very slim, maybe about 150. That leaves us with Devoe and Fisher; both could fit that description."

"Don't forget about Nickerson," Rick added. "He in conjunction with Jenkins' wife is still a suspect. We still don't have any DNA reports from the McIntyre murder. As much as I pushed the lab, there is no way they can come up with anything yet for a couple more days."

"You mean they can't do it instantly like CSI on TV? What a shame." Donna said sarcastically, which prompted a laugh or two.

"You know, Rick, I am sure that the guy with the machete was not Nickerson. I know what Nickerson looks like, and I'm almost positive he was not the guy I saw in the woods at Indian Lake."

"Well, I guess that remains to be seen, Jim." Rick said with resistance, not wanting to give up on Nickerson as the perp.

"Why McIntyre?" Stenson wondered aloud. "How does she fit into the picture? And why the hell is he leaving us his calling card, a white wooden tee? And we might have had the unfortunate luck of adding Slater to the list, if he hadn't been clever enough to arm himself. You did a good job, Jim." Slater nodded modestly.

"By the way, we got nothing from McIntyre's car. No prints; nothing that can help us identify the perp." Redmond said. Martin added: "She has a sister in Dartmouth, and she doesn't know of anyone that might have wanted her dead. So, as far as motive goes, we are in a cul-de-sac. We still have to explore her papers, appointments, finances, insurance, and also have to check to see if she was into gambling or drugs. Until we do that, we have nothing. Personally, I think it is a waste of time."

"Nevertheless, Dave, we'll have to follow up on that. Now here's what we do immediately." Rick elaborated. "I am going to pay Jenkins' wife a visit. Dave, I want you and Jim to talk to Devoe, see what you can come up with, and if that doesn't result in anything positive then I want you both back at Indian Lake, but before you go follow a paper trail on McIntyre. Stenson, you and Donna go to see Fisher. Find out where the hell he was when Jim was approached last night. If anything productive comes out of the interviews, I want to know immediately. And I don't want any of you to fuck around! I think we are getting close, so I don't want any of you taking chances. This person is a fuckin' dangerous lunatic and might be getting antsy, whoever he is. Okay?"

Each rose up from their chairs and desks respectively, with renewed energy, and paired off as the group disintegrated.

. . . . .

Rick approached Lisa Jenkins' house just as she was closing the front door and about to leave.

"Ms Jenkins. Do you have a minute?" He asked as he got out of his car.

"Oh, detective…a" She replied, surprised by his presence, and trying unsuccessfully to remember his name.

"Redmond." He reminded her.

"Yes. Detective Redmond. I'm sorry. I forgot your name."

"That's okay. You're not the first, and probably won't be the last. Do you have a minute, please?"

"Well, I suppose I can spare a few minutes. I have no pressing engagements." She said smiling.

Once inside, Lisa led him into the living room. "Can I get you something to drink, detective?"

"No. Nothing for me, thank you, but you go ahead."

"Please." She said, gesturing to a chair for him to sit.

He took her up on the chair offer and pulled out a notepad as he sat. Lisa sat on the sofa across from him. "I suppose you know that we had arrested Nickerson and charged him with your husband's...your late husband's murder." She nodded. "We have proof that the murder weapon used to kill Mr. Jenkins and Harris and his son belonged to Nickerson."

"What?" Lisa gasped. "How can that be?"

"He identified the weapon himself." Redmond waited for a response from her, but none came. "Are you sure about the time that Nickerson came here?"

"I'm positive about the time. I was listening to CBC and *The Current* just broke for the news. It was right after that, a little after nine when he got here."

"So, he just showed up? With no notice or anything?"

"Actually, he called before he came."

"Really? He called?"

Lisa nodded. "He always called first. He didn't want to arrive and find Geoff here."

"Then it's possible that he called you from his cell phone driving back from the golf course, isn't it?"

"No, not at all possible." She answered.

"Why not?"

"Because I have caller ID. He called me from his home phone."

Redmond thought that if she had anything to do with her husband's murder, she would lie about it. "What time did he call?"

"It must have been just after 8:30. *Information Morning* was still airing."

"Why didn't you tell us this before, Ms Jenkins? Why wait until now."

"I suppose it was because you didn't asked me about it before."

Redmond decided to pursue a different avenue. "Did Mr. Jenkins collect any weapons?"

"Weapons?"

"Like...uhm...say a machete, for example."

The question provoked laughter from Lisa. "No, absolutely not. He abhorred violence, and anything that symbolized violence. He wouldn't tolerate weapons of any sort in the house." She said emphatically.

"What about Nickerson? Did he have any weapons?"

"I have no idea. If he does, he never told me about them."

"Do you have any insurance policy on your husband?"

"My god! I think you are going too far, detective. I don't like what you are insinuating."

"Do you?" He asked again annoyed at her response.

"Yes, I do. We each have - *had* a policy of about six and a half million dollars. If I died, he would be the recipient of the insurance, just as I would...as I am if...when." She said dropping her head into her hands emitting an involuntary sob-like sound. She lifted her head; her cheeks were stained with tears. "If you think that I would kill my own husband for money, you are terribly disillusioned. I would hate to be you, detective."

. . . . .

Jim Slater and Dave Martin, both in casual civvies, knocked on AJ Devoe's door, rousing him from bed.

"I'll do the talking, Jim. You see if he looks like the guy you saw last night. See if you can pick up anything."

Devoe opened the door wearing silk pajama bottoms and a type of smoking jacket that would make Hugh Hefner proud.

"Yeah?" He asked, his eyes barely open and his hair sleep-disheveled. There was no indication that he recognized Slater. If he did, he was one cool character.

They showed him their badges, and he invited them inside, leading them directly into the kitchen. "I already spoke to you guys. There's nothing more that I can tell you."

"This is about another matter." Martin said, as Slater observed Devoe, trying to determine if he was the man with the machete that he met in the woods. He was unsure; his voice did not seem to ring a bell.

"You guys want a coffee?" He asked running water to fill a pot.

Martin looked at Slater, who shrugged. "Sure, if it's no trouble." Martin said observing the dirty dinner dishes in the sink, no doubt from the previous night.

"No trouble at all. Now what can I do for you?" He asked measuring the coffee grounds, putting it in the basket and hitting the start button.

"Where were you last night and be specific, Devoe?" Martin asked.

"Depends on the time, I suppose. What's this about?"

"Just answer the question, Devoe. Let's say from eight o'clock on."

"That's easy. I was at the Old Triangle around seven or thereabouts, and ended up at the Split Crow until I came home."

"And what time might that have been, when you came home?"

"After midnight."

"And I suppose someone can confirm that you were there during those times?"

"No question about that. I met a friend at the Triangle, and then we went to the Crow, and spent all of our time there together."

"Do you have a machete, by any chance?"

"No, but I do have a Japanese ceremonial Samurai sword. Does that count? It is an Orchid Katana sword. I bought it for less than $1,000, a great price."

"May we see the sword, please?"

"Definitely. It's in the living room hanging on the wall. Mind if I pour myself a coffee first?"

"Sure. Fill your boots." Martin said.

Devoe poured three coffees, took a cream blend from the fridge for his coffee and stirred it through. He then led them into the living room, carrying his coffee and pointed to the sword in question. The sword hung at an angle on the west wall. The length of the handle protruding from the scabbard, which was deeply lacquered in blue, was about a foot. The handle was made of blackened iron, with an Orchid and Butterfly decoration inlaid in silver, brass and copper. The length of the blade, which was just wider than an inch at its widest point, was about two and a half feet. Martin looked to Slater, who shook his head. Devoe reached up to take the sword down and Martin told him, "Don't bother. We can see it from here. That's quite a sword. Do you have any others?" "No. One is enough. This one is authentic and a beauty. I'm still getting use to having it on the wall, can't stop looking at it whenever I am in the room."

Martin and Slater turned to each other, took a drink of coffee, raised their eyebrows and shrugged. After getting the name and number of Devoe's friend, Martin and Slater left for the Indian Lake Golf course. ."

. . . . .

Driver decided to slow down his activity, fearful that due to the frequency of the murders it might be difficult to solidify an alibi for each of them, if he was placed in the situation of having to. The bitch would have to wait. He did not want to make any mistakes; he wanted to avoid being connected to those he killed at any cost. Last night was too risky. He wondered if the black man he met in the woods at Indian Lake could recognize him, and what was with the gun? That was weird. He sure was jumpy...but then why wouldn't he be? Who wouldn't be edgy when confronted with a machete? He laughed to himself. He got lucky. I am sure he wasn't suspicious whatsoever. He had no reason to be. I was just in the woods doing my job. He laughed out loud. I don't think I have to worry about him. After all, would a man who pulled a gun on me, a worker, report the incident to the police? I don't think so. Christ! At first, I thought he was going to shoot me. But I think he was as frightened as I was. If only those golfers weren't still playing. It was almost dark when they showed. They must be crazy. I sure would like to have seen what kind of damage the machete would have done. I bet I could have taken his leg right off. There would have been a lot of blood. He would have bled out quickly. But the yelling might have drawn unwanted attention. Well, all said and done, I've had quite a few exciting days. Now it is time to cool it. I have other issues to be concerned with. What is my goal? If I hope to get what I want, I will have to focus. And the most important thing to focus on is the money. I will need several million more before I can disappear. Then it won't make any difference if they know who I am and what I have done.

. . . . .

The morning was already in the low 20s with the sun high in the sky and it looked like it might hit 30 degrees Celsius by mid-day. Stenson and Donna walked from the station along the Citadel, down Duke Street and through Scotia Square to take the pedway to Fisher's office in Purdy's Wharf. "After we talk to Fisher, what do you say we stop at Ray's at the food court for a Lebanese lunch?" Stenson suggested to Donna.

"Hey, that sounds good to me. How about taking lunch to go and eat it down at the waterfront?"

"I can't turn that down. You've stroked me in the right spot."

"Yeah, right. Your stomach." She gibed.

The sun shone through the glass-enclosed pedway refracting the light in a colored pattern on them as they passed Barrington Street and advanced towards Purdy's Wharf. When they arrived at Investment Securities, the receptionist, Linda Belford, greeted them as if they were old friends. Her simple V-neck black dress emphasized every asset that she owned, and she possessed plenty of them. Her long slender body was Pilates' fit. She was the perfect combination of balance, beauty and strength. Stemson had difficulty in taking his eyes off her. She made Donna feel fashionably uncomfortable, resulting in her turning to Stenson with raised eyebrows and a shrug, as if to say 'what can you do, can't have everything?'

Moments later, after being announced, Belford sashayed from her desk and directed them to Fisher's office. Belford exchanged a meaningful glance with Fisher and then she returned to the reception desk.

"Detectives, have a seat, please. I'll be with you in a second." Fisher said, shuffling papers on his desk into a pile. Stenson and Donna sat down at the table in front of the wall of windows looking out over the harbor. Shortly after, Fisher joined them as if he were attending a client investment meeting. A pitcher of water sat on the glass tabletop as if he had been expecting them; next to the pitcher was small dish with lemon slices on it. He poured three glasses of water and asked, "Is this a business or personal visit?"

"Business." Stenson said smiling as usual.

"Of course. I am sure a detective's salary does not leave a great deal left for investments." He said unable to resist and responding to Stenson's smile with a contemptuous smile of his own.

Stenson ignored his comment and said. "No doubt you have read today's paper regarding the death of a woman at Dartmouth Crossing."

"Yes, I heard something about it. What does that have to do with me?"

"We have reason to believe that her murder is connected to Geoff Jenkins' killing." Donna said.

"I see. So, every time someone is killed in this city, you will pay me a visit. Is that it?"

"Do you know this woman?" Donna asked, taking a photo out of her folder and handing it to him.

Fisher took the photo and studied it briefly. "No, I can't say that I do. Is this the woman that was killed?"

Donna ignored his question. "We would like to know where you were when she was murdered."

"So the answer to my question is yes." Fisher said in his typically arrogant way. "And that would have been when?"

"That was just after noon yesterday." Donna said abruptly.

I will have to check that out with Linda before I can answer that, but I can guess that I was probably at lunch." He replied.

Stenson then asked, "What about last night, say about eight o'clock, or thereabouts? Where were you, Mr. Fisher?

"I was home last night. No doubt about it."

"Was anyone with you last night? Anyone that can confirm your whereabouts?" Stenson continued.

"No. I was alone working on my computer, wrapping up some work and checking the market results."

"So no one can verify that, Mr. Fisher?" Donna said accusingly.

"What part of 'I was home alone' did you not understand, detective?" He responded.

Changing the subject, Stenson said. "That should just about wrap it up. I think we're finished here." He started to get up from the chair, and then stopped. "Oh, by the way, do you happen to own a machete, Mr. Fisher?" He said catching Fisher off guard.

Fisher said after a brief pause, his face eliciting surprise said, "A machete? Oh sure." His disdain returned. "And I also own several spears, a bow and arrow and a poison blow gun, a compete arsenal of African weapons." The sarcasm was not lost on Stenson and Donna and it incited their laughter.

"Does that answer your questions this time around … at least for the time being?"

"Thank you for your *usual* cooperation, Mr. Fisher." Donna stung him with sarcasm equal to his own as she stood up.

"We'll show ourselves out." Stenson said and they left the Investment Securities office, but not before checking Fisher's lunch schedule for the previous day. Belford expressed annoyance as Stenson copied Fisher's lunch hour times of the previous day in his notepad.

After picking up a chicken pita sandwich and bottled water from Ray's, they walked down to the waterfront found a spot to sit amid the festive summer activities. Buskers dressed like the 60s hippies played guitars and other instruments with their cases laid open on the ground soliciting Donations from the audience, as unicycles were pedaled along the harbor walk. Tall ships that had gather four times over two decades floated proudly in their allotted berths with visitors ogling them in awe, a spectacle to say the least. Vendors of ice cream, beaver tails and food barked out to potential customers to test their wares. Stenson and Donna sat eating their pitas, and after a few minutes of absorbing the festive environment, became oblivious to the celebratory atmosphere.

"Can you believe that arrogant asshole? He has no respect or consideration for people whatsoever." Stenson said.

"Stenson I am surprised at you, calling a upright citizen like Fisher and asshole. I expect more from you." She said tongue in cheek.

"Expectations are over rated." He said ignoring her playful tone.

"Oh my, so serious, Stenson."

"There is no hiding anything from you, is there?" He said smiling. Donna laughed and struck him hard on his arm with her open hand.

"What is your take on him? Could he be our man?"

"Which question do you want me to answer first?" Stenson replied.

"Why do you always answer a question with a question, Stenson?" She asked.

"You mean like you just did?" Donna slapped his arm hard again and he laughed. "I don't know. He seems to have a good alibi, but still may have been able to pull it off. Did you notice the way that he looked at his receptionist, and how she looked at him?"

"Yes, like they had just finished having sex." She said with a grin. Stenson raised his eyebrows and likewise responded with a broad smile.

They finished eating lunch and disposed of the remains in a garbage bin. They made a few positive comments about the street performers before leaving the waterfront. "Ah, Halifax in the summer, there is nothing like it." Stenson said, and they walked slowly back to the police station.

Chapter 37

It was hot and humid on the walk back to the station. The forecast proved to be accurate as the temperature reached the high 20s. Fortunately, the air exchanger at the station was running on high, keeping the air clean and cool. Stenson and Donna were at their respective desks, Donna writing the notes from the Fisher interview, and Stenson typing his up on the computer, which he added to his laptop version of the murder book. When they finished, they met to revisit Jenkins' notebook as previously planed.

"Let's look at his calendar first." Stenson suggested. The entries in the murder book included the calendar search going back to the beginning of the year. The calendar on Jenkins' cp was a Google calendar and had repeated schedules with his clients, as well as scheduled payments.

"We checked on all the companies and people for whom Jenkins was consulting. They were all legit, nothing unusual. Fees were made on time and all of those involved were quite pleased with the results. Jenkins was pissed off by a few people who had rejected his request to do work for them, but, according to the rejection emails, they all had good reasons not to have any work done at the time and had no bones to pick with him."

"Okay, Donna, that precludes the consultant component. We, at least *some* of us, have ruled out Nickerson as a possibility and love interest as motive. We cannot ignore the fact that Jenkins was worth millions. The likelihood of death being committed for money is a very real one, and who is the one to gain the most?"

"His wife. Lisa Jenkins." Donna answered.

"Correct."

"But what about the other murders? How do they fit in?"

"Diversions, plain and simple. They have had to be random killings to mislead us." Stenson explained.

"I don't see how Lisa Jenkins, if she did it, could have done it alone. And why would she do it? She has money. There is no indication that her husband was going to leave her."

"You are right, Donna. She had everything she needed, and she's not stupid. Any attempt to get all of the money for herself would only lead us to suspect her, obviously. No, it doesn't make sense that she would do it. Even if she wanted to, I don't think she has the temerity to club someone to death. And I don't see her running around randomly killing people. Yet, I can't help but thinking that the entire thing is about money."

"We're starting to repeat ourselves, Stenson. Does that mean we are up the creek without a paddle, trying to convince ourselves that we have one?"

"Fuck it, said the squirrel." Stenson said, usually when he implied 'the hell with it'. "In any case, Donna, It means that we're zeroing in on what we think this is all about. Let's take another look at Jenkins' financial files."

. . . . .

Lisa arrived at Nickerson's house about an hour after
Redmond left. He was out on bail and also suspended from
work without pay until he was either convicted or proven
innocent of the charges against him. Lisa barged in without
knocking. Phil looked as if he slept in his clothes, if he slept
at all.

"What the hell is going on, Phil?" She said, keeping her
distance.

"Oh god, Lisa, I am glad you're here. The police are blaming
me for Geoff's death."

"I know. Jesus! You look terrible, like death warmed over."

"I haven't been able to sleep or eat. The police have my golf
club and they told me it was used to kill Geoff and the others
that were killed at Indian Lake."

"How is that possible? You were with me. You didn't..."
She found it hard to complete the thought. "Tell me you
didn't kill Geoff, Phil. Tell me the truth."

"How can you even ask me that, Lisa? You know better. I
was with you. You told them I was with you didn't you?"

"Of course I did. I told them the truth." She said looking
directly into his eyes. "Did they find your prints on the club?"

I don't remember them saying my prints were on it. I'm not
sure. I'm not sure about anything right now. I don't want to
go to jail, Lisa."

"Is that why you called me here?"

"Partially, but I just needed to talk to you. I'm going through hell. I think they really want to pin the murders on me."

"Get a hold of yourself, Phil." She said, going to him but not wanting to touch him. "The first thing that you have to do is clean up so you don't give the appearance of being homeless. You're a mess, Phil."

"How would you look if you thought you were going to jail for something you didn't do. It's nerve racking. Do you realize how many innocent people are in prison? The police don't give a shit who they convict, as long as they get the case out of their hair. I'm really scared."

"Do you have a good lawyer?"

"I have a lawyer. I don't know how good he is though. I've never needed one before."

"The police came to see me again too, just a while ago. Detective Redmond thinks I might have had something to do with it. Can you imagine that, killing my own husband? And for money, as if I would do that. The whole idea is so obscene."

Phil responded softly and smiled sheepishly. "They're blaming me because they think I did it for you, because I would then have you to myself."

Lisa looked at him with incredulity. "Would you have done that – to have me?" She asked.

"Well, to tell you the truth, Lisa..." he paused and then went on, "I couldn't kill anyone under any circumstances, for any reason. Don't hate me for saying that, but I just couldn't." He moved toward her to take her in his arms. Lisa thwarted his advances, pushing him away.

"No, Phil. I can't. It's over."

"What are you talking about? We were good together; you know that."

"Phil." She emphasized. "It's not going to happen. There's no *us*, Phil. It is as simple as that. With Geoff … gone … I just don't want to continue."

Didn't you say we were good for each other, Lisa? Didn't you say that?"

"Yes, I probably did say that, but that was sex talk. It's not how I really feel, and *especially* how I feel right now."

"I'm sorry you see it that way, Lisa. Really sorry." He said with the same eerie calmness that he experienced when Redmond was interviewing him, sending a chill through her entire body.

. . . . .

Jean sat at her desk in her home office cleaning the gun after having used it for target practice. She bought all the cleaning accessories needed from the attendant at the shooting range. She took his advice to maintain it so as to avoid any malfunctions. After completing the cleaning, she put the gun back in her purse. She kept it in the same small purse that she carried everywhere she went, even though it did not always match the outfit she wore. She was happy with her progress in shooting the gun; her accuracy improved each time she practiced. Jean was completely obsessed with the weapon and knew that she would never surrender it. It was not so much what the handgun could do, or the power that it offered its owner, but its small compact size, beauty and its efficiency. Jean saw her Kahr PM9 as a work of art. And so it was. She wondered how she could think that way about a weapon that could kill another human being. Then as an afterthought, she considered it not as a weapon of death, but rather one of protection.

The phone rang; she picked up on the second ring. "Jean here." She said, and listened to the voice on the other end. "You're right, it is not a good time." She listened again and this time more carefully. "You say a 25% return? How is that possible in this economy?" After she heard him say that the window of opportunity might only be open for a brief period, she said, "Well, maybe we should meet to discuss it. How about tomorrow morning?" Jean jotted down the time for the meeting on her desk calendar. She could not resist a good business proposition.

. . . . .

Stenson and Donna looked over Geoff Jenkins' paper and through his computer files seeking a financial link to his demise.

"What specifically are we looking for?" Donna asked.

"Well, I know what we are not looking for."

"And that is?"

"I don't think we need to look at money coming in. The two most important issues we want to look at are how much money overall Geoff had, and how much he was paying out, and to whom."

"How's it going guys?" Redmond said approaching them.

"Oh yeah, good. Real good. We still have nothing." Donna said. "How'd it go with Jenkins' wife?"

"She is a real piece of meat." He said suggestively.

"What!?" Donna reacted in surprise at Redmond's response.

"Sorry about that." He said. Donna frowned and Redmond realized that he was dangerously on the threshold of a sexist remark. "Whatever, I got nothing out of her except confirmation that Nickerson was at his apartment when he called her before going to her house. That really cuts down on the window of opportunity. No weapons in her house whatsoever."

Stenson maintained his focus on Jenkins' computer but still replied. "I guess we're gonna have to drop the charges against Nickerson, aren't we?"

"I'm afraid it looks that way." Rick said with disappointment. "But I think we should let him sweat a bit. If he sweats enough, you never know, he might just give us something to go on."

Donna retorted, "You just like to make it hard on him don't you, Rick, just love to see him sweat?" And laughed.

Redmond shrugged. "I've got nothing against him."

"Maybe not, but I think you see him as an easy mark."

Rick backed off.

Stenson looked up at Donna, raising his eyebrows at her bold remark. "Tolerance down a little bit today, Donna?"
Donna eased off a tad, almost apologetic. "I suppose you could say that. This case is getting to me."
"If it's any consolation, Donna, I think we are making headway." Rick reasoned. "Anyway, I want to talk to Jean Jenkins. See if she can shine any light on what we already have." Rick starts to walk away, then stops. "By the way, do either of you have any thoughts about the murder weapon? How Nickerson supposedly had it when the murder was committed?" After a moment of thought, Stenson shrugged and shook his head. Donna responded likewise. They heard Rick mumbling to himself, 'Sure is a fuckin' puzzle," as he walked away.
"Maybe Rick has something there – talking to Jean Jenkins." Stenson said. "According to this," he said referring to Geoff Jenkins' computer screen, "Jean is one of the recipients of her brother's insurance policy."
"Say what?"
"It's not a large amount relative to the one held by his wife, about one million dollars."
"Is it part of the same policy that goes to his wife"?
"No, it is an entirely different policy." He said.
"That's odd isn't it?"
"Not necessarily. According to Rick's meeting with her, Jean had a very strong relationship with her brother. They were very close. He sorta looked after her...emotionally, more so than financially. Apparently she has lots of her own money."

285

"And that's it?" She asked.

"You want more?" He said laughing.

"Yes, I want more. I want everything you got." She said softly.

"Whoa!" He said, raising his hands up, palms facing her and his mouth widening in a huge grin.

"I didn't mean it that way, you fool." She said slapping his arm. "I mean more information, more on the computer."

Stenson loved to tease her. "Sure that's what you meant. Right." The moment passed. "Actually, there is more. Jenkins paid out huge amounts of money in lump sums in 2007, 08' and some in 09', as you already know."

"Yes, the money in 09' went to ..."

"Investments Securities." They said simultaneously.

"How much are we talking about?" Donna asked.

"Roughly, it adds up to about nine million dollars invested."

"Whew! Now that's a lot of hamburgers."

. . . . .

Redmond drove an unmarked police issue to Jean's house. He decided not to call her in advance, but rather go unannounced. He sat in the car in front of her house thinking. Is it possible that Jenkins' sister had something to do with her brother's death, he wondered? Two things occurred to him; if she was involved, what was her motive? And she would have had to have an accomplice, a man, and a big man at that. As he sat and pondered, the image of a large man, perhaps, AJ Devoe,

Michael Fisher, or someone else, came to mind. How he would love to come face to face with that man. *Combined with images from his "tough guy" competition of years ago and the man who had committed the murders flooded his brain. He saw himself standing in front of the perp, who stood taller by three inches and outweighed him by at least 25 pounds, both ready for battle. Redmond stared into the glowing red eyes of the perp who stared back undaunted by Rick's presence. Both moved forward, staring the other down, as fighters at a weigh-in. But this time, Rick could hear the cheers of the fight crowd, and knew that the perp had to go down. The perp pushed him and Rick retaliated. He drove an uppercut into the perp's stomach, just below the rib cage, forcing a gush of air out of his mouth and he heard an audible 'oof'. Rick backed away to allow him to recover from the blow. The perp moved in and awkwardly threw a left hook which barely grazed Rick's chin. The perp followed with a right hand that landed heavily on Rick's collarbone, sending him reeling. Rick recovered quickly, even though the pain remained, and sidestepped, avoiding two more hooks thrown by the perp. Rick was in his glory, fighting for his life against all the perpetrators of the world. He threw another body blow with his right that landed solidly, momentarily stopping the perp; Rick followed with a left hook to the head that staggered his opponent. The blow sent sweat flying from the perp's face. Rick knew he had him. He moved in and threw a flurry of punches to the perp's midsection, forcing him to lower his guard to protect against the body blows. Rick then moved up*

287

to his head throwing a flurry of headshots that rocked the perp back against the ropes. It was only a matter of time now before he would take the perp down. Rick instinctively moved in tight throwing lefts and rights to the perp's body, sapping his strength, and again followed with massive punches to his head, which snapped back with each punch thrown. The perp's knees buckled and he went down, but Rick continued his barrage of punches on the felled perp. He was not aware of the arms pulling him off the perp. Redmond took a deep breath; sweat was pouring down his face. He shook his head to remove the images, and then slowly opened the car door and satisfied with the destruction of his opponent walked up to Jean's front door. He rang the doorbell and waited. There was no answer. He pushed the bell again several times and waited for Jean to open the door. There was still no answer, and Redmond went to his car and returned to the station.

. . . . .

AJ Devoe was listening to the wistful sounds of Nora Jones singing *Don't Know Why* and sipping on a rum and coke when he heard a knock at the door. Before he answered the door, he checked his appearance in the hallway mirror; he ran his hands through his hair and tucked his blue cotton designer shirt into his dark blue pants. He was more shocked than surprised to see Jean Jenkins standing at his doorstep. He stood there with his mouth open.

"Well are you going to invite me in, or just stand there like an idiot?"

"I'm sorry. I don't know what the hell I was thinking – just surprised, I guess. Come in, please, Jean." She went in; walked directly into the kitchen and plopped herself down in a chair at the table, looking out over an overgrown flower garden.

"Your garden needs tending to." She said.

"Oh well, yes, it does." He continued after an awkward pause. "Jean, I am so sorry…"

She cut him off, not wanting to hear anymore. "That's okay. Thanks. That's not why I am here exactly."

Jean and AJ had been friends for a long time. Both came from old money. Jean did not exhibit her wealth in the same way that he did, although his display was not as obvious to others as it was to Jean. Still there was a bond. While Jean wore classic, but very conservative expensive clothes, AJ would not be seen in anything less than trendy and very expensive outfits. He traveled exclusively to warm countries where he could buy an occasional expensive memento, and maintain his tan skin tone at the same time. Also, he reeked of money. Jean on the other hand, only traveled with a purpose, when she traveled, which was not often. She did not care to have her skin baked by the sun. To prove it, her skin was quite pale even in the summertime. They met through Geoff, who often brought her to AJ's parties. They seemed to hit it off immediately, having an understanding of each other.

"You look your usual classically drab self, Jean." He said.

"And you look your usual jet-setter, celebrity self, AJ." She retorted. Neither remark was made in a derogatory or judgmental way. Mostly, they were brutally honest with each other yet always devoid of hurting the other's feelings.

"Can I get you something to drink, Jean?"

"What exotic drinks do you have, nonalcoholic, of course?"

"Nothing unusual. How about some mango juice?"

"That will do just fine, AJ."

While AJ was pouring her juice, Jean asked him bluntly, "Do you know anything about what happened to Geoff?"

"I haven't the slightest idea, Jean. I can't imagine anyone doing that to him." He said without hesitation.

"No." She said. "It doesn't make sense, does it?" She drank some of the juice and put the glass down. AJ could tell how sad she was, how Geoff's death had affected her.

"I wish there was something…" He did not finish the sentence, but Jean comprehended what he was saying.

"Have you ever invested any of your money with Investment Securities, AJ?"

"With Mike? No." My money has been in bonds and GICs forever." He said. "Besides, I really don't intend to ever invest with friends."

"No matter what?" She asked.

"No matter what." He responded. "But that's me. I would never tell anyone else how to handle his or her finances. Why do you ask? Are you planning on investing some money?"

"Just wondering. Geoff did, you know."

"Yes, he did, a lot too. He told me. He said Lisa was his beneficiary."

"Of course she is. That makes sense." She said queerly.

"You don't think that Lisa had anything to do with it do you?" Jean adjusted her hat and then turned to look at him. "I don't know, AJ. I don't know what to think. I really don't." She stood up as if preparing to leave, her purse hanging at her side. "There is going to be a memorial in two days. Will you come?"

"Of course I'll come, Jean, I'll definitely be there."

"I just hope by then this nasty business will be over with." Jean turned to leave, and AJ stopped her. "Jean?"

"Yes?"

"If there is anything I can do…"

"Yes, AJ. If there is, I'll let you know. Thanks." She said appreciatively and left. AJ never thought to ask Jean why she came to see him, although he had a fair idea.

Chapter 38

The spirit of the entire department was somewhat subdued. Barnes had called in Redmond for a progress report and demanded a quick solution to the murders. He was getting flack from the mayor, as well as the RCMP, who were threatening to take over the investigation if they, his department, didn't get results within a week. Groups from throughout the city were alarmed that the police were unable to come up with a suspect and make an arrest. The pressure was on. The media wanted answers, but Barnes was putting them off. He was also transferring the pressure he felt to Redmond. He was the chief, but he was unwilling to take responsibility for the investigation. He was not going to let the buck fall on his desk. Redmond would take the hit; he would be the scapegoat. If necessary, Barnes would hand over the case entirely to the RCMP, if only to get everyone off his back. In all of the years as a policeman, he never experienced the likes of this situation. He even went as far as threatening Redmond with a demotion, telling him that if he did not solve the case, he would put someone else that could in the position. Redmond had returned to his desk dejected. He was never placed in a situation like this before, and he didn't like it one bit. Never before was his job in jeopardy. He had to advance the case quickly before Barnes decided to call in the RCMP. He wanted to talk to Jean Jenkins but decided it was too late today. In the meantime, he would see if Slater and Martin had anything new to report. He called Slater's cell. "Hey, Jimmy boy, how ya doin'?" Slater's body tensed at the word 'boy'. He heard it throughout his youth and every time that he heard it since he was overcome with a rage that demanded he strike back aggressively. However, he learned to control his fury, bit the bullet and chalked it up to white insensitivity.

"Doing fine, Rick." He said through his teeth. "It's good havin' a partner with me."

"Any activity?" Rick asked.

"None whatsoever. No one prowling the woods, except me and Dave."

"Well don't get too used to spending your work hours on the links, cause we're hoping for a break soon."

"Did something come up that we should be aware of?"

"No, nothing really, just hoping. Now don't you guys get sunstroke walking around the course. We can't have ya out of commission. Okay?"

"Right you are, Rick. Anything else?"

"No, that's it. I just wanted to check on you. By the way, stay there until everyone is clear of the course. Talk to ya later." Rick hung up.

He called Stenson on the intercom. "Is Donna with you?"

"Yes, she is." He said.

"Can you both come into my office?"

"Sure thing, Rick. We'll be there in a minute."

Stenson and Donna brought Jenkins' financial information with them and the three explored the inexplicable investment payments made over the three-year period, with no obvious returns or dividends from the investment banker.

"As of this point, Rick, we believe that Fisher is our prime suspect. He fits the size of the person that wielded a machete in the woods with Jim. He has, we believe motive, greed, and most of all he is an arrogant bastard who seems to have the balls to carry out the crimes. Now, all we have to do is figure out a way to prove it."

"And also to determine if he did it alone or with an accomplice." Donna added.

"We don't have a lot to go on, Stenson. If we had something a little more concrete, we could get a warrant to search his house and office." Rick said. "How solid is his alibi? Does it look like we can shake it loose?"

Donna spoke up. "I think it's a little sketchy myself."

"His receptionist backs him up, but it is clear that he could very well have been free at the times of the murders." Stenson said.

"Let's place him under surveillance. If we scrutinize his every move, he might give us something to go on, maybe give us a reason take out a search warrant." Rick proposed.

"I wouldn't mind tailing him, especially since I've interviewed him a couple of times. Besides, I think he is just taunting us and daring us to catch him." Donna offered.

"That's a good idea, Donna. I'd like Slater to partner up with you. He talked to the guy in the woods, and it's possible that he could recognize him. If he does, we'll know we're on the right track. I'll pull him off the Indian Lake duty and you can

start the first thing in the morning by staking out his house -
early." Rick emphasized. "You will watch him closely, every
move he makes. And, Donna," Rick emphasized once again,
"I want you to call in every hour. I don't want any mistakes.
Is that clear?"

"You got it, boss." She said smiling. "Call in every hour,
make no mistakes, and take no chances. If necessary, call for
back up."

Stenson smiled at her confidence. Nevertheless, he was
concerned for her well being. If Fisher was, indeed, the one
they were looking for, he was extremely dangerous. But
Stenson was not prepared to support the surveillance team
with his presence, as much as he wanted to. He knew Donna
was careful and was not joking about calling for back up, if it
was required.

Rick called Slater to advise him of the plan, and then left the
station, taking the murder book with him. Slater was elated
with the new and more meaningful assignment. He knew that
if they were correct in their suspicions, he would have another
go at the perp.

Stenson and Donna remained behind to double check the
investment figures and tie up loose ends. Once finished they
closed up and Donna invited him to her place for a drink.

. . . . .

The sun was hovering over the horizon with a single long
cloud, tinted red and orange, passing through its center. The

cloud would turn grey within minutes and it would soon be dark. The evening was warm and expected to remain so overnight. Stenson was deep in thought as he drove behind Donna's Toyota on the way to her apartment. He was weighed down by not being able to solve the puzzle of Nickerson's golf club. How could it be in two places at once, he wondered? Fisher, Fisher, Fisher. What was it that Rick said? *'Nickerson supposedly had it when the murder was committed.'* Supposedly. Yes, *supposedly*. Goddammit. That's it! He supposedly had it. He had a club all right, but it wasn't his. It couldn't have been. He had a club identical to his, but *not* his. Stenson almost ran into the back of Donna's car blinded by his revelation at the interchange just before turning on to the Bedford highway. He honked his horn wildly. Donna jumped out of her car. "What is it?"

He rolled down his window. "I think I got the answer. I'll tell you all about it when we get to your place."

As promised, Stenson explained his theory to Donna. "The perp, maybe Fisher, replaced Nickerson's golf club with an identical one, took his and used it to kill Jenkins and Harris. He then went back to retrieve the replacement club from Nickerson, leaving Nickerson's real club in the woods at Indian Lake, and without a club to call his own." He said. Stenson was smiling again.

"Stenson, I think you've got it right. And it seems so obvious. Perhaps that's why we didn't think of it before."

"Let's not jump the gun. If I'm right we still have to find the replacement club, *and* the machete."

"A search warrant would solve our problems." She said. "Do you think he would keep the weapons? Would you?"

"It would make sense to ditch them. That's what I would do. That way there would be no proof whatsoever to tie him to the murders."

"I think keeping an eye on Fisher could possibly break this case wide open. I'm glad Jim will be with me."

"Remember, Donna, keep your cover, and be careful not to let him see you. If Fisher's our man, he knows who you are, he would, no doubt, recognize Slater as well, and he's obviously very dangerous. You've got to give him space, and make sure that he doesn't spot you."

"I promise." She said with sincerity.

Stenson felt a need to protect Donna. He felt an overwhelming responsibility for her; he was her mentor since she became a detective and partnered with her for the most part. She was a good detective and he knew she could take care of herself.

"You will keep in touch with me while you're shadowing him, Donna, won't you?" Stenson asked her.

"Sure, if you want me to."

"I want you to."

"What are you going to be doing, Stenson?"

"I don't think you really want to know, Donna." He said, displaying his usual warm smile. "But I do have plans."

"If you are planning on doing something illegal, Stenson, you'd better think twice before doing it." She warned.

"Donna, all I need is for you to tell me about Fisher's movements. I want to know where he is every minute. Okay? It is very important that you do that."

"How can I refuse when you ask me like that?" They both smiled.

Chapter 39

Fog hung over the city, a thin gray blanket sealing in the damp cool air that drifted in from the Atlantic Ocean. It was not the pleasant conditions that were expected during the summer in the ocean playground, as to which Halifax was often referred. For those who worked indoors, it was of no consequence. The sidewalks were wet with drippings that fell from the moisture-laden leaves. Most of the streets of the city were lined with trees, keeping it cool during hot sunny days, or wet on days like today.

Jean was undecided on bringing an umbrella with her as she looked out her window seeing the wet sidewalks that, oddly enough, amused her. She went though a checklist; credit cards and checkbook were there, and her files from previous investments were in a brown manila envelope tucked inside a soft leather brief case. She knew that if she made a large investment, a transfer of funds would most likely be in order. Also, it was a more sensible way to make a transaction she thought. She adjusted her hat and then opened her purse to see that she had her constant companion with her; it was there, with a full magazine inserted.

As Jean approached and parked in front of Fisher's house on a quiet section of Henry Street, Donna, who sat in her old Toyota with Slater, called Stenson.

"Stenson, we're parked down the street from Fisher's house, and guess who is visiting him?"

"Don't make me guess, just tell me."

"Jean Jenkins. She is going inside now."

"Did Jim get a look at Fisher?"

"No. He's too far inside the house, not enough light. Couldn't get a look at him."

"Okay, Donna thanks. Let me know when she leaves." Stenson hung up and walked to the elevators in the Purdy's wharf building.

He rang the bell at Investments Securities knowing very well that Fisher would not be there. Linda Belford opened the heavy solid wood door, as she always did. She wore a black dress with red and brown strips along one side of the overlay bodice. The bottom of the dress stopped several inches above her knees, emphasizing her long slender legs. Her heels were about three to four inches high and open at the toes. Her dress seemed more than appropriate for the office. She looked sophisticated; she looked stunning. She gave Stenson a warm smile. "Detective, how are you? Come in. You might be a little disappointed though. Mr. Fisher is out of the office. He has an appointment."

Hmm, he thought, so Jean Jenkins is his appointment. "Not disappointed at all, Ms Belford." He said, intending it to be a compliment. Her smile said she accepted it as one.

"Perhaps I can help you. And please call me Linda." She said a little more professionally, but still no less alluring than before.

"Yes, perhaps you can, Linda."

"Would you like something to drink, Detective?"

"Water would be fine." He said. "And you may call me Stenson. Everyone does."

"Water it is, and Stenson it is." She walked through a doorway to the right of the reception desk where a small counter with a sink and a small fridge was located in an alcove. She took two bottles of water from the fridge, picked up two glasses and returned to the reception area. "Shall we take this to my office?" She asked.

"Your office?" He responded somewhat surprised.

"I am more of a partner than I am a receptionist, but investors would rather deal with men." She smiled smugly and in control. "Come." Linda headed toward Fisher's office, and turned right down a short hall to another corner office that was almost the same size as Fisher's, just slightly smaller. "This is it." She said as she sat behind a desk and extended her arm out, offering him a chair. He sat. "Michael and I each own a fifty percent interest in the company. I do the books and receptionist, and he does the schmoozing with the clients." Stenson studied her for a moment. She said nothing. Clearly she was confident and at ease during the silence. "You know we are treating Mr. Fisher as a suspect for at least three murders and possibly a fourth." Stenson waited for her reaction and it came quickly.

"What? Michael wouldn't hurt a fly. Besides, he accounted for his whereabouts when the murders occurred." She said in his defense.

"You did vouch for him, didn't you? Sort of."

"What the hell do you mean by that?"

"It seems, Linda, that his alibis are full of holes."

"What are you talking about? I told you where he was."

Yes, you did tell us. You said he was at a meeting, he was working at home and he was at lunch. During those times, without you knowing it, he could easily have been at the crime scene. In other words, his alibis are not ironclad."

"I don't know what to say." She knew it was possible that Fisher might have been elsewhere during the times he was out of the office.

Stenson attempted another ploy. "Why do you think he did it, Linda?"

"Come on Stenson. That's a leading question and totally absurd. I'm positive he didn't do it. Killing someone would be so unlike him. He's so caring. I can't possibly imagine Michael harming anyone – *ever*." It did not go unnoticed by Stenson that she leaned forward, squirming, and uncomfortable in her chair.

"Does Mr. Fisher keep any weapons here in the office?" Stenson asked, trying to push her buttons.

"Weapons? This is an office, not a war zone. What kind of question is that?"

"I'm sorry, Linda, but I have to ask; after all, we do consider Mr. Fisher a suspect. By the way, since you do the books, has there been any large investments made during the last six months?"

"I'm sorry too. As you can appreciate, that's a private matter. We can't divulge that kind of information without first getting consent from our clients." She said with an artificial smile and brushing her hair away from the side of her face with the back of her fingers.

"Sure. I understand. Do you mind if I take a look around his office?"

"My god! Of course I mind. You can't just come in here, make all kinds of accusations about my partner and then demand to search through our personal things, clients papers and what have you, in search of god knows what. If you want make a search, you will have to have Michael's consent or get a warrant." She said with righteous indignation.

"Okay. I thought I'd ask. Thank you for your help, Linda. I hope I didn't offend you." Stenson said, mending fences, but not really caring that he offended her. Linda mocked a smile as she glared at him.

. . . . .

Fisher offered Jean a drink, but she declined. He took her into his small home office and they both sat. They went way back as *sort of* friends but were not really that close; they were acquaintances, more than anything. Michael was a ladder-climber, and tried to keep up with the likes of Geoff and AJ. Jean recognized just how hard he tried. He was never able to impress Jean as much as he hoped to, but she was not one to be easily impressed. Nevertheless, she was impressed by his

303

investment skills. She made a fair amount of return on the money she invested with him over the years, and he so convinced her that he could easily turn a profit that she was willing to gamble a lot more on his say so.

"What do you have for me, Michael?"

"This is really good, Jean, really good."

"I assume that it's good, or I wouldn't have come. She said, not entirely convinced.

"This is the one that I have been waiting for my entire life, Jean. It is unbelievable, mind-boggling. You won't regret it. I am putting every cent I have into this deal. This is the kind of deal that turns millionaires into billionaires."

"Yes, yes." She said impatiently. "And it is what?"

"It is common knowledge that Warren Buffet has invested $230 million into BYD for a 10% stake."

"Buffett did that? And BYD - they are?" She asked.

"Auto makers." He said as if he were referring to the Holy Grail.

"Auto makers?" She repeated.

"They are a Chinese company that's building hybrid and electric cars. A mid-size hybrid can go 100 kilometers on battery alone or 360 miles in the hybrid mode with gasoline, and an all-electric car was introduced in China recently. The intention of BYD is to see electric cars fill the roads where quick-charge stations are as readily available as gas stations today."

"And for this, you want me to throw away my money - on electric cars? In this economy, you want me to put my money on an automaker, when the auto industry is taking a dive? You think I'm crazy, Michael?"

"No crazier than Buffett, Jean. BYD plans to sell both the hybrid and the all-electric car in the U.S. starting in 2011. The economy will have turned around. There will be a lot less competition since some of the major auto players are folding, and with Buffett's help everyone will want a green car that will save our planet from toxic emissions and save millions of dollars that would have been spent on gas which is sky-rocketing." He waited for her reaction, and when none came, he continued. "There is a small window of opportunity that will close shortly. It is now or never, Jean. It's going to be huge. However, we are not looking at pennies here." Michael sounded like an evangelistic revivalist.

"How much are we looking at?" She asked cautiously. She was still concerned about making a rash decision. Jean never invested that way, impulsively.

"It is not a small amount. I am putting in everything I have, at least one million. If I had more money, I'd put in more. They are only excepting a minimum investment of $25 million. Since Buffett joined BYD, everyone wants in. BYD doesn't want to waste their time with small investors – at least not yet."

"You want me to put in $25 million?"

"No, no. It's going to be a joint investment in a single sum from Investments Securities. So far, I have almost $5 million. I need another $20 million. I anticipate picking up another $5 million from a few of my other clients. So far, an additional

$3.5 million has been spoken for. All of the funds will be pooled and everyone will receive a percentage of the profit proportionate to the amount that they invested."

"And that's where I come in, is that it? You want my portion?"

"Yes. You can invest as much as $20 million or as little as $15 million." He said simply and waited for her reply.

"And when do you need the money?"

"No later than five days from now, but the sooner the better. I can guarantee that $20 or $15 million will return at least $100 million in two to three years. You'll never be able to do any better than that, anywhere. This is not a penny stock where you will get a ten to one return." Michael said trying to close the deal. "By the way, I will be talking to Lisa to see if she is willing to switch over Geoff's investments. The more we put in, the better for all of us.

"You're putting in $1 million?"

"Everything I have. My partner is throwing in everything she has. If I can re-mortgage this house and invest the money, I will. My reputation is on the line, Jean, as is my entire business. I'm not holding anything back. In three years, I expect to have quadrupled my money. I will then sell half of the investment for double what I invested, and still have double working for me, with expectations of quadrupling again."

"I have to think about it. $20 million is a lot of money."

"By all means think about it. This investment should not be taken lightly."

"And Buffett went in big, did he?"

"Yes, he certainly did. And others are following suit. There is not much time left."

"Okay. You've sold me, Michael."

"Wonderful, Jean. I don't want to be rude, but when can you get the money to me? Time is of the essence."

"How about tomorrow? I will make a bank transfer to Investment Securities first thing in the morning."

"That's fine, Jean. I'll then be able to meet the deadline with our pooled funds. I'll need you to sign these papers authorizing me to invest the money for you. As soon as the deal is completed, I will send you copies of the transaction indicating the percentage that you will have invested." He said placing several documents in front of her.

Jean adjusted her hat, pulled up her sleeve and took the pen from Fisher to sign the documents.

Outside in her car, Donna and Jim continued their vigilance. "If Fisher is our man, do you think you would really recognize him?" Donna sipped water from store-bought plastic bottle. Jim watched her drink. "Why do you buy that water? It cost nothing to get it out of the tap."

"It's easier, I guess."

"Easier than filling it up at home from the tap?"

"Cut me some slack, will ya' Jim."

"I was just wondering, is all." He watched her drink more water. "Ya know there are billions of those water bottles that go into the dump a year and it takes about a hundred years for them to decompose." He couldn't resist.

"You're getting on my nerves, Jim. Give it a rest." She demanded.

Jean left Fisher's house. He closed the front door behind her. "Hey, she's leaving. There she goes." Donna said as Jean got into her car and drove off. "I wonder what that was all about." "It's been about an hour or more now. Shall I call Rick to report in?" Jim asked.

"Yeah, good idea; use the car phone. I'll call Stenson on my cell and fill him in as well."

Jim told Redmond that Fisher had a visit from Jean Jenkins, and that they would remain in place to watch and follow Fisher, if necessary. Redmond told him to keep their position, and keep him informed of any movement on Fisher's part. At the same time, Donna spoke with Stenson, giving him virtually the identical information. "Where are you, Stenson?"

"I just finished having a nice talk with Linda Belford, Fisher's partner."

"Partner? You mean receptionist?" Donna said surprised.

"Not just a receptionist, Donna, definitely a partner. It is a 50/50 operation. She was offended when I asked to look through Fisher's office."

"Now why doesn't that surprise me? If it was me, I wouldn't let you look either." She laughed. "So what are your plans?" "I'm sitting tight until I hear from you. Let me know when our boy leaves the house."

"Heyyy…you don't have to wait long, Stenson. He just came out of his house in a mad rush. He doesn't look happy. Wait a second." Donna says to Jim: "Did you get a look at him? Is he the same guy you saw in the woods?"

"He's too far away. I can't tell. He looks so different. I can't be certain."

"Stenson?"

"Yeah."

"Jim wasn't able to positively ID Fisher. So, that doesn't help much. Fisher is on the move; he's getting in his car. We have to go."

"Let me know what his destination is, okay?"

"Will do. Ciao." She hung up, started her car and followed Fisher at a safe distance.

. . . . .

Stenson walked to his car that he left illegally parked on Lower Water Street. He removed the parking ticket from under his windshield wiper and threw it on the dashboard. He drove up Duke Street and went left at the Citadel. He then drove west on Sackville until it dead-ended at the Camp Hill Cemetery, which, in 1844 replaced the city's first cemetery known as the Old Burying Ground that had been established almost 100 years earlier. After Stenson turned right on Summer Street, he stopped his car, to the annoyance of drivers behind him, to ponder those who were buried there, the elite of Nova Scotia and veterans of World War 1, notably black veterans whose graves in a segregated section of the cemetery were marked by nothing more than flat white stones, but that situation had recently been rectified. Stenson shook his head at the thought and then resumed driving and took an immediate left on Jubilee Road which he followed until he came to Henry Street. He took a left and slowed down as he approached Fisher's house, making sure that Fisher's car was not in the driveway as he drove past. Stenson turned his car around and parked in Fisher's driveway. He didn't care if anyone saw him; he behaved as though it was his house. He walked casually to the end of the driveway along the side of the house, looking for a back entrance. He found one. He took a pair of gloves out of his jacket pocket and put them on. He tried the door, but it was locked. It was a simple lock that didn't require tools to open. He slid a credit card down between the door and the jam, and the lock released. Stenson looked around before he went inside, expecting to see signs of an alarm system. There were no signs of any type of system. Stenson opened the door and found himself in the kitchen. "Hello." He called out just to be safe. Stenson didn't like surprises. He took a furtive look around the kitchen, and called out again as he walked through an archway that led into the dining room. "Hello, Michael? Are you home?" There was no response and no movement in the house. No one here, he thought. He skipped a dining room search, and went into the large living room that was separated from the dining room by a long hall, which led to the front entrance and at the other end was a second entrance to the kitchen. He did a quick visual search of the living room and decided that there was nothing there of interest. He walked back into the hall and towards the front entrance where there were doors across from each other. He opened one door to a small well-organized office. A computer sat on the desk. Stenson wisely decided not to start it up. He touched almost nothing so as to leave everything undisturbed and consequently his presence there undetected. On the desk, Stenson saw a document that had been signed by Jean Jenkins. He took note that her signature gave Fisher authorization to invest a huge sum of money for her. He did not want to spend too much time in the house, so moved quickly out of the office and checked the closed door across the hall. It was a closet that held outdoor coats, an umbrella, hats and nothing more. Stenson went through it thoroughly looking for hidden compartments, but found none. As he walked down the hall toward he kitchen door, he saw another door to his right. He was about to open it when his phone rang, startling him. He almost jumped out of his skin. "Stenson here." He said.

"It's me." Donna said. "Fisher's in his office. Something's going on. He's running around like a banshee. He was on the phone the entire time driving to his office. I would love to be in his office right now."

"Maybe you wouldn't. I told Linda, his partner-receptionist, that we suspected him of committing three murders."

"Stenson, you didn't!"

"I had to get things stirred up, force him to make a move. I think it's working. By the way, I found out what Jean Jenkins was doing at his house."

"What? How did you find that out?"

"To answer the first question, she is investing a huge amount of money with him…and how you ask? I am inside Fisher's house right now."

"Stenson! You're crazy."

"Right. Just let me know if Fisher leaves the office."

"Okay. But…" Stenson hung up.

Stenson opened the door and found a set of stairs leading to the basement. He found a light switch on the wall at the top of the stairs. He turned the lights on and went down the stairs into a low-ceiling, room with a dirt floor. The basement was damp and musty, and wide open. A new furnace and oil tank sat in one corner on a cement platform. There was an old rickety workbench against the wall reaching about half the length of the house. A variety of tools, some rusted, and some new, were scattered on the table. Watching where he stepped, Stenson went to the bench to examine the tools; he found nothing unusual. He walked the length of the bench to his left, but nothing caught his attention. He returned and walked to the other end of the bench and found, leaning against the foundation wall, and partially hidden by the bench end, a golf club identical to the one that was used as the murder weapon. "Eureka!" He shouted. He looked again and next to the club, partially stuck in the dirt floor, was a machete. "My god! I hit the jackpot." He was going to take the club and machete with him, but decided that that would not be a sound decision. If he took it, there would be no way to prove to whom it belonged, or where it was found. He pulled a small kit out of his pocket and quickly dusted the handles of the weapons, and with clear tape, lifted prints from both of them. He deposited the tape in a small plastic container. He then took out a small digital camera, and took several photos of the club from different perspectives. "Fisher's our man." He said aloud satisfied and then left the basement. He traced his steps into the kitchen; took a long look around, started to leave and stopped. He made a decision. Stenson took a small brown bag out of his pocket, considered several places in the kitchen and finally decided on one; he stuffed the bag in a cupboard, securely hidden behind some packages of food. He went out the back of the house after locking the door that he had opened with a credit card. The sun had burned off the fog and the light was blinding. Stenson put on a pair of sunglasses as he walked to his car and drove off with a larger than usual smile.

Chapter 40

Fisher paced in front of his office window, pausing to look out over the harbor. Several boats sailed in the light breeze as if they had no particular destination. The sight of the boats pacified him somewhat. Without turning from the view of the harbor, he said quietly to Linda, but no less cruelly. "What the fuck do you mean they suspect me?"

"Just as I said, Michael. They are onto you. Detective Stenson told me that he thought you committed all three murders. I told him it was impossible."

"Why would he think that?"

"How would I know? He never said."

He turned around to look at her. "What else did you tell him?"

"I'm not stupid, Michael. I told him nothing. He wanted to look through your office, at the files, the books, among other things, I suppose. I wasn't about to let him do that."

"Okay. We have to move fast, before they bring in a search warrant. Call Jean Jenkins. Tell her we need the money today."

"What reason shall I give her?"

"Tell her the window of opportunity is closing; we only have until five o'clock today, otherwise we'll lose the chance of a lifetime."

"You think she'll buy that, Michael?"

"She already bought it, Linda, lock, stock and barrel." He said smiling arrogantly. "After you call her, make the bank transfers arrangements – for every dime."

"What about Geoff's money?" She asked making sure that all the Ts are crossed.

"I'm one step ahead of you, baby. I've completely transferred all of his money." He said pleased with himself. "The airline tickets?"

"Done. We have two seats together on the red eye, with only one stop. What about the houses?"

"They are sold and closed, and the money is in the bank. Got exactly what we asked for. Everything is running on schedule. Every cent that comes in after we're gone will be automatically transferred."

"I can't believe it; there's less than a day to go." She exhaled a breath of air that relaxed her body entirely. She felt the stress that she carried over several years dissipate.

"We're almost there. All the planning we've made is now going to pay off." Michael pulled her into his arms and held her tightly. She stiffened ever so slightly, and pulled back.

"I have to make the calls, Michael." She stepped back.

"We'll have all the time in the world for us later. I don't want to make any mistakes now."

"You're right. We have to tie up all the loose ends today. Go." He said. "Do your job, love. I also have a few jobs left. We'll meet at my house tonight, and leave from there, as planned?" Linda nodded, smiled and left his office.

While Linda called Jean Jenkins and the bank, Fisher called at least ten more clients. He told them of the BYD deal, hyping it for all its worth. Two of the clients bought in and would transfer their money within the next few days. The others were no-go, too concerned about the economic conditions. Fisher was no longer worried about a deadline, since all of the money that he received would be automatically sent to his new offshore account. He estimated the amount to be about $40 to $45 million. His dreams were about to be realized.

. . . . .

Stenson pulled his car to the curb on Brunswick Street, bordering the east side of the Citadel. He rolled his window down and sat at a parking meter in thought. He knew he couldn't use the prints he found on the golf club and the machete. They would never be allowed in evidence since he came upon them illegally. The pictures would be of no help either. What to do, he thought? He looked up at the Citadel, which overlooked the Halifax Harbor, one of the deepest ports in North America. The fort was once used to protect the city from attacks coming by sea. But that was long ago. Now, aside from being a tourist attraction, the Citadel was notorious for being a nighttime gay cruising spot. On occasion, a gay bashing on the hill had been reported, and once a foreign sailor died after he fell into the waterless 20-foot moat that separated the hill from the fort. As lovely and powerful as it looked, the fort offered no answer. Stenson wished it was over. The case was taking its toll. He thought about Donna and the possibility of a personal relationship, but quickly dismissed the idea. They worked well together professionally and he wanted to keep it that way. After more thought, he finally made his decision. He punched in a number on his cell phone. After about five rings, the phone was picked up.

"Yeah?"

"Hey."

"Who's this?"

"It's Stenson."

"Hey, man, long time. What's up?"

"Not much. Just taking it easy. You?"

"Ditto, man. Just playing it cool; trying to get by, you know."

"Look, man, I've been working this case, a real tough one."

"Tell me about it. It's been all over the news for the past week. Never seen anything like it. So? What's it got to do with me?"

"Nothing, actually. Well…"

"Well then, why the call, man?"

"Zero, I need you to do me a favor."

. . . . .

"Lisa? It's Michael. How are you holding up?" He said in no specific direction. His phone was on speaker.

"As good as can be expected, Michael, given the circumstances."

"I know this is not a good time, Lisa, but something extraordinary has come up, and I thought you should know about it." He described the BYD stock deal to her and explained that Jean had signed on for a sizeable sum. He told her that he has transferred all of Geoff's investments into the company and expected that the stock would triple or quadruple within a minimum of two years.

"The reason I'm calling now is twofold: I want to make sure I have your approval to transfer Geoff's investments, and to let you know that the stock will be available for only another day or two."

"Is it going to be a sure thing, Michael?" With…with Geoff gone, I don't want to take any financial risks."

"It's a no-brainer, Lisa. I'm putting in everything I have. You won't believe the amount Jean is going with."

"Do you think I should go ahead with some of my money?"

That's up to you. Even though it can't miss, in my opinion, something could happen. After all, it is only a company. However, the risk is very small, miniscule, compared to the upside."

"Definitely transfer Geoff's money over, Michael. If I decide to invest more tomorrow, what should I do?"

"If you do decide to go ahead, then all you have to do is make a bank transfer to Investment Securities, and I'll take care of everything else for you, okay?"

"Sounds good to me." Lisa said with the most excitement she had mustered for the past week. "And thank you, Michael."

. . . . .

Stenson arrived at the station and immediately typed up the notes from the meeting with Linda and transferred them to his flash drive, which would later to be transferred to his personal computer. He made no mention of his visit to Fisher's house obviously.

Donna rang him up and, said she tried to reach Redmond, but his line was busy. She informed Stenson that Fisher was leaving the office. "Stay with him." He told her and hung up. Once he finished his notes, he went to see Rick. Redmond was just getting off the phone. "Donna called. Fisher's on the move; he just left his office."

"She's got to stay on his ass."

"I told her that, Rick."

"Well, Stenson," Rick said clapping and rubbing his hands together as though he had just won the lottery. "We've got cause for a warrant. We got the fucker."

"Who? What?"

"Fisher. He was seen buying drugs from a dealer. We've got the bastard."

"Really? What happened, Rick?"

"An informant called. He told me he saw a dealer selling drugs to Fisher. He wouldn't give his name. He said he works for a couple of us here, but wouldn't reveal their names. Then he hung up. A mysterious bastard he is, to say the least. He was adamant about the purchase, said he saw a guy delivering drugs to Fisher's house."

"Is that enough to go on to get a warrant?"

"We'll find out. I applied for one with Judge Kearney. He said that if he gives us a warrant, we had better come up with something. I think I can push it a bit more, if need be, so that if searching his property turns up empty, we'll be able try his office."

"Let's just hope that in the meantime we can come up with something that can link him to the murders."

"One thing at a time, Stenson. Let's see how real the drug allegation is. The warrant will be ready first thing tomorrow morning. In the meantime, we keep a close eye on him, and hope we don't have to deal with any more surprises."

The phone cut into their discussion and Rick picked up.

"Redmond."

"Rick, Fisher just arrived home. Slater and I are down the street. Do you want us to stay here?"

"For the time being I do. We'll have Martin and Stenson relieve you in about an hour or so. Just so you know, I've applied for a search warrant for Fisher's property, so keep a close watch on him. If anything looks suspicious, I want you to nab him."

"How did you get the warrant?" She asked

"I'll give you the details when you come in. Later."

Redmond said without waiting for an answer and hung up.

Chapter 41

The early evening saw the fog moving in over mainland Halifax, muting the light from the sun, which would not set for at least another hour and a half. The peculiar light brought a sense of quiet dread. It seemed that life on the streets came to a halt. Donna and Slater, sitting in the car, waiting and watching, instinctively felt the uneasiness as they awaited their relief. They sat there quietly. Donna sensed this evening as one that brought on the emergence of a madman running out of a house and down the street, screaming and waving a weapon in his hand, after having shot someone while in an insane state. The thought left her with a shudder. She tried to erase the image from her mind. Her stress had reached its limit.

Inside the house, Fisher was in his bedroom packing two suitcases. He opened a drawer of one of the tables that was separated by the bed, took out a .38 revolver, and put it inside a leather carry on bag. He picked up his cell phone from the tabletop, released the charger cord from the phone, and dialed a number. "Hi. You planned on coming over for the car?" The response was positive. "Now is a good time. I may not be here later." He listened for a moment and then said, "Oh yes, use the right away from Edward Street and come in through the kitchen." He remained focus as he listened. "Good. See you soon." He closed the flip cover of his phone and put it in his sport jacket pocket. One thing more, most important he thought, the laptop computer. He left the baggage in the bedroom, with the exception of his carry on, which was deep enough to house his laptop and went downstairs to his office. He was unhooking his laptop when he heard the kitchen door open. Fisher went into the kitchen where Dan Lee was waiting for him. "Danny, ole boy, how ya doing. Good to see you." Fisher shook his hand and patted him on the shoulder pleasantly.

"I'm doing just fine, Fish. You?"

"I'm getting by, considering the present state of the government." The both laughed at what was a running joke between them.

"So you got a car for me." Lee said as opposed to asking.

"Do I have a car for you. Can I put you in the driver's seat today?" Fisher joked and they laughed again.

"You're in great spirits, Michael."

"Yes. Because I am about to give my car away for practically nothing to my very good friend."

"Are you sure you want to do this, Fish? You're giving it to me for about the tenth of what it would cost me to buy."

"Of course I do ole buddy. I couldn't think of a better person to have it." Fisher said slapping him on the shoulder.

"I brought cash. I hope that is okay."

"What? No checks; no credit cards. Oh well, I guess cash will just have to do, won't it?" He laughed.

They filled out and signed the transfer of ownership of Fisher's BMW. Fisher gave him a receipt for the cash. Dan Lee was now the proud owner.

"The car is out front. It's yours, just drive it away, Danny." Fisher said handing him the keys. Lee left by the front door, and Fisher went back into his office. Lee quickly walked to and got in the car, and proudly started it up. He sat there for a moment listening to the hum of the engine. It was almost dark when he pulled out of the driveway and drove in the opposite direction of Donna's parked car.

"He just got in the car." Slater said. "There he goes." Neither got a good look at Dan Lee and so mistook him for Fisher. It was too dark and too distant for them to realize that it was not their quarry. Donna started the car and followed the BMW at a safe distance.

"Call Rick and tell him we're on the move, and not sure where we're going. Tell him we'll contact him when we arrive at whatever our destination happens to be." Slater made the call, informed Rick of their status, and was told that he and Donna would be relieved a bit later.

Instead of driving directly to his house on Shirley Street, Lee decided to try his new car out. He headed for the Bi-Centennial Highway where he could lean on it a bit to see how she handled. There was still enough traffic flow from the rush hour that Donna could easily follow the BMW closely without being noticed.

. . . . .

Stenson decided to research Linda Belford and came up with very little information. She was clean, not even a DWI. She graduated high in Business Management at Dalhousie and was top of her class in Investment Management and Portfolio Management courses. From there, she went to work for Investments Securities. There was no record of when she had become partner or had invested in the company. One oddity he came across was her father's death. His name was Thomas Scanlan. According to the obit, his wife who predeceased him was Stella Belford; his daughter Linda apparently used her mother's maiden name. An additional search turned up that Scanlan was killed in a head on car collision. According to the article, the insurance company fought the lawsuit, treating the collision as a suicide, suggesting that his death resulted from losing his entire life's savings in a stock company that had gone bankrupt. However, the insurance company lost the case, and a huge sum was paid in compensation. It was thought that the insurance company attempted to use Scanlan's financial loss solely to keep from paying off a huge claim. Linda's mother had died years before, and so Linda was the recipient of the award. Hence the money, perhaps, to buy into Investments Securities, Stenson figured.

He jotted the information on Linda into his duplicate murder book and did another transfer of the data onto his flash drive, for what it was worth.

. . . . .

Linda parked her car on Edwards Street and went into Fisher's house using the kitchen entrance. "Michael?" She called from the kitchen. "Are you here, Michael?"

Fisher walked out of his office and into the living room. "I'm in here, baby." He said, putting down the carry on bag that now contained his laptop.

Linda, wearing the same dress that she had on in the office, walked into the living room. "How is my hard-hearted Driver?" She said softly, using a nickname that he earned from driving balls a long way on the golf course. She smiled suggestively and moved her body tightly against his.

"Mmm, love when you talk dirty. You're a hot turn on, baby." He kissed her on the neck, and moaned.

She gently pushed him away. "Everything set to go?"

"The only way it could be better is if we were in Morocco right now."

"Where are your bags?"

"Two are upstairs." He said and pointed at his carry on. "This one I'll take on board."

"Get your bags from upstairs and we can get started. Our flight is in two hours."

Fisher took the stairs two at a time to get his bags. While he was upstairs, Linda took out an airline ticket from her purse, pushing aside a .22 caliber handgun. She opened Fisher's leather bag to put to put his ticket inside, and as she did she saw his gun. She smiled at seeing his gun, took it out of the bag and saw that it was loaded. When Fisher returned with his bags, he saw Linda holding the gun and his bag open.

"What the fuck are you doing?" He said viciously.

"What the fuck am I doing? I put your airline ticket in your bag, and this is what I find? The question is, what the fuck are *you* doing?" She said lifting her hand with the gun in it. "You are amazing, Michael. Did you plan on leaving this in your bag to take through security?"

"No. Of course not, I was going to dump it."

"Where? When?" She demanded.

"Never mind. Just give it to me."

She laughed at him. "Uh-uh. Look. Now I have the cold steel rod, Michael. What do you think?" She said, licking her lips, her mouth partially open and her tongue in the corner of her mouth suggestively.

Fisher moved against her, feeling the heat generated from her body. He made no attempt to take the gun. "You really know how to excite a guy, don't you, baby?"

"I do." She said, looking into his eyes. She held the gun against his forehead, the steel cold against his skin, as she pushed her pelvis against his groin. "Now I see why cops carry guns – so much power – so erotic."

"You want to fuck now, before we leave?" He said almost begging.

"Sure." She said smiling. "Let's fuck."

As Fisher cupped her breast, she let out a soft moan, pulled the trigger and the gun exploded into his left temple; it was slightly muffled by the barrel being pressed tightly against his skull. The blood spurted and bone and flesh were driven out the back of his head, and Fisher fell backwards to the floor. "Fuck *that*, Michael. That was for daddy, you asshole, for stealing the money he gave you in trust to invest and for turning him into a broken man. That, you slimy fuck, was for killing him." She said gasping for breath. Linda wiped the gun down and placed it in his open right hand. She looked all around quickly, more excited than frightened. Did I touch anything, she wondered. She went into the kitchen, wiped the doorknob off on both sides of the door and left unhurriedly. When she got into her car, she checked her tickets; there were two, one to Morocco and one from Morocco to Belize with open dates. Her itinerary read Halifax to Montreal to Morocco. A second itinerary read Morocco to Belize. Both were in the name of Linda Scanlan. She sat calmly for a few minutes, put the tickets and itineraries in her purse, and thought about how to get rid of her own unregistered gun. She decided to toss it on the way to the airport. Linda then drove away.

. . . . .

Jean left her house, disturbed by the chain of events. How could she possibly get involved in an investment scheme without checking it out? She never spent so much money on any deal in the past without months of research and investigation. Why now? She wasn't thinking. She was distracted by Geoff's death, and justifiably so. Also, she did not feel right investing money so soon after Geoff had been killed. It seemed selfish. She felt ashamed. She had a great deal of money and did not care, certainly at this point, about making more. That was not the way she wanted to operate. She decided not to go ahead with the transaction with Investments Securities. She thought it would have been thoughtless to go ahead with the deal. She was on route to Fisher's house to tell him face to face that she was backing out. It was only the right thing to do

. . . . .

Dan Lee turned off at the Bayer's Lake Centre. He stopped at the Nova Scotia Liquor Commission. He planned to buy a bottle of wine to celebrate his new acquisition. Donna and Jim pulled up next to him and when Lee exited the car, she realized that it was not Fisher at all. Donna left her car as fast as she could. "Lee!" she shouted at him before he went inside. "What are you doing with Fisher's car?" "What?" He smiled. "You must be kidding. I just bought this beauty from him, minutes ago." "You bought it? Shit!" Donna ran back to her car. "Call Stenson. Tell him to go to Fisher's house immediately. We were duped. Tell him to hurry." She started her car, put the police light on the dash and drove off with little concern for the heavy traffic at the shopping center.

As soon as Stenson got the message, he and Martin took the shortest route to Fisher's place, driving a police car with the siren blaring and lights flashing.

. . . . .

Jean Jenkins parked in Fisher's driveway. She did not see his car and hoped that she didn't miss him. She rang the doorbell and waited. She saw the lights on in the house and thought that he might still be at home. She rang again, but again there with no response. She turned from the door when she heard the siren and saw the flashing lights. She stood waiting as the police car pulled up to the curb. Stenson and Martin ran up the driveway. "What are you doing here, Ms Jenkins?" Stenson asked breathing hard.

"Why detective, I was just going in to see Michael, but I don't think he's home. He didn't answer the bell. What's the problem?"

"I'm not sure there is a problem. But it would be a good idea if you left right now."

"What's going on, detective?"

"That was not a request, Ms Jenkins. Leave right now. Move!" Stenson ordered emphatically.

Jean looked out towards the street. "I would leave if you moved your car. It's blocking the driveway." She said with as much unpleasantness as she could gather.

Stenson gestured with his head asking Martin to move the car. "Yeah, sure." Martin said obnoxiously.

By the time Jean got in her car, Donna had driven up screeching to a halt behind the squad car blocking the driveway. Martin was unable to clear the path for Jean who sat in her car watching and waiting.

"What's the story here, Donna?" He asked a bit annoyed.

She explained what happened and said, "It looks like he might still be here."

"We can't just waltz in there without a reason, or a warrant."

"Is that Jean Jenkins in the car?" Donna asked.

"Oh yes, it is. She was here to see Fisher, but Fisher didn't answer. Just a minute." Stenson walked to Jean's car and asked her if she still wanted to see Fisher, and of course, she did.

They went back to Fisher's front door, rang the bell several times and when there was no answer, Stenson pounded on the door. Finally, he tried the door and found it unlocked. Stenson went in first, his hand on his holstered weapon.

"Mr. Fisher?" He called. Jean was right behind him.

"Michael? Michael, I need to talk to you." She said.

Stenson drew his gun and first checked the office – nothing. He then went into the living room followed by the others; he saw Fisher's body supine on the floor with a pool of blood around his head like a red halo.

Chapter 42

The house was cordoned off with yellow police tape. Redmond had arrived and took over the investigation. Dan Lee was brought into the station for questioning, since he was the last person to see Fisher alive, with the exception of the killer. A forensic team arrived and was working inside as well as outside, looking for evidence. The medical examiner considered that Fisher's death had to be a homicide due to the angle of the bullet entering the left side of his head and exiting on the right side. The only other solution, if it were to be deemed a suicide, was laughable at best, because the victim would have had to have a wrist that was double jointed in order to shoot himself in the left side of the forehead with his right hand. Suicide was really not considered, especially since the victim had his bags packed was about to catch a plane within two hours of the shooting. Forensics found no prints on the gun, which had been placed in the palm of Fisher's open hand. The medical examiner completed inspecting the body and then covered it up. Redmond sat in the living room interviewing Jean Jenkins who seemed to be unusually cool considering that someone she knew had been murdered.

"Had you been inside before Detective Stenson arrived?"

"Not at all. I rang the bell and there was no answer. I was about to go back home when the detectives drove up."

"What were you doing here?"

"I had business with Michael. I changed my mind about an investment and came to tell him that I was backing out."

"Why didn't you call, Ms Jenkins?"

"It would have been rude to call." She said as if he should have known the answer.

"Did you hear any sounds, perhaps a gunshot?"

"No, I didn't hear a thing. I arrived, rang, and there was no answer and no movement or noise that I could tell." She said impatiently.

"Okay, Ms Jenkins, I think you can go now. Don't leave the city; we might need to talk to you again." Redmond said, dismissing her.

"Don't leave the city… what a thing to say. Do you think I'm a criminal that's going to flee the country?"

"Yeah, yeah." Redmond said disgusted with her response.

"One thing, detective. Did Michael have anything to do with Geoff's murder?"

Redmond looked at her stone-faced without saying anything. Jean was resigned to the fact that she would not get an answer. Redmond watched Jean as she rose from the chair, adjusted her hat, and left the house.

. . . . .

During the house search, a brown bag containing cocaine was found in a kitchen cabinet. Redmond concluded that Fisher most likely knew the killer since there was no evidence of a forced entry. He also thought that, because of the cocaine, the killing was drug related. At Stenson's insistence and with his help, the basement was searched. The hunt turned up a golf club identical to the one used in the golf course murders. The machete was found sitting next to the club. It would no doubt take several days to sort out all of the details. The intention was to collect Fisher's DNA and compare it to the DNA found in the glove left at the murder site at Dartmouth Crossing. It was to be determined later that the golf club had both Nickerson's and Fisher's fingerprints on it. Redmond concurred with Stenson's theory that Fisher had switched the clubs on Nickerson; leaving him with the one he bought and then he returned to take it back, leaving Nickerson's set of clubs without a driver. Only Fisher's prints were found on the machete, confirming the suspicion that it was Fisher who confronted Jim Slater in the woods at the Indian Lake Golf course. The theory, which could not be proven, was that Fisher was there, at the golf course, looking for another victim, begging the question why? Slater was convinced that Fisher was the man he encountered at the course, but still could not positively ID him. Everyone was in agreement that Fisher was the serial killer and the evidence confirmed that belief. The follow up now was to find the perp who killed Fisher. Although it was considered unlikely that the search for his killer would be forthcoming. It was established that the cash found on Fisher was the same amount that Dan Lee said he paid him for the car. Dan Lee was checked for gunshot residue and the results were negative. He stated that Fisher was alive when he left, and Donna and Slater reported that they didn't hear any shots before they followed Lee, putting his murder within a 45-minute window. Lee was released without being charged.

A one-way airline ticket to London, England was found in Fisher's carry on bag. It was clear that he was on the run. Chief Barnes spoke with the press to do some damage control. He gave the media only information that suited him and his department.

The next day's newspaper headline read:

GOLF COURSE SERIAL KILLER SUSPECT SLAIN

It was ironic that the suspected killer of four people, three at the Indian Lake Golf course, was himself struck down by an intruder, just moments before he had planned to flee the city and escape to Europe. The police would not say if they had any leads or a suspect responsible for the murder, but that it might have been a drug buy gone badly.

A spokesperson for the HRM police force said that Michael Fisher, 44, of Halifax was himself a suspect in the golf course murders and they were in the process of gathering evidence to that effect. It is believed that the motive for the alleged serial killings by the investment broker was an attempt to cover up the defalcation of millions of dollars from his clients.

However, they cautioned that it would take weeks or possibly months of investigation to determine the amount of money lost and the names of the clients who were defrauded.

The story continued on with background information about Fisher and his company, Investments Securities. The media projected a sense of relief by the general population of Halifax that the serial killer had been identified, captured, and was dead.

. . . . .

The department held a brief celebration at the station; Redmond went home early, reasonably satisfied that they had solved the golf course murders' case. All of Fisher's bank accounts would be frozen in the morning and his books would be gone over with a fine-toothed comb. It would take weeks before it was discovered how much money was peculated from his clients. Redmond also felt that it was only a matter of time before they found the drug dealer who, they believed, killed Fisher. At home, Redmond poured a double shot of rum over ice and added cola, and then plopped down in an easy chair, turned on the TV to watch the Toronto Blue Jays play a baseball game against the Boston Red Sox. Tonight he would not worry about finding Fisher's killer. That was the least of his worries. For now, he would relax.

Stenson followed Donna to her apartment. He knew that Fisher's murder had nothing to do with drugs. Although, if he were to tell Redmond that he hid the drugs in Fisher's house after entering illegally, not only could he be charged with planting evidence, but also the golf club and machete found in the basement would undoubtedly be inadmissible as

335

evidence used against Fisher, if anyone chose to contest it. Stenson was reluctant to tell Donna about the drug plant, even though she knew that he had been in Fisher's house without authorization and suspected that he may have had something to do with it. He decided that it was best that she didn't know for sure. Donna had good instincts and did not succumb to Fisher being struck down by a drug dealer. It seemed too convenient.

"Do you really believe Fisher was killed by a dealer?" She asked him. "It just doesn't seem plausible." She added.

"No. It doesn't seem logical to me either." He said, looking out over the Bedford Basin, attempting to make sense of Fisher's death. Both felt uneasy about the results, and although they celebrated, they did not feel victorious nor did they think this was the end of it. "There is no rhyme or reason for what happened to him. I suppose we'll have some answers once we go through his books. Which reminds me, I don't think anyone contacted his partner, Linda Belford."

"If she doesn't contact us tomorrow, we'll definitely contact her. I am sure she will have heard the news about Fisher." Donna said as she poured a drink for herself and one for Stenson. He took his drink.

"Who do you think killed Fisher?" She asked him.

"I have no idea, but my guess is that it was someone he knew and possibly linked to the murders." He answered.

"A partner perhaps?"

"Perhaps."

"Why did he kill those people, Stenson?"

We're more likely to find the answer to that question in the next few weeks. Again, I would venture to say it was for the money."

"You think he killed all of them for money?"

No, not all of them. I suppose he killed some of them to mislead us."

"Hmm. Even the boy?"

"I think he murdered the boy out of necessity. Although, there was no doubt that he intended to kill the boy's father."

"Now what, Stenson?

Stenson took a long look at her and then sipped on his drink and said, ""You know what?"

"What?"

"You know what I'd like to do?"

"What would you like to do, Stenson?" She replied with a smile.

"I want to treat you to a drink downtown. Sort of to celebrate a small victory, even though we are far from finished."

Donna lifted her eyebrows. She expected something different. Gradually her mouth formed into a broad smile exposing her even white teeth.

"Oh?" She said disappointed. "I thought we would call it a night. However, I'm game." They pushed all thoughts of the case behind them and left her apartment.

. . . . .

The following morning, just before noon, an Air France airplane landed in Casablanca. The passengers disembarked and passed through customs uneventfully. The air was humid, and the temperature scorching, close to 35° Celsius. Linda Belford wore a white dress as a blast of heat hit her when she exited the airport in search of a limo that she had pre-booked. She was taken directly to The Kenzi Tower Hotel, which was located on Boulevard Al Massira al Khadra in the new city and only minutes away from the Medina. She looked forward to taking advantage of the Spa services available at the five-star hotel after spending the night flying. Linda was bi-lingual in French and English, so she felt comfortable in Morocco, whose predominant language is Arabic, but where French was commonly spoken. But even more importantly, the country had no extradition agreement with Canada.

Within two weeks she had sorted out the bank transfers that was routed through London, a numberless account in Switzerland, and then finally to Banque du Maroc. She discovered that instead of the anticipated $50 million dollars, her account now contained just under $10 million, which had been transferred before all of the accounts had been frozen. The amount did not deter her. It was enough. She was not greedy. Morocco was her first stop, but not her last.

www.ingramcontent.com/pod-product-compliance
Lightning Source LLC
Chambersburg PA
CBHW061929170626
46813CB00006B/2345